fixed up

JESSICA LEIGH JOHNSON

To Leslie—
my Disney travel buddy ☺

[signature]

✝
FROST & FAITH
· PUBLICATIONS ·

Identifiers: ISBN 9798987438008 (paperback)

ISBN 9798987438015 (ebook)

Cover design by Roseanna M. White/Roseanna White Designs

Edited by Robin Patchen/Robin's Red Pen

Edited by Lora Doncea/Edits by Lora

❀ Created with Vellum

For my husband.
I am so proud to be your awkward librarian.

one

NEVER AGAIN. *Never. Again.*

I repeat the words over and over as I drive home from my blind date. My *last* blind date.

Ever.

I thought it'd be fun to have a guy of my own so I didn't have to spend every Friday night alone while my roommate and her boyfriend went out, but I've changed my mind. I don't need a man that badly. I'll pick up a new hobby to occupy my lonely nights. Knitting has always intrigued me. I think I'll try it.

Although, ever since Nora started dating Milo, she's happier than I've ever seen her. I wouldn't mind being that happy too—if I could find the right guy. But so far, none of the guys Nora has set me up with have come close to hitting the mark. Especially Todd, the guy I spent the last two hours with. Why Nora thought he would be a good match for me is anyone's guess.

My foot presses down on the accelerator as I speed home. Once I park in front of the fourplex where Nora and I live, I hop out and run across the lawn as fast as my Birkenstock-clad feet will allow. The warm summer wind blows strands of auburn hair in front of my face, and I don't bother wiping them away. I'm a woman on a mission.

By the time I reach our second-floor apartment, I'm almost out of breath, but I can't let that stop me. I have to tell Nora that I'm done with all the matchmaking.

But when I walk in and Nora's face erupts in a massive grin, I almost regret what I have to tell her.

She springs from the couch. "So...how was it?"

I cross the brown-and-orange linoleum entryway, pass the small kitchenette, and march into the living room. I stand across from her and lightly grip her upper arms. "He has aquariums."

Nora's grin fades, and her dark eyebrows scrunch together. "Meg Rowland, for Pete's sake, cut the guy some slack."

I release her, then fall back onto the faux-leather couch behind me. "I did. I spent more than an hour at dinner cutting him slack—yards of it. I listened to him talk on and on about his job, while he never once asked about mine. Did you know he owns a pet store?"

Nora sits beside me, crossing one leg over the other. "That's where I met him. Milo wants to get a dog, so we went to Todd's pet store, only it turns out they don't sell dogs there."

"No. They sell aquariums. That's probably why Todd owns the place, so he can get an employee discount to buy more aquariums. His apartment is full of them." I can still see the glowing blue lights whenever I blink, like they're seared into the backs of my eyelids.

Nora exhales and leans back into the cushions. "If he was so awful, how did you end up at his apartment? That seems a bit premature for a first date."

"Under normal circumstances, yes, I would agree. But my last few dates didn't make it past the half-hour mark, and I knew you'd be disappointed if I came home early again. When Todd mentioned he had a huge collection of National Park stickers at his place, I thought, why not? Maybe they'd be interesting. But when we got there—"

"You discovered the aquariums."

"Nine aquariums, actually. Floor-to-ceiling."

"So then what? You left?"

"What else could I do?"

She flings up her arms. "You could've taken the time to get to know him. Maybe you guys have something in common, but now you'll never know. Todd could be a really great guy, yet you rejected him over the littlest thing."

I raise an eyebrow. "Did I mention he has an eighteen-year-old African bullfrog named 'Homey' in one of his aquariums? That thing is *not* little." Besides, Nora should know how I feel about pets with no fur. "Why prolong something that's destined for failure? I gave Todd more chances than I normally would, but when a guy has obvious red flags, it's not right to string him along. Some things are deal breakers."

Nora shakes her head. "You need to pare down your list of deal breakers. You have too many."

There's no use arguing with Nora because she'll never understand. She thinks that I try to find reasons to reject men before they have a chance to reject me, like some sort of self-preservation tactic or defense mechanism. But she's wrong. The guys she's introduced me to have been total mismatches, and Todd has been the worst one yet. I smile at her, trying to soften my expression as I announce my decision. "I appreciate all the effort you've put into finding me a man, but I think we should take a break from the matchmaking for a while."

Nora frowns. "What? You can't give up now. I still have a few guys in mind for you."

Her disappointed expression tugs at my heart a little, but it's time to face facts. Nora has set me up on six blind dates in the last two months, and not one of them has led to a second date. "Nora, for as much as you know about me, you don't seem to have a clue what I'm looking for in a man. I doubt you could ever find the right guy for me."

She places a hand to her chest. "I'm hurt. I think I've been spot-on with my selections for you. You're the one who sabotages relationships before they even start. You're too picky."

Too picky? "Let's review." I hold my hand out in front of me and tap my fingertips, listing men's names off one by one. "Nate from the gym called me 'dude' the entire night, Lucas wore two necklaces—two!—and Derek says pro-*noun*-ciate, which we all know is not a real word."

Nora grabs my hand to stop me. "Do you hear yourself? Do you know how insignificant those things are in the big picture?"

I shrug. "*Dude* is not a term of endearment, I should be the only one wearing jewelry, and I don't want to be the smartest person in the relationship."

She scratches her chin. "Well, that cuts out Gideon, my delivery guy at the salon. He's super funny, but I think he has pierced ears, and you'd probably spend your entire date correcting his grammar." She presses her lips into a thin line and taps her index finger against them. "Hmm..."

Oh no. She's *hmm*-ing again. I can almost see the matchmaking cogs spinning like a roulette wheel in her head. On whose name will the ill-fated marble land next?

Nora points her index finger in the air. "What do you think of Jason from the bank? Remember him? He's that loan specialist I met with about opening my own salon."

"No way. Don't even go there."

"Why not? He's smart. He knows a lot about investing and saving. I think he could be a great match for you."

I laugh. "I could never have romantic feelings toward Jason."

"But he's so nice."

"Yes, and he sounds like a frog."

Nora freezes. Her unblinking gaze gives me chills. "You're kidding me."

"Kidding you? About the frog voice?" I shake my head. "No, I assure you, I am not. No one's voice should sound like that unless they're being strangled. Plus, he has rug hair."

Nora covers her mouth with her hand and slides it, ever so slowly, down to her chin until she's pulled her lips into the perfect frown. Like a painted-on clown frown. Then she tilts her head to one side. "Dare I even ask what *rug hair* is?"

Does she need to? It's self-explanatory. "His hair is super thick, and it's cut sheer across the top like a rug. Can you imagine running your hands through that hair or listening to his frog voice rasping sweet nothings in your ear every night? I certainly can't. Oh, and he's way too short. I'm only five-six, yet when I stand across the bank counter from him, I can stare him directly in the eyes without looking up. Next to him, I feel like a *Brobdingnagian*."

"A *what*?"

"You know, from *Gulliver's Travels?* It means a person from the land of Brobdingnag. Everything there is giant-sized, as opposed to—"

"Enough already!" Nora makes a giant *X* in the air with

karate-chop hands. Her cheeks are flushed and her eyes are bugged out. "I've heard enough of you tearing these poor guys apart. So what if he's on the short side? If you want to be happy, you'll have to let some of those things go, or else you'll be alone for the rest of your life."

I stare open-mouthed at her. She looks ticked. But this is important. This is my life we're talking about, and I won't settle. I straighten my spine and lift my chin. "I'm totally fine with being alone."

"No, you're not, Meg. You're just saying that." Nora's gaze holds me hostage. She's reached her limit with me. That much is clear. But how can she possibly relate to my man-finding problems? She met Milo at work. He walked in one day, asked for a shampoo and trim, and they were both smitten. Love at first sight. If only it were that easy for everyone.

"Do you know what I think the problem is?" she continues. "You're setting your standards so high, no man could ever measure up. You have all the power. If you cut things off after the first date, no one can break things off with you because you've already beaten them to it." A few seconds pass, and her rigid expression softens. "I realize you don't want to get hurt again, but if you want to find love, you'll have to take some risks."

I look down at my hands, then drag my gaze up to meet hers. "That's not what I'm doing. Not even close." Okay, maybe it's a *little* close to that.

Nora takes a slow, deep breath. "I'm only trying to help because I care about you and I want to see you happy."

"I know, and I appreciate it. I really do."

"But you still want me to stop fixing you up?"

I press my lips together while I mull that over. Since I'm the only one who really knows what I'm looking for, it's probably best that I take control of my love life for a while. What's the rush anyway? I'm only twenty-five. Maybe a dating hiatus will be good for me. It will give me time to explore that knitting idea. I only have one hobby—reading. Imagine how much fuller my life would be if I had two.

Decision made, I bob my head once. "I'll take it from here. Consider yourself released from all matchmaking duties."

Nora's brow hikes upward. "So...you don't want a boyfriend?"

"Not right now. I'm good. Maybe I'll meet someone on my own, but if not, then I'll remain single. I am totally fine with that if it means I don't have to endure another blind date."

"If you say so."

"I do. And now, will you promise never to fix me up again?" I extend my hand toward her. I wait a moment while she angles her head first to one side, then the other.

"I still have one last guy in mind, and I think he might be the one."

"Nora, please! No more fix-ups. You have terrible taste in men, Milo excluded."

She sighs, then takes my hand. "Fine. No more men."

I shake her hand like I've just sold her a really nice used car. "Thank you. Now, doesn't that feel good? Like a weight has been lifted from your shoulders?"

"Yes, I feel amazing," she utters sarcastically. "Now we're back to you tagging along when Milo and I go out. What could be better?"

I toss my hand out to my side. "Hey, I'm fine with third-wheeling it. It's better than being stuck in a relationship with someone who keeps his roommates in glass containers."

Before I go to bed that night, I decide to get cracking on my new hobby as soon as possible. I pull my phone from the nightstand and order five thousand yards of wool yarn —enough to make three adult-sized sweaters. I feel lighter than I have in months. Finally, no more blind dates. No more struggling through awkward conversations with strangers. And no more dating someone just to avoid being alone. I'm content in my singleness.

I do a celebratory kick-punch judo move in the air. "No more aquariums," I whisper-shout. "No more rug hair! No more frog voice!"

"I can hear you," Nora calls from her room.

Whoops. Sometimes I forget we share a bedroom wall. I plop onto my mattress. "Sorry. I'll go to sleep now."

But I'm not sorry about not settling. If a guy doesn't meet my standards, then he isn't worth my time. I refuse to compromise.

Besides, singleness is a virtue, isn't it? Or maybe that's patience—which is okay, too, because I happen to have an abundance of patience. I'll wait for the right guy to come along, no matter how long it takes. I have nothing but time.

Time...and a whole lot of yarn.

two

I SPEND a good part of the next day sitting at the kitchen table with my laptop open, watching a knitting tutorial online. I learn how to cast a row of stitches onto my left needle, then transfer them onto the needle in my right hand. I can't wait until the yarn I ordered last night arrives because at the moment all I have is bright yellow. It'll have to do for now.

After completing one row, I realize a sweater may have been too big a project to take on as a knitting novice. I decide to make a scarf instead. And then I change it to a hot pad. I start on a second row of stitches, but the conversation I had with Nora yesterday is distracting me. I mess up one of my loops and have to start the row over.

I can't help but wonder if I was too hard on Todd. If I'd given him twenty more minutes of my time, would we have found some common ground?

Probably not. There weren't enough National Park stickers in the world to cover up the stench of fish food in his living room. I'd have to place them directly over my nostrils, and even that might not block it out completely.

Maybe I'm an idealist, but whenever I picture my future home, the home I'll one day share with my husband and kids, it doesn't have a single aquarium in it. And after only a few seconds in Todd's apartment, I could tell that would be a major source of conflict for us. I have no intentions of budging on the aquarium issue, and he definitely isn't going to, so it's probably best that we parted ways when we did. The two of us simply aren't meant to be.

But what about all the other guys Nora had set me up with? Was I too quick to dismiss them? They didn't have aquariums, but they had other qualities that I found equally objectionable. I know what I'm looking for in a guy, and I absolutely know what I'm *not* looking for.

Besides, it's not like I've rejected every single man I've ever gone out with. Only the ones Nora has set me up with, which is basically all of them...except one. She's never met Braxton, my ex-boyfriend. He is the only man I've ever been able to picture myself with long-term. He's practically perfect. I never would've broken up with him. Too bad he decided to break up with me.

It's taken me two years, but I can finally say with confidence that as perfect as Braxton was, he's not perfect for me. That's mainly because he didn't love me, which is kind of a big red flag. Even so, I suffered months of heartache over him and shed an incalculable number of tears before coming to that conclusion. To this day, the pain of his rejection still stings. Sometimes I wonder if he regrets ending things. Part of me hopes he does. A big part of me.

Since our breakup I've seen him a handful of times, though not recently. And because my mom is still friends with his mom, she always makes sure to keep me updated on his life. But it's been ages since she's shared any news with me on the Braxton front. It seems like he's been MIA for the last few months.

With a regretful sigh, I trade my knitting for my phone. It's not wrong to wonder what Braxton's up to these days. It doesn't mean I'm pining for him or anything. It's pure, friendly curiosity, that's all. I check his social media profile to see what might be taking up his time. Maybe he packed up and moved across the country. Maybe he's in a full-body cast and can't leave his bed for six weeks. Or maybe he impulsively shaved his eyebrows and has to wait until they grow back before venturing out in public again.

When his profile page loads onto the screen, my contented single-and-satisfied attitude goes up in a puff of smoke. There, filling up my entire phone screen, is a horrifyingly beautiful picture of Braxton with his arms wrapped around some woman named Talia, and the words *We're Engaged* scribbled in an artsy, black cursive font across the top of the photo.

Engaged? Since when has he been dating this Talia person? I've never heard of her. And I'm no stranger to Braxton's social media posts. I check them from time to time, like someone who *isn't* cyberstalking someone else. Is there a reason he's been keeping her a secret from the rest of the world? Or is their relationship really that new and, apparently, fast-paced?

This news shouldn't bother me so much. Braxton and I have been broken up for two years. There's no reason for the nausea that rolls over me now. It's not as if I expected us to get back together, but I sure as heck didn't think he'd meet someone so soon. Okay, maybe two years isn't soon— but I didn't think he'd meet someone before *I* met someone. Now he's engaged, and I don't even have a boyfriend.

Maybe I misinterpreted the post, or maybe it's all a big

joke. I search through the other social media apps on my phone, and they each tell the same sad story. The news is all over the internet. I can't even look at my phone without it shoving Braxton's engagement back in my face. So I turn it off. I'm talking hard shutdown.

I spend what's left of my Saturday afternoon in cut-off sweatpants, sprawled out on the couch with a jar of chunky peanut butter and a spoon, watching *13 Going on 30*. What I really need is someone to shake a dollhouse filled with magic sprinkles on my head so I can fast-forward through life and wake up in the future with a hunky hockey-player boyfriend and an exciting job in advertising. A dollhouse like that could solve all of my problems.

Oh, but my life can't mirror the movie exactly. I'd have to skip the part where the guy from my past gets engaged to some other woman. That's pretty much what I'm dealing with already, and I hate it. So maybe this isn't the best movie for me to watch today.

I stop the movie, slide from the couch, and put the peanut butter out of sight. Just as I close the cupboard, there's a knock on my door.

Now what?

I open my apartment door an inch, leaving enough room for one of my eyeballs to peer into the hallway. My mom stares back at me. *Great.* She's pushed a square Tupperware container as close to the door gap as she can. "I made cookies."

I pull the door open all the way and frown at her. "Why?" Not that I need a reason. I take the container and hug it to my chest.

"I thought you might need some comfort food. I heard about Braxton and Talia."

"And you've already had time to bake cookies?"

"I saw the announcement first thing this morning." She sighs and gives me the most pitying look. "I get a notification every time he posts something. You didn't think I'd stop following him just because you broke up, did you?"

Of course not. Because if she unfollows him, how will she pry into his private life? Since I'm an only child, my mom has no one else's life to fixate on. Lucky me. "I appreciate the concern, but I don't need cookies." And yet, I'll still devour this entire container before Mom leaves my apartment. Not because I need comfort food, but because my mom makes the best chocolate chip cookies ever. Hands down.

Mom pushes past me and makes her way into my living room.

"Why don't you come on in?" I follow her to the couch, where she's already rearranging pillows, making herself at home. Then she sits with her head tilted to one side and a pouty expression on her face. She looks up at me with sad eyes. "How are you doing with all of this, Megan?"

"I'm fine."

Her head shifts to the other side. "How are you *really* doing?"

Now she has me where she wants me. I drop onto the couch beside her and sigh. "I just don't get it. Braxton and Talia can't have been dating that long. How could they possibly be engaged?"

"Why does it matter? You're not jealous, are you?"

"Of course not! It's been two years. I'm more than over him. But it's still hard to see him moving on and getting engaged when I don't have someone of my own."

Mom pats my knee. "Just try to be happy for him. Personally, I'm glad he's marrying Talia and not you. You and Braxton never felt right to me. I was relieved when he broke up with you."

"Mother! I cried for weeks over him."

She holds up her hands. "I'm just being honest. You're better off without him."

Am I, though? What have I done in the last two years that's been the slightest bit noteworthy? There's no reason to say that my life is in any way *better* than it was when we were together.

Braxton and I grew up in the same neighborhood. Our dads worked together at the same hospital. And while I'd had a crush on him throughout middle school and high school, it had taken him a little longer to decide he liked me as more than a friend. It may have had something to do with how awkward I was in my adolescent years. I was a late bloomer.

We didn't actually date until right after college, when we'd reconnected at a mutual friend's graduation party. When he asked me out that night, I couldn't believe it. Braxton had asked *me* out. Me! I was twenty-two, had just started my first real job, and the guy I'd crushed on almost my entire life finally wanted to date me. It all felt too good to be true.

And apparently, it was. We dated for six months. During that time, I was mentally planning our wedding while Braxton was busy discovering that I was "too difficult to be with." He spent the last half of our relationship trying to figure out how to break things off without causing a rift between our families. I'd say he succeeded, given the fact that our dads still play golf together every Saturday.

At least someone got a happy ending out of the deal.

I cross one leg over the other and pull a cookie from the container. "I don't think this engagement will last," I say to my mom between bites. "Braxton is just wrapped up in the newness of this relationship because it's still exciting and passionate. That will wear off eventually, and then we can all go back to normal. Everyone will be single and happy."

Mom taps the screen of her phone, which is sitting on my coffee table, opened to the page with Braxton's announcement. "He has two-and-a-half months until his wedding. The newness had better hurry up and wear off, or it looks like you'll be the only single one left."

Two-and-a-half months? I didn't realize they'd set a date, but there it is on my mom's phone screen in small print below the picture: August 14.

I shake my head. "Why the big hurry?"

Mom shrugs. "Ten bucks says Talia's pregnant."

"Mom! Just because they've thrown together a quickie wedding doesn't mean anyone's pregnant." The woman could be so limited in her thinking. "Besides, Braxton isn't like that. He takes things slow. Like I do."

"Apparently not in this case." Mom gives my knee a squeeze. "It's natural to feel a little upset by this news. Braxton was your first love, after all. But he seems happy, so you should try to be happy for him."

"I'll try." But it would be a lot easier to do if I were happy too. Maybe I'll just have to fake it. I'll leave a really excited-sounding comment beneath his post, using three exclamation marks followed by a bunch of smiley-faced emojis wearing party hats. Then he'll assume the news of his engagement doesn't bother me at all.

"Your dad and I have always liked Braxton," Mom says, interrupting my happy post planning. "But I think you can do better. Braxton has long hair. It isn't right for a man to have long hair."

"Heaven forbid a man lets his hair grow a fraction of an

inch over the top of his ear."

"I should come along in the night and snip it off for him while he sleeps."

"You could get arrested for that."

She waves off my comment. "I think the judge would see it my way. It's in bad taste for a man to grow out his hair."

"Mom, you've got to stop letting little things bother you so much. You're too easily annoyed."

"Allow a woman her pet peeves."

"I'll allow you *some* pet peeves, but you're limited to five. Five pet peeves. Pick the most critical, and let the rest go."

"Let's not be ridiculous."

"I'm serious. You use pet peeves as a way to judge others who don't measure up to your standards without admitting that you're judging. You have to stop." Oh my. How many times has Nora said that exact thing to me? I shudder.

Mom concedes with a dramatic sigh. "Fine. But do yourself a favor and don't waste another minute thinking about Braxton. Find someone who makes you happy."

See, that's the problem. I've been trying and failing for two years to find happiness with someone, and so far all I have to show for it is a lot of wasted time.

Suddenly, a sick feeling hits my stomach. If Braxton, who has known me for years, couldn't love me for who I am, how will anyone else? If a guy were starting from scratch trying to figure me out, he'd be at a serious disadvantage. It would take time for him to fully understand me, and only then could he decide if he likes me or not. Am I worth the effort?

Or am I too hard to love?

three

IT'S WEDNESDAY AFTERNOON, and I'm lying on the couch with an ice pack on my head to thaw my brains. They are completely fried, and without them, I'm useless.

Work today was exhausting. I don't often say that after a shift at the library, but today is the exception. For a full two hours, the building was literally overtaken by a herd of crazed second graders from one of the local elementary schools. It's the last week of school in the district, and for some reason the teachers thought a field trip to the library would be a great way to keep the kids occupied. But everyone knows kids can't focus on anything during the last week of school, let alone stay quiet. Had no one thought of going to the park? Our city has loads of them.

Somehow I survived the intrusion without being trampled, but now all I want to do is lie here with my feet up on pillows and dream about a peaceful place. Like a lake on a foggy morning, or the library—on a normal day. *Ding.* My respite is cut short when my phone alerts me to an incoming text message. I extend my arm toward the coffee table, groping for my phone. I pick it up, even though I know better than to pick up my phone while resting. It's my mom.

You'll never guess what came in the mail for you today.

I haven't used my parents' address since college, so it can't be that important. Probably a credit card application. When I don't reply, Mom texts again.

It's an invitation to Braxton's wedding. I assume you'll want to go.

I jerk to a sitting position. The ice pack falls off my head and lands in my lap as I frantically stab my index finger against my phone screen, texting back.

What? Are you sure you read it right?

She wastes no time getting back to me.

Of course I did. I'm capable of reading a simple invitation.

I don't reply. Sending invitations means that Braxton is taking this wedding thing seriously. He means business. Now that he's gone and invited actual people to his wedding, it actually has to take place. And he invited me! And that means I have to go. No way can I decline. That would be like admitting defeat, like admitting that Braxton's wedding bothers me. I have to show him that I approve of it, that I *celebrate* it. That I'm happy he's found someone better than me to spend his life with because... because...I've found someone better than him to spend *my* life with.

Only that part is a little tricky because I have *not* found anyone better than him. But I will. I still have time. I have two-and-a-half months to find my perfect match, and I know someone who can help me with that right away.

Nora.

As if I'd said her name out loud, she appears in the hall outside her bedroom with a puzzled expression on her face and a brown plastic bottle in her hand. "Did you use the last of my Tahitian hair oil and not tell me?"

This is not the time to worry about such trivialities. "Not that I recall."

She waves the bottle in the air. "Well, someone did because it's empty. I can only buy this stuff at the beauty supply store downtown, and I don't have time to go back there before Milo and I go out to dinner tonight. I think we're dining outside on the patio at Metro Plate, and you know what this humidity does to my hair. I can't go out with frizzy hair."

My shoulders sag as I exhale. "All right, I think I might have some frizz-control spray you can use." I spin my legs around so that I'm facing her. I look her straight in the eyes and plead with her. "But before I get that, I need to ask a really big favor of you."

Her eyebrows hike up a notch. "What favor?"

I grit my teeth. This is a total blow to my ego. "Braxton and Talia have sent out wedding invitations, which means it's highly unlikely that this was all just a publicity stunt to gain more social media followers. He's actually getting married."

"I'd say that's probably a good assumption."

"He invited me to his wedding, so now I have to go, and I can't go alone. I need a date. I have to show Braxton that I'm not as difficult to love as he said I was, because obviously someone loves me."

"And who would that someone be?" Nora says.

I duck my head a little. "The person you find for me." I fold my hands prayer-style. "And it can't be just anyone, but someone who I can fall in love with and eventually marry so that Braxton isn't the only one who lives happily ever after."

Nora takes a long moment to absorb what I've said. I can tell she's mulling it over by the way her tongue traces her lower lip, followed by her top lip, and then the lower one again. She is giving this a full-lip-circle deliberation.

"Hmm."

"Hmm...what? What's *hmm* for?"

Now she's nodding. I know I'm in for something because she's really enjoying drawing this out. Finally she speaks. "I seem to remember making a promise—no, a vow—never to set you up with another man as long as I live. Are you asking me to go back on that vow? What kind of person would that make me?"

I lower my head in shame. "Go ahead and milk this. I can admit when I'm wrong."

"You can? So you're saying you'd rather *not* spend the rest of your life alone? And you're *not* perfectly content being single?"

What am I supposed to say to that? If the Lord intends for me to be single, I'll have to be content with that, won't I? But deep down, I know I don't want to spend the rest of my life alone. Not if there is actually someone out there for me. I take a deep, calming breath and let it out slowly. "I'm saying I may have been premature in asking you to cease the matchmaking efforts. Will that be enough? Or do I need to grovel as well?"

A sly smile spreads across Nora's face. "I would like to see some groveling."

"Fine. I am prepared to swallow my pride." I close my eyes for a moment and place a hand to my chest. In my most sincere voice, I say, "Nora, you were right. I put too much stock in first impressions, and I need to stop finding fault with every guy I meet. I have *some* faith in your taste in men, and I would be honored if you'd help me find one. Please."

"Okay!" She smacks her palms against her thighs in enthusiasm. "I know the perfect guy. His name is Garrett Atkinson. He's twenty-six, super good-looking, and he's a Christian."

My pulse kicks up a notch. "Keep talking."

"He's an accountant, and he recently started working at Milo's firm. He and Milo have really hit it off."

And just like that, my hope evaporates. "Another accountant?" Can the world handle that level of excitement? I know I can't. "Got anyone else up your sleeves?"

She frowns. "What's wrong with Garrett? You haven't even met him yet."

I toss my head back and groan. "But he's an accountant."

"So is Milo. What are you implying?"

"Nothing against Milo, I promise. He's perfect for you because he's your exact opposite. You're creative and free-spirited. You style hair for a living and you take huge fashion risks that actually work for you. But me? I'm a librarian. I like books. I wear long cardigans over leggings, and Birkenstocks with socks. The last thing I need is the male version of me. What kind of guy makes a career out of numbers and math?" I shake my head. "They say opposites attract, so I'd like to meet someone a little less bookish— maybe a white water rafting guide or a wildland firefighter. Do you know anyone like that?"

She clucks her tongue. "You asked for my help, and I'm helping you. You have to trust me."

"Fine. I'll go out with Garrett. But if he ends up being

the most boring man on the face of the earth, can I at least say I told you so?"

Nora waves a hand through the air. "Sure. But you won't need to because he's perfect for you." She does a little celebratory dance. "I'm so glad you decided not to give up on love. And thank you for letting me be a part of your journey. I know you won't regret it."

I regret it a little bit already. Dating is scary. It's so much easier to stay at home and not risk rejection and humiliation. But now Braxton is engaged, and I'm determined to show up at his wedding with a man on my arm and a smile on my face—a real smile, inspired by genuine feelings of love. No fake boyfriend schemes for this girl. I want the real deal, and I have two-and-a-half months to find it.

Even if it means being fixed up with an accountant.

That night, I sit on my bed with my Bible opened to Proverbs like I do every night. I hope that by reading these thirty-one chapters over and over again, some of the wisdom on the pages will soak in and I'll be transformed into someone more like Jesus.

Thanks to Braxton, I know how and where I fall short of being Christlike. He kindly listed my not-so-attractive qualities in one long diatribe when he broke up with me. He said I'm self-focused, too easily annoyed, I complain too much, and I don't filter my thoughts before speaking them aloud.

I've been working on those things ever since. I've studied the book of James several times, pored over the pages of Ecclesiastes, and practically memorized Proverbs

31. But after reading how "wise" people talk, how they behave and treat others, I realize I still have a long way to go.

When I finish the chapter, I close my Bible and pray for God's help. I ask him to grant me humility and compassion. I pray, like always, that I will learn to consider others better than myself. It's a daily struggle and sometimes, at the end of the day, I feel like an utter failure.

But tomorrow will be a new day. Hopefully God will extend me the grace to get through it without royally screwing up.

Nora has been acting as the liaison between me and Garrett for a week and a half. They've texted back and forth, coordinating schedules and choosing venues, as if she's the one going on the date instead of me. It's annoying, and at the same time relieving. I don't know what a guy like him and a girl like me would possibly have to talk about, so I'm glad Nora's handling all of the pre-date communication. I wouldn't want to run out of conversation topics before we even meet.

But now that the big night has arrived, it's up to me to make it a success. I won't have Nora to lean on, and I don't exactly have a stellar track record when it comes to first dates. I'm seriously tempted to back out. As I'm sitting on a stool in our shared bathroom, I tell Nora just that.

"Meg, you have to go. I have it all arranged." Nora stands behind me, brushing my auburn locks until I'm pretty sure a third of my hair is now attached to the brush instead of my scalp. She gathers the shoulder-length strands into her clenched fist and reaches for a hair band to hold it all together.

I wince. "Do you have to pull it so tight?"

"You want it to look nice, don't you?"

"I'm not sure it matters. You're the one who's so excited about this guy. Why don't you go? It's your favorite restaurant, right?"

She gives my hair a hard yank. *Ouch!*

"You said you wanted my help finding you a man."

I rub my scalp. "I said I wanted to meet the *right* man."

"And I think he is the right man."

We are getting nowhere. We've had this same conversation-slash-argument every day for a week. It's time for me to go out with Garrett, probably have a terrible time, prove to Nora that accountants and librarians do not mix, and then move on to someone better suited for me.

Nora spins me around in my stool in front of the bathroom mirror and examines my face. "You look beautiful. He won't be able to take his eyes off of you."

"So you think he's going to stare at me? What if that makes me uncomfortable?"

Her shoulders fall. "We're done here. Have fun. Or don't. Just please give the guy a chance, okay?"

I turn back to face the mirror. My makeup does look good. Nora has a way of applying eyeliner that makes it look so natural. A trick of the trade, I suppose. I smile at my reflection, then look beyond myself to connect with Nora's gaze. "I'll give him several chances because I know that will make you happy."

"Thank you. Try to have a good time. Milo and I are going to dinner and a movie, but I'll have my phone with me. Call me if anything comes up."

"I will." I take a deep, cleansing breath, then let it out

slowly, watching my reflection as my chest falls with the release of air. I can do this. I will rock this date. Garrett doesn't sound like my ideal guy, but at least going on this date will be good practice for the next one. And who knows, maybe I'll be pleasantly surprised. Maybe Garrett will turn out to be my Mr. Right.

four

GARRETT and I plan to meet at the restaurant at six. It's downtown and parking is limited, but I'm lucky to find a spot along the street outside the building. After I parallel park, I check my makeup in my visor mirror, then get out and shut the door. There's a tall man standing at the right of the restaurant's big glass double doors. He looks about my age, with wavy brown hair and a tiny hint of an afternoon shadow coloring his jaw. He's wearing nice jeans and a light blue button-up shirt, untucked, and he has oxford slip-on shoes—perfect for early June in Minnesota. If this is what accountants look like these days, then I've seriously misjudged them.

Well done, Nora.

When I approach, he pushes away from the brick wall and takes a hesitant step toward me. "Meg?" He rubs his hands on his pants.

My tension eases a bit seeing his uncertainty, and I look up and offer him my most friendly smile. "Yes, I'm Meg. You must be Garrett."

He nods. "It's nice to meet you."

"You too." I hold out my hand.

He gives a nervous laugh and then takes my hand—well, not actually my whole hand, just my three longest fingers—and shakes gently, as if he's a French maid waving around a feather duster just for show. I want to shout, "Put some effort into it, man. My grandma can squeeze my hand tighter than you!"

But I refrain, which takes an enormous amount of effort because one of my biggest pet peeves is weak handshakes. I expect a man to shake like a man, even if he's shaking a woman's hand. I'm not afraid of a little strength, a little muscle. In fact, I welcome those things.

I welcome them so much that I refuse to accept his offering and non-verbally challenge him to a re-shake. Before he can let go of my fingers, I latch on to his whole hand, like a shark clamping its jaws down on a surfboard. I take it all in. I squeeze his palm with my fingers and jerk his arm up and down in a handshake that would make my war-veteran grandfather proud. I can just hear him say, "Now that's what I call a handshake."

But from the look on Garrett's face, that's not what he would call it.

I release my death grip on his palm and gesture toward the door. "So, should we go inside?"

"Uh...I guess?"

As we walk into the fifties-diner-style restaurant, Garrett is side-eyeing me like he's afraid I'll suddenly sprout claws and pounce on him like a lioness and shred him to pieces. It's pretty clear we're not going to get over the awkwardness I caused with my non-ladylike show of strength. Now what am I supposed to do? I promised Nora I would give Garrett a chance, but he looks like he's about to bolt. If only I could rewind time and behave a little more gently.

The hostess greets us at her podium and leads us to a small booth for two in the middle of the dining area. Garrett sits, but I hesitate. I've made things weird already and need Nora's help if I'm going to salvage this date. I excuse myself, making up some story about needing to use the "little girls' room." Hopefully Garrett finds that cute and innocent, because I really need to crank up the femininity factor.

I slip into the hallway, pull out my phone, and dial Nora's number, praying she picks up. When she does, I sigh in relief. "Oh, Nora, thank goodness."

"Meg? Why are you calling me? Didn't Garrett show up?"

"He did. But the date is already ruined, and it hasn't even started."

"Whoa, calm down. What did you do?"

"Why do you assume I did anything? Well, maybe I did, but it's not my fault. He has a weak handshake."

There is a long pause, and then I hear Nora's loud exhale like a strong wind blowing through my phone's tiny speaker. "I'm gonna go out on a limb and say that's a bad thing."

"It's a terrible thing! Garrett's over six feet and looks like he weighs at least one-ninety, yet he took my hand and gave me a dainty, limp handshake. I was like, 'No way does a man shake my hand like that.' So right when he was about to release, I went in for a second squeeze."

"You what?"

"I squeezed his hand again after the initial squeeze. I resqueezed. It was so awkward, Nora. He probably thought I wasn't ready to let go, like I wanted to touch him some more." I cover my face with my free hand. "I want a do-over."

Nora chuckles. "I think that's what you just did."

"I'm not talking about a do-over handshake. I want a do-over date. I need to reschedule. Help me come up with an excuse to get out of here. Call me in five minutes and say you're my mom and you need an appendectomy. Then maybe Garrett and I can try again next weekend."

"No. No more do-overs for you. You can fix this. Just go back out there and pretend like nothing happened. Don't worry, he probably didn't even notice."

"Oh, he noticed."

"Maybe so, but once you move past this awkward moment, I'm sure things will go fine. Just get back to him. If you're gone too long, he'll suspect something's wrong."

I exhale a puff of air. "All right. I'll do everything I can to act normal. Thanks, Nora. I won't call you again."

I end the call, slide my phone into my purse, and make a beeline for our table. When I sit down, I'm all smiles. "Sorry about that. It was Nora."

"Nora? I thought you had to use the restroom."

"What? Oh, right. She called me while I was in there."

He smiles. "I see. I suppose she wants to see how things are going. She's not the only one. My brother has been blowing up my phone since you left."

I blink. I cough. "What? You didn't just say that."

"Say what?"

"That your brother was *blowing up* your phone." I use air quotes. I can't help it.

He stares at me with a blank expression.

"Sorry, I just hate that phrase." I also hate air quotes. "It's one of my pet peeves." And so are air quotes.

And just like that, I've become my mother. *Somebody*

shoot me now. I reach for the glass of water the hostess must have set on the table while I was pretending to use the restroom and take a long, slow sip. I need something to do with my mouth other than speak, since that clearly isn't working so well for me. When I allow my eyes to look up past the rim of the glass, I catch sight of Garrett staring at me beneath a furrowed brow. It's been that way for a while now. I set the glass down, swallow the cold water, and smile at him. "So, how do you think things are going?"

"Excuse me?"

"Tonight. On our date. How do you think things are going so far?"

He sits back and crosses his arms. "I can't really say how it's going. You just got back from the bathroom. It's only been five minutes."

"Oh. That's true." I drum my fingers on the tabletop. "So, let's see...what do you plan on ordering? I hear this place is known for their burgers. At least that's what Nora tells me. She and Milo come here a lot. They have all kinds of creative topping combinations, all named for Minnesota celebrities and fictional characters." I flip the page in the plastic-coated menu and peruse the burger options. "Oh, the Babe the Bleu Cheese Ox Burger sounds yummy."

He grimaces. "It's not made from actual ox meat, is it?"

"An ox is just a steer that's been trained to work. It's all beef." I love it when I have the opportunity to spew random knowledge at people. It's one of the things I look forward to about getting my master's degree someday and becoming a reference librarian—helping other people find ways to acquire knowledge about a vast array of topics. If Garrett were interested, I'd explain to him the history of oxtail soup. But given the look on his face, I don't think he wants to know.

Garrett taps his index finger against the table while he stares down at the menu. "I imagine oxen meat would be tough. Chewy." The face he makes when he says the word *chewy* is almost comical. Like it would be an imposition for him to use his jaws for anything strenuous.

What are jaws for, if not for chewing? Those bulging muscles on the side of his face aren't merely ornamental. Except on Garrett, they are rather decorative. I can't help staring at his jawline, which is angular and strong. I have to admit, I like the look of it—of his whole face actually. If I were to grade him, which I often do on first dates, I'd give him two bonus points for having a nice face.

Wait, what am I doing? *Focus, Meg!* I shake my head, breaking my trance and refocusing on the issue at hand— the ox burger. "I'm sure it's just a name. The actual meat is probably regular ground chuck. From a regular cow."

"I really don't think I want a burger."

"What if the burger was made of moose meat? Or elk? Would you eat it then?"

"If I knew about it ahead of time, sure. I'm not opposed to eating wild game."

"Do you hunt?"

"No."

"Why not? This is Minnesota."

He scoffs. "Not everyone in Minnesota hunts."

"Everyone in my family does."

"Well, I'm not a member of your family, am I? In my family, there aren't any hunters that I know of."

"Do you think it's wrong?"

"No, I just didn't grow up hunting." He clamps his lips tight. And with that, the conversation is closed. He stares at his menu a moment longer before setting it down. "I think I'll just go with the sirloin steak."

"That's made of beef too."

Ooh, that did it. I thought his jaw muscles were bulging before, but now I'm seeing them in all their glory.

"I never said I didn't eat beef." He speaks through gritted teeth. "I also never said I wanted a burger. You're the one who brought up burgers in the first place." His cheeks flame red.

So he has a temper—one which I seem skilled at igniting. I'll have to tread lightly from here on out if I want this date to last longer than my last one.

five

AFTER TWENTY MINUTES of strained conversation, the waitress brings our dinner. My bleu cheese ox burger looks amazing. It turns out it's just made from regular old beef. I only ordered it because after talking about it for so long, I couldn't think of eating anything else.

Garrett finishes most of his grilled chicken, but leaves a generous cut of what he calls "fat" on the edge of his plate. Apparently our pre-dinner conversation had turned him off from beef in any form. I probably should've kept my mouth shut, but sometimes my thoughts have a way of pushing themselves out of my mouth, no matter how hard I try to hold them in.

When the waitress stops by our table, she notices that our plates are mostly empty. "Are you two ready for dessert?"

"No!"

It's not clear who shouted *No* first, but I'm pretty sure he shouted loudest. I look at him, shock and embarrassment burning my cheeks, and he stares back at me. Am I really that hard to be around?

"Oh-kay," the waitress says. She places a slip of paper facedown on the table. "You can bring that to the register when you're ready."

"Thank you." I smile at her and watch her walk away. As Garrett and I sit in silence, discomfort expands in my chest. Clearly he doesn't want to spend any more time with me, and I'm not exactly ready to agree to a second date with him. This one has been enough.

"Maybe we should just call it a night," he says, picking up the bill.

"For sure. Not that I didn't have a good time, because I did." So I lie a little, just to be polite.

"Yeah, we should do it again sometime." His eyes grow wide, and he shakes his head with lightning speed. "Wait, I mean...that was just a reflex response. We probably shouldn't do it again, no offense."

"None taken." I shrug it off. I'm the picture of nonchalance. "Not every blind date is a winner." *Reminder to self: Tell Nora, "I told you so."*

I make sure I'm the first to stand up, and he quickly follows. Like a gentleman, he pays for the meal even though I offered to split the bill with him. And like the considerate person I am, I wait for him by the door until the transaction is finished. On the way out to our vehicles, we both agree on one thing—that if our friends think we'd be good together, they don't know us as well as they think they do. So that's something we have in common. Probably the only thing.

Garrett's truck is parked in front of my car. He pulls his keys from his pocket and climbs up and into his vehicle. Before he closes the door, he says, "So, um, have a good evening."

"I will. You too." I barely spare him a glance. I'm too

busy trying not to get clipped by a passing car while digging through my purse, searching for my green beaded snake chain that's supposed to make my keys easier to find. I pull out my wallet, lip gloss, and hand sanitizer and hold them in the crook of my arm while peering into the dark, empty depths of my purse. Nothing. Then I glance through my driver's side window into my car, and...oh. There they are. Right in the cup holder where I set them while doing a last-minute makeup check in the mirror. Back when I still had a sliver of hope that this date might be something other than the disaster it turned out to be.

I'm beginning to miss the ignorant state of bliss I was in moments ago when forced awkward conversation and having nothing in common were the worst things I could say about this evening.

I feel like an idiot standing outside my car while traffic whizzes past me, so I pray that Garrett will hurry up and drive away. Then I can call Nora and ask her to come and pick me up. I have an extra car key in our apartment. But I can't get into our apartment without Nora because my apartment key is on my keychain. Which is locked inside my car.

My heart thuds. I need to calm down. I casually glance at Garrett's truck, and I can see in the reflection of his side mirror that he's watching me. *Look away! Shoo! Nothing to see here.*

Then his door opens, and he steps out. "Anything wrong?"

"No, I'm good. Everything's fine."

He ambles toward my vehicle. "Seems like you might be having some car trouble."

"Not really. I'm sure my car will run just fine...once I get inside and get my keys."

"You locked your keys in your car? Is that even possible these days? My truck unlocks when it senses my thumb on the handle."

"Wow. Thanks for that super interesting story." I fake smile at him. "My car isn't as fancy as yours. And, I didn't lock it, okay? It locked itself. I left my keys in the center console, forgot about them, and then when I walked away, it must've locked. The security system has been acting up for a while."

He grimaces. "Man, if my truck did that, I would make sure I always had my keys with me before walking away."

"Well, you're obviously smarter than I am."

He folds his arms across his chest and leans against my car's hood. "Why haven't you taken your car in to get fixed?"

I can't help exhaling loudly. I want him to hear my annoyance. Does he think I'm dumb and haven't thought of all these things already? "I just haven't had the time. If I ever get into my car again, I will take it in first thing Monday morning. I've been wondering what to do with that extra thousand dollars I had lying around, and now I know."

"Are you mocking me?"

"Maybe. Are you trying to annoy me, or is this the way you are all the time?"

He sighs. "Here, maybe I can get it to open." He steps toward my door and jiggles the handle several times. Then he moves on to the back door. Unsuccessful, he drops his hands to his sides. "You're right, it's locked."

I press my hand against my forehead. I can't deal with this for one more second. "Thanks for trying, but I'll be fine. Nora can pick me up. I have a spare key at home."

"I'll wait with you until she comes." He gestures toward

a black metal bench a few yards away. "We could sit there or go back inside the restaurant."

Back inside? And extend the most uncomfortable date I've ever had? *Please, Lord, help me. Let this evening end while I still have some dignity left!* I smile, hoping that the horror I feel inside isn't splattered all over my face. "I'll be okay. I appreciate the offer though."

He places his hand on my shoulder and semi-pushes me toward the sidewalk. "Let's at least get out of the road where it's safer."

"Sure." I can do that. My frayed nerves can't handle being so close to oncoming traffic much longer.

I dial Nora's number while Garrett stands beside me on the sidewalk. Three rings later, the call goes to voicemail.

"No answer?" Garrett asks.

"I think she and Milo are at the movies. I'll have to wait until they're done."

"Another two hours? No way. I'll just give you a ride to your apartment."

"No!"

He frowns.

"I mean, no thank you. You don't have to do that."

"Look, I know we didn't exactly hit it off, but I hope you don't think I'm the kind of guy who would leave a woman stranded alone outside."

"I really don't know what kind of guy you are. You didn't give me a whole lot to go on during dinner other than the fact that you don't hunt and you're repulsed by oxen. But if you're worried about me, I'll go back inside and wait. I'll grab a cup of coffee, drink it really slowly, and you can leave with a clear conscience."

His lips twist to one side, then the other. "I don't feel right about that. Just get in my truck. I'll drive you home."

"I appreciate the offer, but my apartment key is on my key ring. I need Nora and her key to get into my apartment."

"Do you have a landlord? Would he have a spare key?"

"Yes, *she* would, if she were home, which she almost never is." But my landlady does live just downstairs from me, so if she is home, it would sure make life easier. "I guess it would be worth a try."

"Great. Hop in."

Just when I thought this date couldn't get any worse.

Other than my directions, we make the drive in silence. When Garrett turns onto my street, I point out the window. "There it is, on the corner. It's the brown, seventies-style fourplex."

"Sounds good." He pulls to a stop, and I yank on the handle, ready to jump the second the wheels stop rolling. Before he even shifts into park, my feet swing out, hit the pavement, and I take off running. I jump over the curb and land in the grass of my front yard.

Freedom!

"Do you want me to come with you, or should I wait here?"

An invisible rope loops around my torso and cinches tight, lassoing me like a steer at a rodeo, stopping me mid-stride. It appears Garrett and I will be stuck together until I can get inside. Otherwise, his overactive sense of manly duty won't allow him to leave. I turn around and try to wave him off. "Really, it's fine. I'm sure she's home. Even if she's not, I'll just wait in the hall and read or catch up on emails." Until my phone battery dies, which will be in about ten minutes. But he doesn't need to know that.

"Let me know if she's there or not."

I feel like I'm with my dad. That's a surefire way to squelch any romantic notions that may have entered my mind. Not that any have.

My landlady, Betsie, lives on the first floor, right under my apartment. She's in her sixties, divorced, and has an elderly mother in town. She's often at her mother's house taking care of things like laundry and paying the bills. But I pray that tonight will be one of those rare Friday nights she's actually home. I knock on her door, then wait. No answer. I knock again, but deep down I know it's a waste of time. I don't hear the sound of footsteps coming from beyond the door. There's no rummaging, no talking, no TV noise—nothing that would indicate someone's inside her apartment. I figured as much when I didn't see her car outside.

With a sigh, I leave the building and head back toward Garrett's truck.

"No luck?"

I shake my head. "Nope. But like I said, you can go."

I follow his gaze as he examines my building. His eyes narrow as he points to a second-story window on the right-hand side. "There's an open window on the second floor," he says. "Is it one of yours?"

"Actually, yes," I say. "That's my bedroom. It gets hot if I leave it closed. And it's not like anyone can break in, since it's on the second floor."

"They could if they had a ladder." He looks at me, and the sparkle in his eyes makes me uneasy. "Do you have a ladder? I could climb up and get into your apartment through your bedroom, then we could get your spare key."

It's not the worst idea, but I don't know where I'd find a ladder. I don't own one.

Again he points, this time to something behind my building. "Is that a storage shed?"

I crane my neck to follow the line of his finger. "I think so, but I've never been inside. I'm not sure if I'm allowed."

"Isn't it on the same property as your apartment building?"

I shrug. "It appears to be, and it has the same siding."

"Huh." He walks toward the storage shed, talking to me over his shoulder. "You should look over your rental agreement. You could be paying a monthly fee to store things in this building, and you're not even utilizing it."

I follow him. "I-I don't need to store anything." Can't he please walk slower? I have much shorter legs than he does.

"Maybe there's a ladder in there." He keeps walking, and I keep running and trying to breathe.

"Wait a sec." I wave at him to stop, but he can't see me. "I don't really know if we should be breaking into a building we don't know anything about."

"I'm just looking for a ladder. No one will care." He stops in front of the door on the side of the small shed and tries the knob. It turns in his hand, and the door opens. "Nice. Now let's see what we can find in here."

Spiders, mice, bats...and probably a dozen other reasons why this is a terrible idea.

six

I STAY OUTSIDE while Garrett rummages around in the dark building. After a minute or two, I hear him call, "Perfect!" And then a second later he comes out, dragging a tall but rather rickety wooden ladder behind him.

My internal danger detector starts going off like crazy. "I, uh, don't think that looks up to code."

He scoffs. "I only need to climb one story. You can hold the ladder if you don't think it's safe." When he reaches the side of my building, he hefts the ladder to a vertical position and then eases the top of it to rest against the siding beneath my window.

He steps on the bottom rung, and I run to the ladder to help stabilize it. Not that I can do much, but it eases my mind the tiniest bit to have ahold of it. I watch with jaw clenched as he climbs one rung, then another. It really is nice that he's doing this, but I can't seem to shake the feeling that it's a big mistake.

My heart beats a little faster as he nears the top. When his hand reaches out to my window, I hear a sickening crack, then a loud, masculine bellow. I jump back and

41

scramble to process what happened. The third-to-the-top rung has cracked in half, and Garrett's foot has slipped to the rung below, causing him to lose his balance. He grasps both sides of the ladder for support, but since I've let go, it's no longer stable.

I freeze in horror as Garrett's shifting weight causes the ladder to slide to the left, scraping against the aluminum siding until it hits the building's corner trim piece. It stops abruptly, but the momentum causes Garrett—now only holding on with one hand—to swing out, away from the building, until he does a complete one-eighty.

"Hang on!" I yell.

Only he can't, because there's nothing secure to hang on to. Garrett lets go, attempting to jump to safety. He lands with a grunt.

I run over to him to check for any injuries. He pulls his knee up to his chest and grips his left ankle, wincing in pain.

"Are you okay?" Dumb question, but it's all I can think to say.

He speaks through clenched teeth. "My ankle."

I reach for it, but he bats my hand away. "Sorry," I say. "Is it broken?"

"Hopefully not."

"What can I do?"

He leans over to glance at his truck, and then looks up at me. "Do you think you can help me get to my truck?"

If he wants me to carry him, the answer is going to be a solid *no*.

"Just grab my hands and pull, and I'll try to stand."

With both of his hands in mine, I lean back to counter his weight and pull as he raises himself to a standing position on his right foot. He tries to put weight on his injured

42

ankle, but lifts his foot instantly. The look on his face tells me that's too painful.

He lets go of me and runs a hand down his face. "I'm going to have to lean on you for support while I hop to my truck. Do you think you can handle that?"

Can I handle that? I'm not sure. I work out twice a week, but I'm no heavyweight. "I can try." I run around to his left side and wrap my right arm around his waist—his trim, muscled waist—while he rests his left arm on my shoulder.

He inhales, and I feel the rise of his chest. "Okay, here we go." He takes one hop-step, and I nearly buckle under the weight.

"Oh, boy. I'm so sorry," I say, looking up at him. "I wasn't ready."

He clenches his jaw, and I'm pretty sure he growls a little when he looks down at me. "Are you ready now?"

I nod. "I think so."

Slowly and painfully—for both of us—we stumble our way to his truck. I get him situated by the driver's side door while I open it, and I hold out my hand, ready to help him in.

He looks down at the floorboard and groans. "I don't suppose you can drive a stick, can you?" He scratches his head. "I won't be able to press the clutch with my left foot."

Of course I can drive a stick. Does he think I'm inept? "No problem."

"Great. Thanks."

Like contestants in a three-legged race, we make our way to the other side of the truck. Getting him into the passenger seat is not the easiest feat, but with the aid of the handle above the door, he's able to heft himself up and in without much heavy lifting from me. I blow out a long breath.

I run back to the driver's side door and hop in. "All right. Where to? Do you want me to head to the ER?"

"No. I'm sure it's just a sprain."

"But how can you know without an X-ray? That was quite a fall. I think we should go to the ER just to be safe."

He shakes his head, exhaling. "I'm fine. I've had sprains before, and I've heard they hurt worse than breaks do. If it doesn't get better in a week, I'll get an X-ray."

That doesn't sound wise to me. Of course I've never sprained or broken anything, so what do I know? One thing I know for sure is that men are stubborn when it comes to going to the doctor, and I'm practically a stranger to Garrett. I'll never be able to convince him to do something he doesn't want to do. "Fine. I'll take you home, then. Where do you live?"

"I'm staying at the Pinewood Inn and Suites in New Brighton."

"You live in a hotel?"

His nostrils flare, and I can almost feel the tension in the truck cab rising.

"Right." I face forward. "No more questions. I'll take you there." I realize he is in a lot of pain, so I try my best to be patient with him. When he hands me his truck key, I insert it without a word and start the engine. Or I try to. Only nothing happens. I look over at him.

Garrett narrows his eyes at me. "You said you know how to operate a truck with a manual transmission."

"I do."

"Then why aren't you pressing down the clutch?"

Oh. Right. "I forgot that part. Sorry." With both brake and clutch pedals pressed, I start the engine, which roars to life. "Here we go." I cover the shifter with my palm and move it to the left and up into first gear. Then I release the brake, press down on the accelerator, and release the clutch. The truck immediately stalls, then slams to a halt. Our bodies lurch forward, then our seatbelts send us crashing back into our seats.

"What in the world are you doing?" Garrett's face is red. His hand grips the door handle.

I bite my lip. "It stalled."

"Yes, I know. You don't know how to drive this, do you?"

I throw my hands in the air. "Of course I do. My dad only drives cars with a stick shift." My mom, on the other hand, only drives automatics, and so do I. But I've watched my dad shift gears hundreds of times throughout my lifetime, so technically I *know* how it's done. I've just never done it myself. Turns out, it's harder than it looks.

"Have you driven a manual—yes or no?"

"Um...technically, no."

He huffs and throws his head back against the headrest. "You're going to destroy my truck."

I shrug. "We could just sit here and wait until Nora calls back."

"I need to get some ice on this." He shakes his head, slumping his shoulders as if defeated. "I'll just talk you through the steps."

I can't help smiling. "Great. This will be fun."

Garrett clenches his fists in his lap.

Clearly, he does not agree.

I only grind the gears seven or eight times on the way to the interstate. Then it's smooth sailing because I get to stay in fifth gear the whole time. I'm getting pretty good at the whole shifting thing. I only had trouble with a few stop signs in my neighborhood. All that stop-and-go was a bit tricky. And then there was the on-ramp to the interstate. While I was accelerating, I stayed in second gear for way too long according to Garrett. He yelled something at me about redlining and five thousand RPMs, but I was too busy looking for semitrucks in my side mirror to listen. I can only focus on so many things at once.

When I finally pull into the hotel parking lot, I look for a spot close to the entrance. I bring the truck to a stop, shift into neutral, then turn off the engine. When we start rolling backward, Garrett reminds me that I need to park the truck in gear. I do remember my dad mentioning that, come to think of it. I shift into first, and his truck lurches to a halt.

"Press on the brake! Don't just shift into first and let go of the clutch while you're moving!" Garrett's chest heaves and beads of sweat dot his forehead.

I turn to him to offer him comfort. "At least we're here, safe and sound."

His lower jaw juts forward and his eyes narrow. He sits there, glaring at me. I stare back at him. We stay like that for at least thirty seconds until finally he exhales and shakes his head. "Help me get inside."

I smile to myself, proud to have won that little staring contest. I would pump my fist, but I don't want to rub it in. He's already in a mood.

With Garrett using my shoulder for balance again, we make our way from the truck to the hotel entrance and through the sliding glass doors. I help him into the elevator, where he instructs me to push the button for the third floor. *Thank you, God, for elevators.* I try to imagine helping him up three flights of stairs. The picture in my mind is not pretty.

When we finally arrive at his suite, he uses his key card

46

to open the door, which leads to a decent-sized living room. He points to the couch, and I guide him toward it. Together, we sort of fall onto the cushions. I have no choice but to go down with him, since his arm is holding me prisoner.

He unwraps himself from me and lifts his leg up onto the coffee table, wincing with every move.

I angle to face him. "Can I get you some ice? Pain meds? Do you need a brace?"

"Yes, ice. There's a bucket in the kitchen. Take it down to the end of the hall. There's an icemaker there." He hands me his key card.

"Gotcha." I hurry in the direction of the kitchen, grab the bucket, then head down the hall to fill it. When I return, I spread out a dish towel, pour ice into it and twist it into a makeshift ice pack. "Here you go." I place the bundle over his elevated ankle.

"Thanks," he says. "Now, can you go into the bathroom and open the little cupboard next to the sink? There should be a bottle of ibuprofen in there. Get me two tablets. No, three."

"Uh...sure." I make my way to the bathroom, flip on the light, and pull open the small cabinet door. Inside I find his razor and shaving cream, some *Icy Hot*, and a tube of antibiotic ointment. I push aside a bottle of hair gel, a thermometer, and a roll of athletic tape, but where is the ibuprofen? I stand back and scan the two shelves. Oh, there it is, behind his deodorant.

Looking at Garrett's personal belongings feels wrong. We barely know each other. I would never, on a first date, be looking in some guy's medicine cabinet. Medicine cabinets are like one-month anniversary territory—at the earliest. But I have to admit I'm relieved not to find anything

47

questionable in here. No red flags. Nothing to send me running as far away from him as possible.

I grab the little white bottle and take it to Garrett. I pop open the lid and pour some pills out in my hand. "You said you wanted three?"

He nods.

"Are you sure?" I turn the bottle over and read the tiny print on the label. "It says to take no more than two pills every four hours."

"I said three." He grinds out the words.

"Okay, it's your body." I select three pills and set them in his open palm. He raises his hand to his mouth, then stops. "I need water. Could you get me a bottle?"

"Of course." I run back to the kitchen, pull hard on the stainless steel refrigerator door, and peer inside. Top shelf, middle shelf, side door. "No water bottles. You must be out."

"I have a twelve-pack in the bedroom. But never mind, they'll be warm. Just use the tap water."

Interesting. Warm water isn't good enough for him. And apparently tap water is only acceptable in emergencies. Just like I thought. Picky.

I find two drinking glasses turned upside down on paper coasters beside the sink. His suite must've been recently serviced by housekeeping—which reminds me, why does he live in a hotel? I'll have to ask later. First, he needs water.

I return to the couch with a half-filled glass and hand it to him. He swallows all three pills in one big gulp, sets the glass down on the coffee table, and leans his head way back until he has a very clear view of the ceiling. Then he releases a huge sigh.

"All better?" I ask.

"No, but thanks for your help."

"My pleasure." Calling it a *pleasure* is a bit of a stretch. It's more like an aerobic workout. I can probably skip the gym this week after all this sprinting back and forth.

I sit on the far end of the couch and pull out my phone. "I'll text Nora and let her know where I am so she can come and get me."

He says nothing in response. I glance at him and notice that his eyes are shut. Right. He's in pain, and he's probably not interested in my plans. So I'll just keep them to myself.

I swipe my screen and punch out a text to Nora.

I'm sending you my location. I'll explain later. Please pick me up ASAP!

seven

I'VE BEEN in Garrett's hotel suite for two hours, and I still haven't gotten a reply from Nora. It's ten thirty. If she and Milo went to the seven o'clock, or even the seven-thirty movie, it's long over by now. Where is she?

The pain meds I gave Garrett must've kicked in because he fell asleep. While he's been sleeping, I've tried passing the time by staring up at the ceiling fan or out the window at the parking lot lights. I don't dare use my phone since I have to save what little battery I have left. I can't even borrow a cord from Garrett because his phone is two models newer than mine, and our charging ports aren't compatible. Of course. Because why would they be? Something actually working out would go against the motif of the evening, which appears to be *complete and utter failure.*

So here I sit. Every once in a while my gaze wanders over to Garrett's sleeping form, and I start comparing him to all of my other blind date failures. He and I earn a combined score of zero in the compatibility category, but not surprisingly, he comes in first place in physical attractiveness. I hate to admit it, but he's even better looking than Nate, the hunk from Nora's gym.

I have to give Nora some credit for her selection this time. Although Garrett's personality doesn't mesh with mine, he's easy on the eyes. While he softly snores, I make a mental list of which of his features are my favorites, only because it helps pass the time.

I already noted his jawline is perfection, but I also decide that his lips are the ideal size. Not so full that they're nicer than mine, but not too thin either. And he does *not* have rug hair like Jason from the bank. He has mid-length, wavy brown hair that looks soft enough to touch—not that I would, or even want to. He's tall, well-built, and has a smooth, somewhat deep voice that sounds *nothing* like a frog. So I conclude that as long as he's not in extreme pain, not eating beef, and not shaking my hand, he's pretty much the perfect man.

As impressive a specimen as Garrett is, I eventually get bored watching him sleep. I clear my throat several times, each time a little louder than the previous time, until he wakes up. His head jerks forward, then he looks at me, eyes wide with shock. After a bit, his facial muscles relax, and his expression morphs into one that says *You're still here?*

"What time is it?" he asks. But before I can answer, he swipes his phone off the couch, taps it, and then groans. He must've thought it was earlier than it is. He hits the screen a few more times, and then starts typing. Whatever the message, it seems urgent.

For a while I think he's forgotten I'm here. Or maybe he's just pretending I'm invisible. He snatches the remote from the coffee table and flips through the channels on his TV. When he settles on an episode of *Deadliest Creatures of the Amazon*, I decide I have two choices: either die of boredom or try to start up a conversation. It's awkward enough that I'm still here when he clearly wanted to be rid of me back at the restaurant. But sitting in silence and watching large reptiles bite each other only makes it worse. I press my lips together and try to think of an icebreaker.

"So what's your biggest fear?" I blurt.

That gets his attention. He turns toward me, eyebrows raised. "Excuse me?"

"What's your biggest fear? I know it isn't heights, because you didn't hesitate at all before climbing up to my bedroom window. But it could be oxen. Maybe that's why you're so hesitant to eat one."

"I'm not afraid of oxen."

"Interesting." I place my index finger to my chin. "If I were you, my biggest fear would be rickety wooden ladders."

He scoffs, shakes his head, and rests it once again against the back of the couch. Only this time, he's facing me and not the ceiling. "Why are you asking me such a personal question?"

I fold my arms and lean back, mirroring his posture. "Well, I am stuck here for the foreseeable future, and I just thought it'd be nice to talk rather than watching meaningless TV."

He nods—or at least tries to, with half his face rubbing against the cushions. "Sorry. Meaningless TV is about all my brain can handle right now. It helps to distract me from my throbbing ankle. But you're probably pretty bored."

I sit up. "Is your painkiller wearing off? It hasn't been four hours or I'd get you more."

His lips turn up in a lazy smile. "It's okay. If you want to talk, we can. But maybe ask an easier question this time? I'm not really a night person."

"Noted." I hum an exhale and try to think of a better question. "I've got one. Tell me about the worst date you've ever been on."

His brow arches. "Do you really want me to answer that one?"

"Why not?" Then realization hits me. "Oh. Right. I think I can answer that one myself."

"It's nothing against you personally," he says, "but the circumstances as a whole. You have to admit, tonight was pretty bad."

I can't help but laugh. "Yeah, I guess it was. You really tried my patience at dinner."

"Me? How so?"

"I could make a list, but if I had to choose one reason, I'd say you were being a mite picky."

He clucks his tongue against the roof of his mouth. "You wouldn't give me a chance to decide what I wanted before insisting that I try a burger named after a fairy-tale ox. I was two seconds from telling you to take a chill pill."

My jaw drops. "A *chill pill?* Are you secretly a nineties teenage girl? If you'd said that to me, I would've left."

"Then maybe I should've said it and saved us both a lot of trouble." He winks, so I know he doesn't mean it, but he's right. Our date could quite possibly go down in history as the worst of all time.

I relax again, more comfortable now that we've started talking. "Okay, I have another question for you."

"Shoot."

"I know you lead a super-thrilling life as an accountant, but if you could have any job in the world and money was no object, what would you do?"

He purses his lips while tapping his index finger against

the couch. "I've always had this dream of owning a lake resort up north."

I can't stop the gasp that escapes my lips. "For real? That's the furthest thing from being an accountant."

He sits up straight. "You didn't say it had to be the same."

"But that's not even in the same category. I was thinking more like a financial advisor or the president of a bank. But a resort owner? Do you know the kind of time commitment that would be?"

He holds his hands up, palms out. "Forget I said anything."

"No, I didn't mean it was a bad thing." He looks so defeated that my heart breaks a little, knowing I'm the reason for it. I resist the urge to cup his face in my hands. "I'm sorry. I'm just surprised that one person could be happy doing such different things. I mean, a guy who spends his days sitting at a desk performing audits and balancing budgets does not strike me as the type of guy who'd be happy fixing old boat motors and stoking a campfire."

"First of all, that's not all I would do if I owned a resort. And second, aren't you being a tad stereotypical? Isn't there some exciting dream job you would do if given the chance?"

I shrug. I've only ever wanted to be a librarian, but saying that out loud only proves how boring and unadventurous I am. "I have another question for you," I say, changing the subject.

He relaxes once again, crossing his arms behind his head and leaning back. "Go ahead. I'm dying to hear this one."

"Why do you live in a hotel?"

His eyes glint with amusement. "I was wondering when we'd get back to that."

"Is it some sort of secret? Are you in the witness protection program?"

He chuckles, shaking his head. "No. Nothing as interesting as that. Actually, I just moved to the Twin Cities three weeks ago when I started working at the accounting firm with Milo. I have a deposit down on a really nice new two-bedroom apartment not far from here—only the building's not finished. They've run into one problem after another. At first, I was only supposed to be in this hotel for two weeks. Then it became three. Now it looks like it'll be over a month."

"What's the holdup?"

"Currently, they're waiting on kitchen cabinets." He shrugs. "Supply chain issues, I guess."

"That's too bad. You must get bored sitting in this hotel every night."

"Usually. But thanks to you, I've had one excitement-filled evening."

I have to laugh at that. "I wouldn't call the night we've been through exciting."

He makes a show of looking at his ankle, propped on the table with a sopping wet towel around it from the ice that has long since melted, and then back at me. "Well, I wouldn't call it *boring* either."

"Very true. As terrible as it was, it *was* rather action-packed. More action than I've seen in months." Definitely more than an average day at the library, not counting when the kids came for the field trip.

Several beats pass as he stares at me with a slight smile on his face. I don't think I've noticed before just how blue his eyes are. They definitely top my list of his best features.

Just then, as if he also realizes he's been staring, he blinks several times, then clears his throat. "So...um, if you hadn't gone out with me tonight, what would you have done? What does a typical Friday night look like for you?"

A buzz of nervous energy infuses my chest. "Well..." How can I answer that question without looking like a total, pathetic loser? I go for honesty but blanket it in vagueness, only sharing the barest of details. "Sometimes I hang out with Nora and Milo." As a pity invite tagalong on their dates. "Occasionally I go out with new acquaintances." A nice way of saying blind dates, which almost always end disastrously. "But most Friday nights I prefer to stay home and read." There's really no other way to say that to make it sound any less boring.

His brow arches. "Read?"

I nod. "It's my favorite pastime."

"Do you have any other hobbies?"

"Possibly." I don't think I should mention knitting, since I haven't technically knitted successfully yet. But if he were to give me another week or two, I could answer that question differently and sound a whole lot more exciting. Well, maybe *exciting* isn't the right word.

"Where'd you say you worked again?" he asks. "The library?"

I fold my arms. "Yes."

He chuckles. "I think you need to get out more."

My jaw comes unhinged and my cheeks flame with heat. "I get out." Did I not just tell him all of the things I did on weekends?

Seeing my reaction, he winces a little. "I'm sorry. I'm not making fun of you."

"It kind of sounds like you are."

"Okay, maybe a little. But it's so easy to get a rise out of you. I couldn't resist."

My pulse picks up, partly because he's right. I can actually feel my blood pressure rising. But also because he talks about me like he knows me—or at least he knows one thing about me, which is more than he knew earlier tonight—and it doesn't seem to make him like me any less. He certainly isn't trying to get away from me like he was not that long ago.

Although a glance at his ankle propped up on the coffee table reminds me that he couldn't leave the room even if he wanted to. But he doesn't look like he wants to. He looks like he's completely content being here with me. And the way he's looking at me...something has changed in his eyes, in his expression. The frown he'd been wearing since dinner has vanished, and now he's actually smiling. At me! As an added bonus, I'm pretty sure he's forgotten about the fact that his truck probably needs a new clutch, thanks to me.

I smile back at him. "You're right, though, I do need to get out more. The only person I hang out with is Nora, and lately she's been pretty wrapped up in all things Milo."

His smile fades as the expression on his face changes into one of understanding. "I'd offer to take you somewhere tomorrow, but..." He bobs his head toward his elevated leg and shrugs. "You know."

"Right. I think it'll be a week or two before you do anything other than sit at your accounting desk, tabulating sums or whatever it is you do."

A sudden banging on the door startles me. "Meg? Are you in there?"

I jump as Nora's voice echoes from the hallway. As always, she has impeccable timing. I've waited for her all night, and just when I'm beginning to make progress with Garrett, she shows up.

"I'll get it." I hop off the couch and jog to the small entryway to open the door. When Nora sees me, her worried expression morphs to relief, and she wraps me in a hug. "You must feel like I abandoned you. I'm so sorry. I shut down my phone during the movie to save battery, and afterward I tried to turn it on, but it was dead."

While Nora behaves like the world is ending, Milo stands behind her, calm as a summer breeze. He nods as he enters the suite. Then, hands in his pockets, he saunters over to the couch where Garrett is sitting, stands behind him, and slaps him on the shoulder. "So, you injured yourself. On a date. That stinks, man."

Garrett scoffs. "Thanks so much for the sympathy."

Milo turns to me. "So Meg, I'll bet you're ready to get out of here."

I clasp my hands as if in prayer. "Yes, thank you. But first I need Nora to let me into our apartment so I can get my spare keys. Then we can go to the restaurant where I left my car." I look over at Nora, who's blinking rapidly.

"You're locked out of your car?" she says. "Is that why you're here?" She yanks on her boyfriend's arm. "Milo, why didn't you tell me that?"

"Because I didn't know." He shrugs. "I didn't ask for details."

I narrow my gaze at Nora. "Why did you think I was here at Garrett's hotel at this hour? And why else would I need a ride? I told you all of this in my texts. And my voicemail."

"But I haven't gotten any of those. My phone is charging in the car. I haven't powered it back on yet."

I jerk my head back. "So you haven't gotten any of my texts from tonight?"

She shakes her head. "Not one."

"Then how did you know to come here?"

Milo raises his hand, then points a finger down at Garrett's head. "You can thank this guy right here for notifying us. He texted me about fifteen, twenty minutes ago, begging me to come and get you."

My gaze flies from Milo to Garrett, whose face has drained of color. "That's what you were so urgently typing? An SOS to Milo to come rescue you from me?"

Garrett's Adam's apple bobs as he swallows. "It wasn't like that. It was more of an FYI, just letting him know you were here." He scratches the back of his neck.

Milo chuckles. "No, dude, it was definitely an SOS."

The longer I stare at Garrett, the more sick he looks. Sure, he may feel uncomfortable now, but I feel ten times more so, and there's nothing he can say to make it better.

I am a fool. I actually started to think we were moving past the catastrophe of our date and were headed toward something as crazy as a second one. But no. I must've read Garrett wrong. I took his friendly small talk for something more than it was—just a way to pass the time until he could get rid of me.

Nora grabs me by the upper arm. "It's late. Garrett needs to rest, and we need to get your car."

"Right," I say. "I'm sure Garrett would much rather be alone. Like he is every night." I swipe my phone off the coffee table and follow Nora toward the door.

"Meg, wait," Garrett says. I turn back toward him. Unable to get up, he rotates his torso to face me. "Thanks for helping me out tonight. I really appreciate it." From his remorseful expression, I can tell he means it.

"It was the least I could do after everything you did to try and rescue me." Even if it was only so he could be rid of me sooner. "I'm sorry about your ankle. I hope it's not broken."

Once Milo, Nora, and I reach the parking lot, I ask if we can forget about my car until morning. Sure, I parked in a three-hour parking zone and I'll probably get towed, but I don't really care. I'll deal with the consequences tomorrow. I'm exhausted and humiliated. All I want to do is go home, bury myself under my covers, and forget this entire night ever happened.

eight

MY MIND IS FILLED with questions during the drive home, but I remain quiet, not wanting Milo to be part of any conversations Nora and I might have. But once he drops us off and we're safe inside our apartment, I pounce on Nora like a kitten on a grasshopper. "What did Garrett's text say?"

She walks into our small kitchen, pulls a stool out from beneath the counter, and sits. "I didn't read it."

"But Milo did. Didn't he tell you?"

She flings her hands out at me. "Why torture yourself? You get the gist, right?"

"I need to know what it said exactly." If I'm going to go to the trouble of avoiding Garrett for the rest of my life, I need to know exactly what he's done to deserve it.

Nora huffs, frustration evident in her strained expression. "He said something about waking up from a nap and you were still there. He asked Milo what was taking us so long."

"Is that it?"

Nora presses her lips together for a moment. "He may have also said...'get her out of here.'"

I wince. "Ouch." A million tiny knives stab me in the heart, one after the other. Although Garrett's words are pretty much what I expect, hearing them out loud is a giant blow to my self-esteem. That's it. He is officially being avoided. Boycotted. *Canceled.*

I'm the world's biggest idiot. How could I have thought Garrett was actually starting to like me? I should've stuck to my old, tried-and-true dating protocols. It's so much easier to focus on a guy's flaws and the things I don't like about him. Then, when he ultimately rejects me—because eventually, they all do—it doesn't sting so badly.

But something unexpected happened tonight when I was with Garrett that caused me to let my guard down. Maybe it was because he was in pain and in need of medication, but there were moments when he opened up to me. He briefly let me see who he was—and I liked it. I liked him.

Oh, Meg. You stupid, stupid girl.

Nora pats the stool beside hers, and I plop down and rest my forehead on the counter. "I am the most unlikeable woman on earth."

Nora rubs circles across my back. "So the date was really that bad?"

"Not all of it." My voice echoes in the space between my face and the countertop. "We didn't have the greatest conversation at dinner, but once we discovered I was locked out of my car, Garrett made sure I wasn't alone. He refused to leave me, and he was determined to get my keys for me."

"I told you, he's a good guy." She gives my shoulder a squeeze.

"But then he fell off a ladder, and now he's injured. Because of me. And he thinks I'm a pest."

Nora lowers her head until it gently collides with mine. "It'll be okay. I'm sure his ankle sprain isn't fatal. And you *can* be a pest. Sometimes."

"I know that." How could I not know that? I've spent my entire life hearing it from basically everyone I've ever met.

I don't know how long I stay in this hunched-over position with Nora rubbing my back, but the longer I sit here, the more I can feel my resolve strengthen. There is no use dwelling on Garrett. He doesn't like me. End of story. Nora has plenty of time to find someone else for me to bring to Braxton's wedding. I have two months. And it's not like I need a ring on my finger by the time Braxton walks down the aisle, though it will sure be easier if I'm happy with someone of my own. And I will be. I'm sure there are plenty of guys in the world who like annoying women who say what they think without filtering first, who do nothing but read and think about possibly taking up knitting.

I will be single forever.

After the ordeal I suffered last night, I give myself permission to be lazy and lie in bed a little longer than usual this morning. It's Saturday, and I have no plans. I'll eventually have to pick up my car, but I'm in no hurry. I'm pretty sure the three-hour parking rule only applies on weekdays. At least that's what I plan to tell the attendant at the impound lot where my car is probably sitting right now.

When I finally do crawl out of bed, I glance at my alarm clock. It's nine a.m. I walk in a sleepy haze to the kitchen to start a pot of coffee. A few minutes later, loud, rhythmic banging sounds come from the other side of the entry door.

"Are you up yet?" Nora's muffled words come from the hall.

"I'm coming." I push the brew button on the coffeemaker, zigzag around the kitchen counter, and run to the door. When I pull it open, I see a very full laundry basket with Nora's relieved face above it.

"I got all the way up here and realized I forgot to bring my key with me when I went down to the laundry room," she says. "I hated to wake you up, but I also didn't want to stand out here all day."

Locked doors? Hey, they happen to all of us. "No problem. I was already up." I step aside to let her through. "Thank you for letting me sleep in, by the way. I'll wash your clothes for you next time."

"I'll hold you to it." She trudges to the couch and plunks the laundry basket down in the middle. She sits on one side of the basket and I join her on the other side. I love laundry days. For some reason, Nora and I have our best talks while separating our clothes into piles—hers and mine. I wonder if it's just some quirky thing that makes our friendship special or if the mere act of folding laundry has the power to draw out a person's true feelings.

With Nora and Milo so head-over-heels for each other, I know she and I won't be roommates forever. I can practically hear the clock ticking on our time together. If and when they do get married, who will I fold laundry with?

"I hope my future husband enjoys folding laundry," I say.

Nora shrugs. "Maybe you should ask him."

"Ask who?"

"Garrett. Ask him if he likes folding laundry." She gives me a teasing wink.

My face flames with heat. "Are you kidding? Garrett is not my future husband. I'm never speaking to him again, remember?" And if I'm never speaking to him again, there's no way I'll ever fold laundry with him.

I hold a white tank top in front of my face to cover up my embarrassment. When I'm sure the redness has left my face, I line up the thin straps before folding it in half. "Anyway, I don't think men are particularly good at folding laundry. It wouldn't be the same."

"Why wouldn't they be good at it? Folding is not an exclusively feminine talent. Guys can do it just as well." Nora tosses a gray T-shirt my way.

"Maybe. As long as my guy isn't the kind who would ball up a pair of socks. You know how some people fold socks inside out and somehow shove them into a ball that is almost impossible to unfold? It's like a Rubik's Cube of white cotton and elastic. Which way is up? Is this the inside or the outside? I can never tell what I'm looking at when I see a balled-up pair of socks. Just one fold is sufficient. There's no need to go to extremes. The future of the world does not depend on whether or not those two socks stay together."

Nora's hands fall to her sides. "Let me guess. Balled-up socks are a deal breaker?"

"As a matter of fact, yes." I take my silky black camisole and fold it in half, then in half again. "If your house catches on fire in the middle of the night and you have to get dressed in a hurry because you sleep naked but don't want to be naked when the fire department shows up, you would lose precious time if you had to un-ball a pair of well-balled-up socks. It might mean the difference between surviving the fire with minimal smoke inhalation or burning up completely."

Nora shakes her head. "If my house is on fire, I'll wrap a sheet around my body and run outside in bare feet."

She has a point. Maybe I should add that to my mental fire escape plan: *Don't worry about clothes. Just wear a sheet.*

Nora carefully creases a short flowered skirt. "Are you sure you don't want to know how Garrett folds his socks?"

"Can we please never mention him again?"

She tilts her head to the side and presses her lips firmly together. "Hmm, I don't know...it might earn him a few points if he folds socks the right way."

I slash my hand through the air, putting an end to this nonsensical conversation. "After the date from you-know-where, followed by that whole text message debacle, he'd have to earn a lot more points than what he'd gain from folding socks correctly. He might earn two more points, max. And right now, he's so far in the red he'll never recover. Besides, he doesn't want to earn points from me. He doesn't like me, and that's good because I don't like him either."

"You're just embarrassed. In time, you'll forget all about it and so will he." She adds a gray fleece hoodie to my pile and pats the soft fabric. "Speaking of embarrassment, I listened to my voicemails and read through all my missed texts last night, and I got the most interesting message from you."

My stomach recoils in my belly. "I have no idea which text you are referring to." But actually, I do have a pretty good idea. The prickly heat of shame climbs its way up my neck.

"I got a text message from you, begging me to pick you up from Garrett's hotel *ASAP*." Nora places a finger to her chin. "Hmm, that sounds a lot like the text he sent Milo. The one you're so upset about. Seems to me you both wanted to be rid of each other, at least at first."

"In my defense, I sent mine while he was sleeping. I was bored out of my mind. And it was much earlier in the evening. We hadn't even started talking yet."

"He may have sent his text prematurely too." Nora moves her hand to my knee. "Listen, Meg, I know Garrett hurt your feelings, and now you're putting up all your defenses. But I could tell from the look on your face when I walked in last night that you wished I hadn't come yet. You were enjoying yourself. Admit it."

"Bwah-hah!" I slap my thighs with both hands. "You must not have had your contacts in. If you saw anything, it was me humoring him while he made fun of my reading habit. You completely missed the part where he ordered me around, demanding that I get things for him."

"He has a sprained ankle."

"Even so, he could've been more polite about it. And then he fell asleep, and I had to stare at him for a very long time."

"Oh, you poor baby. I'm sure that was taxing."

"Very. And don't even get me started on the dinner portion of our date." I make a show of shaking my head repeatedly. "Garrett checked several of my pet-peeve boxes, and that's not the kind of box-checking a woman wants when she's looking for a man."

"So you annoy each other?" Nora's lips turn up into a mischievous smile. "Seems like you two make a perfect pair."

"A perfect pair of annoying people?" That sounds a lot like my parents, and the world can't handle another couple like them.

Nora tosses a pair of khaki shorts at me, then stands. "Here, *Miss Perfect*. This is the last of the laundry. By the way, I'll be running errands in the afternoon. If you come with me, I'll take you to get your car. Oh, and remember we have to be at Milo's by five thirty."

"Milo's?"

Nora places her hands on her hips. "His cookout. Did you forget?"

"Of course not." But I sort of did. A little. "Who else will be there?"

Nora clears her throat, smiles, and says, "People." Then she makes a beeline for the kitchen.

Wait. That wasn't exactly an answer. Fueled by determination, I follow her into the kitchen and stand behind her while she fumbles through one of the base cabinets. "Nora," I say sternly, "*which* people, exactly, will be there?"

She emerges from the cabinet with the blender cradled in her hands. She sets it on the counter, then turns toward me. "You know—the usual." She waves her hand through the air as if that fills in all my blanks. Then she opens the freezer, pulls out two frozen peeled bananas and a bag of something green, and dumps them into the blender before slapping on the lid. She flips the switch, and immediately the loud whirring and grinding fills the air around us, making it impossible to carry on a conversation.

I have grown accustomed to this spontaneous smoothie-making habit of Nora's. Any time she wants to escape an uncomfortable conversation, she suddenly finds herself in desperate need of a smoothie. Doesn't matter if we have fruit in the apartment or not—she'll make it out of lettuce and ketchup if she has to. The blender is loud, and it can run all day. I know this because I bought the industrial strength model, so it's pointless to stand here and wait it out.

Shaking my head, I return to the living room. I grab my clean clothes and carry them to my bedroom, freeing Nora to turn off the blender and preserve her hearing for another day. I'm not about to badger her. I'm pretty sure I don't want to hear the answer to my question anyway.

By some miracle, my car is still where I parked it the night before, sitting right outside the restaurant where Garrett and I first met. There's no boot on the tire, and all of the glass is intact. My only punishment for parking there all night is a little white ticket on the windshield which I will gladly pay, knowing it could've been a lot worse. I feel ecstatic for about five seconds. Then I remember that I have a cookout to attend in a couple of hours, and there's a questionable guest roster that Nora refuses to talk about.

During my drive home, I tense up just thinking about it. But why should I? I can be stubborn too. Maybe I won't attend the cookout. Ha. I've spent the afternoon running errands with Nora, it's quarter to five, and I'm wiped out.

As soon as I walk in the door, I tell Nora this, and she balks. "You're not leaving me alone with Milo's sister-in-law," she says. "I can only talk about the effects of pregnancy on the bladder for so long. You have to come."

About fifteen minutes before we're supposed to leave, I try faking cramps. But Nora and I have lived together so long, she quickly calls my bluff. "Nice try. That's not for another week."

Drat.

So at five twenty-six, I find myself sitting in the

passenger seat of Nora's car while she drives to Milo's. The entire time, I'm silently praying my seatbelt will spontaneously malfunction and lock into place forever, not allowing me to get out of my seat. But when we pull up in front of Milo's house, I click the big red button and the buckle pops right out of the locking mechanism. No resistance whatsoever. I've never been more frustrated with a car part for doing its job.

As nervous as I am to be attending this gathering, I know at least I'll eat well. Milo has been hosting cookouts twice a month since the weather started to warm up—around late April. That's when he first got his ceramic egg-shaped grill. The man obsessively watches online videos about grilling and then tries the recipes out on us. I'd never had prime rib or brisket in my life until this past spring, and I have to admit, I'm a fan. Milo is becoming quite the grill master—but I'll never tell him that. I don't want to inflate his ego. I also don't want him to stop experimenting. It's best to let him keep striving for perfection.

The cookout crowd varies from time to time, but there's a core group of us who show up on a regular basis—Nora and me, the old neighbor couple from two houses down, and Milo's brother, Wyatt, and sister-in-law, Michelle. I invited my parents one time, but that will never happen again. My dad went home after that night and immediately plunked down $1,400 online to buy an egg-shaped charcoal grill for himself, but he hasn't used it once. My mom has resented Milo ever since.

Nora manages to squeeze her small sedan between two other cars, and then we walk around the corner toward the fenced-in backyard. The savory smell of grilling meat fills the air, and my stomach growls in response. What amazing thing has he whipped up this time? I can almost hear my taste buds cheering.

Nora pushes the wooden fence gate forward, and we walk through. I reach back to latch it on the other side, then turn around and stop in my tracks. I recoil as if someone has tossed a bowling ball straight to my gut. It's just as I feared. Seated at the umbrella table by himself, looking almost too good to ignore, is Garrett.

nine

I SWIPE my talon-like hand at Nora before she can get away, and I manage to hook the loose fabric of her shirt. I tug her backward. "I *knew* he would be here."

Nora turns around, nothing but doe-eyed innocence staring back at me. "Of course he's here. He's Milo's friend."

"But I'm trying to never see him again."

Nora frowns at me. "Don't get mad at me. I didn't invite him."

"But when I asked you who was coming, you couldn't tell me. You just had to make that banana and...what was it...*parsley* smoothie?"

"It was kale. And it was excellent, by the way."

I roll my eyes. "Come on, Nora. You didn't want me to know because you knew I wouldn't come."

"You're right. I think this whole situation is silly. Garrett is new to the area, and he needs to make friends."

"Does he have to make friends with us?"

She bats my hand away until I finally release her shirt. "He's a very sweet guy. You're the only one who has a problem with him."

"Correction—he has a problem with me."

"Be nice to him," Nora hisses. "I'm going to see if Milo needs any last-minute help. I'll probably be in the kitchen if you need me—which you shouldn't." She practically runs away from me, leaving me alone and exposed.

I look around for anyone to talk to besides the obvious lone man at the small table to my right. The other guests are coupled off, engaged in their own conversations.

Story of my life.

Garrett must sense my unease because he flags me down with his waving hand. "Meg."

So much for my plan to avoid him forever. I force my lips into a smile and wave back. "Hey, Garrett, so good to see you. Okay, talk to you later." I start walking toward some vague destination behind him, and almost make it past his table.

"Meg, I would really like to talk to you. Can you spare me just a minute of your time?"

Wincing, I turn on my heels to face him. "I was actually on my way to..." Nowhere. Darn it. "Can I get you anything? A drink, maybe? Some munchies?"

"This won't take long. You can either sit here with me for two minutes, or I'll follow you inside." He gestures toward his foot, which is propped up on the chair across from him. "Are you going to make me follow you?"

That familiar still, small voice taps at the door of my conscience. I know I should at least hear Garrett out, no matter how stupid I feel in his presence. I take a deep breath and release it on a prayer. *Please help me get through this without making things worse.*

I take a few slow steps toward his table, pull out the empty chair beside him, and sit. I nod toward a pair of crutches that are propped up against the table. "I see you went to the doctor."

He shakes his head. "Not yet. I have an appointment on Monday." He wraps his fingers around the foam hand grip of one of them. "These bad boys are on loan from one of Milo's neighbors. Apparently their teenage son is really into skateboarding. They had an assortment of crutches and braces for me to choose from. If I ever sprain my wrist or blow out my knee, I know where to go."

"Cool. It's good to have neighbors with benefits." I cringe when my words play back in my head. My meaning might have gotten lost in translation.

He gives me a weird look, one of those squinty-eyed, furrowed-brow looks that says, "Do you hear yourself when you talk?"

I clear my throat. "Anyway, you wanted something?"

He straightens in his seat. "I wanted to apologize. For the text. I was in a lot of pain last night, and I probably wasn't thinking clearly when I woke up."

I wave my hand. "Not a problem. We can blame it on the pain and put the whole thing behind us." That's all I want to do. Put it behind me, gather up what's left of my bruised ego, and never think about it again—never think about *Garrett* again. But with him sitting a foot away, that's difficult to do.

"Also," he says, his voice lowered, "I may have been a little hard on you when you drove me home."

"A little?" I nearly shout the words, but I can't help it. My heart rate ratchets up just thinking about how I'd almost merged into a semi while Garrett bellowed instructions at me. "I could've done without your constant commentary." I press my lips together to stop any more words from slipping out. I've already made one comment too many, and if I've learned anything from the book of Proverbs, it's that wise men—and women—hold their tongues. So I will try to hold mine. I'll hold it with my teeth if I have to.

Garrett slants one eyebrow. "I'm sure you did the best you could, given the circumstances."

"I did."

"Next time, though, just be honest with me and tell me up front that you've never driven a truck with a stick shift."

His words flip a switch inside me, and I feel my defenses rise. At this point, my teeth forget all about holding my tongue. "What good would it have done to tell you? You never would've gotten back to your hotel if I hadn't driven you."

"So you're saying lying was okay under the circumstances?"

"I didn't lie. When you asked me if I knew how to drive it, I said yes because I really thought I could. I understood the basics, having observed the process many times."

"Obviously you didn't understand the process enough to execute it in real life. It wasn't until you'd already ground the gears to a pulp that you finally admitted you'd never actually operated a manual transmission." He shudders. "I still cringe when I think about it. I've never heard my truck make those sounds before."

I clench my fists and my jaw at the same time. We're already back to butting heads again. What did that take, sixty whole seconds in each other's presence? Why do we bother trying to see eye to eye? It's obvious that unless Garrett is taking a heavy dose of painkillers, he and I will never get along.

A glance over my shoulder tells me we've attracted an audience. The man and woman from down the street are staring at us, concern etched on their faces. I have to remove myself from Garrett's presence before they come over to intercede.

"Not that I don't love a good debate," I say, "but I should see if Nora needs help in the kitchen." I brush my palms together, then push against the edge of the table. I force myself to smile at Garrett, then do a little curtsy-type move for some reason I'll never know.

Garrett presses his hands against the armrests of his folding chair like he intends to stand up. "Wait. That didn't go how I planned it."

I hold up my hand at him like a stop sign. "Let's just forget about it then. It's obvious that I push your buttons, and you *definitely* push mine."

"So, that's it? We're just going to leave things unresolved?"

I shake my head. "Don't worry about it. Consider it resolved. It's all good." I give him two thumbs up for extra reassurance. Hopefully, the night before can finally be laid to rest, never to be resurrected.

I dash across the patio, up the wooden steps of Milo's deck, and through the open door that leads into his kitchen. I push the slider shut behind me, press my back against it, and breathe a heavy sigh. "Thank goodness."

"Meg!" Nora glares at me from the other side of the kitchen island. "What are you doing in here?"

I cross to the island and stand opposite her. "I thought you might need help with the…" I glance down, taking note of what Nora holds in her hands—packages of buns. I clear my throat. "I thought you might need someone to open the bun bags, but I see you've got it all under control."

Nora huffs. "Did you leave Garrett alone?"

I lean my elbows against the countertop. "Believe me,

I'm the last person he wants to talk to right now." I leave out the part where he literally called me over to his table because he wanted to talk.

"You're hopeless." Shaking her head, Nora rolls a giant watermelon across the counter. "Since you're here, you might as well cut this. But when you're done, you have to go back outside." She slides an oval-shaped stainless steel tray toward me. "Put the slices on this."

"Will do." I pull a knife from the knife block and center the watermelon on a cutting board. I have to hand it to Milo —his kitchen is very well organized. Everything is exactly where I expect it to be, which makes finding things a snap.

While I slice watermelon, Nora fills a large pot with water. "I'm going outside to mingle. Let me know when the water's boiling so I can add the corn."

"I can do that." And once the water boils, I'll offer to cook the corn myself. That will buy me eight more minutes. I'll do whatever I can to stay inside as long as possible.

Just before six, Milo slides open the glass door and pokes his head into the kitchen. "The brats and burgers are done. How are you coming with that corn?"

I smile at him. "It's ready and waiting. And I made Kool-Aid in case you run low on beverages. The pitcher is in your refrigerator. I also found a few cans of baked beans in your pantry, so I cooked those too." I push the large stoneware bowl full of beans across the island counter. "Here you go."

His eyebrows arch high on his forehead. "Wow, thanks, Meg. And please, make yourself at home in my kitchen."

"I will. Thank you." I realize he probably meant that sarcastically, but those eight minutes flew by, and I needed more excuses to stay in the safe shelter of his quiet kitchen. Now that the food is ready, I'm completely out of stalling tactics. My respite has come to an end, and it's time to face the harsh reality that Garrett is outside and I'm about to join him. No way will Nora let me hide inside all evening.

I take a deep breath, lift the corn platter with two hands, and make my way toward the door, which Milo has left open for me. Outside on the patio, the picnic table is set up like a buffet, so I set the corn down next to the bowl of baked beans. "There we go."

"Are we all ready to eat?" Milo asks.

An affirmative round of murmurs passes through the small group gathered around the table.

"Then let's bless the food, and then we can—"

"Oh, wait, I forgot the Kool-Aid." I throw my hands in the air. "I'll go back in and get it."

"It's fine, Meg." Nora grabs my arm and pulls me back. "We have plenty to drink here."

Milo asks God's blessing over the food, and then everyone begins dishing up. Nora fills a plate for Garrett and delivers it to him at the umbrella table and then sits beside him. When Milo finishes serving the meat from the grill, he joins her.

Now where am I supposed to sit?

Maybe I'll step out of my comfort zone just this once and make a new friend or two. That nice older couple seem safe enough, and they already showed their concern for my well-being. I think I'll befriend them.

With a new sense of purpose, I carry my plate over to the white-haired man and his wife and take a seat in a nearby folding chair. "You guys don't mind if I sit here, do you?"

"Of course not," the man says. "My wife and I were just

remarking on all of the different bird species that Milo has at his birdfeeder."

"Really?" I crane my head to the right. Beneath a canopy of maple leaves, a wooden bird feeder hangs from a long branch. All I see is a robin and a smaller brown-and-white bird perched on opposite sides of the glass seed reservoir, pecking at tiny seeds.

"We live only a few houses down, and I only ever see blue jays," the woman says. "They're such territorial creatures. They scare all the other birds away."

I finish a bite of three-bean salad, then offer her a sympathizing frown. "That's too bad." I know a bit about the various bird species that inhabit central Minnesota, but I'm not a bird person—not enough to relate to their disappointment. So I try to put myself in their shoes by thinking of something more personal to me: books. If my library had one thousand volumes, but they were all copies of the same book, I probably wouldn't enjoy working at that library, and I definitely wouldn't look forward to reading as much as I do now. Thinking of it that way, I can understand why maybe they'd get tired of seeing nothing but blue jays day in and day out.

After another twenty minutes of nonstop bird talk, I decide it's time to mingle a little more, widen my circle. I wipe my mouth with my napkin and lift my empty plate as I stand. "Well, it's been nice sitting with you," I say. "I'll keep an eye out for those white-breasted nuthatches."

I notice Milo's sister-in-law, Michelle, has just gone for another helping at the picnic table, so I run over to her and try to strike up a conversation. I gesture to her rounded abdomen. "Looks like it won't be too much longer. You must be so excited."

She groans. "I was...for the first two weeks or so. Then

the morning sickness set in. That was four months of torture. And now that that's finally over with, my back is starting to hurt. I've been having sciatic pain, and I'm only seven months along. Doesn't that seem a little early to you?"

"Um, I've never been pregnant before. I'm not sure what's normal and what's not." These questions are way beyond my limited knowledge of pregnancy. "I'm sure we have some books at the library that might help you find some answers. I work on Monday. I could set some aside for you. Or you could browse our online catalog."

Michelle leans against the edge of the table and digs her fists into her lower back. "Oh no, don't worry about it. I have books. I can also call my doctor. I'm more or less just thinking out loud."

Apparently, Michelle really needs someone to talk to about her pregnancy if she's desperate enough to talk to me. So I decide to offer her a listening ear while she rambles on for at least twenty more minutes about her birth plan, her aversion to anesthesia, and her decision to breastfeed for the first year. When the conversation turns to the topic of labor and delivery, I have to step away. I'm squeamish about blood and other bodily fluids, and I try not to think about them. Maybe that's because the images I conjure up in my head are even worse than reality. So when Michelle mentions something called a *mucous plug,* I almost pass out.

Thankfully, as the sun sinks lower on the horizon, the people around us begin standing up, tossing their trash, and preparing to leave.

Nora joins me as I gather dirty plates. "Did you have fun? I saw you talking to Jim and Joan."

"The bird couple? Oh, yes. We had a fascinating conversation."

"And you talked to Michelle? I'm sure that was equally fascinating."

I place my fingertips to my lips. "I'd rather not discuss that conversation."

Chuckling, Nora shakes her head. "I take it you're ready to go. Or do you want to stay longer?"

"I'm more than ready to leave. Just let me get my phone. I think I left it in the kitchen." I start to retreat toward the house.

"No rush," Nora says. "It'll take a minute for Garrett to get into the car."

I whip my head around. "Who? Into what?"

Nora's smile can only be described as annoyingly satisfied. "We're giving Garrett a ride home. He shouldn't have to wait until Milo finishes cleaning up. I knew you wouldn't mind."

I grab my phone from Milo's kitchen, then sneak out the front door and down the porch steps to Nora's car. I can't chance a run-in with Garrett in the backyard. What if we have to walk through the fence gate at the same time? What if I say, "You first," and then he insists, "No, after you," and neither of us will back down, and we continue to argue until everyone else has gone home, and the sun has set, and it starts to get cold...no. I will avoid confrontation at all costs.

When I get to Nora's car, I'm relieved to see that she and Garrett haven't gotten there yet. I can snag the back seat, knowing he'll need the passenger seat for his long legs. I can lay my head back and pretend to be asleep so I won't have to engage in conversation. Or maybe I can become totally engrossed in an e-book by the time they get into the car. I have over a hundred on my phone that I haven't even started yet.

I'm still trying to figure out how to occupy myself—or at least how to appear occupied—when Nora opens the passenger door, sticks her head inside and gives me a look. It's one I'd seen on my mother's face many times back when I was a child, and usually it came after I'd misbehaved. So now Nora is my mom in this scenario, and I'm a five-year-old who's just eaten a bunch of candy and flushed the wrappers down the toilet, only not all of them went down and remain floating in the bowl for my mom to discover the next time she needs to use the bathroom. Oh yes, I am familiar with that look.

Nora stares at me, blinking for emphasis. "You could've helped."

I place my hand to my chest. "I'm sorry. I didn't realize Garrett couldn't handle crutching it twenty yards to your car."

She rolls her eyes, then pushes herself back out of the car. I wait in silence as Garrett hands her his crutches, grips the upper door frame with his right hand, and lowers his long, lean body into the passenger seat.

"Are you good?" Nora asks him.

He swings first his left leg in, and then his right. "Yep. I'm all set. Thanks."

"Great. I'll just be one second. Hang tight." With that, Nora closes the passenger-side door with Garrett and me trapped inside the car together, then she runs back toward Milo's house. As she passes through the gate and disappears, I want to bang on the windows and scream after her. *"You can't do this to me! I know what you're up to, and it won't work!"*

But I don't do that. I keep my mouth shut and look out the window on the opposite side of the car. Not much is happening in Milo's neighborhood. A man across the street bounces atop a green lawn tractor, using what's left of the daylight to finish mowing his lawn.

The silence inside the car grows thick as morning lake fog. Nora probably thinks that if she leaves us in here long enough, we'll eventually have to talk. But she's wrong. I won't break. I can outlast anyone playing the *Let's See How Long We Can Go Without Talking* game.

But apparently that is a game Garrett has never played before. Either that or he gives up easily. After a couple of minutes, he turns toward me. "So, what are we going to do about this ..." He gestures between us. "We can't seem to be together for two minutes without you getting mad at me."

I dare to look at him for the first time since our verbal sparring match in Milo's backyard. "You get mad at me too."

He shrugs. "Yeah, but I get over it."

"Well, I can't turn my feelings on and off as quickly as you, so I'm planning to pretend you don't exist. You can do the same with me if you want. I won't be offended."

He huffs at me. "I could do that, but I'm not five years old. Come on, Meg. We're adults. Yes, I should've been more patient with you about the driving, and yes, I could've been more selective with my words when I texted Milo. I just wanted to go to bed but felt obligated to stay with you because you were still there."

Still there. Like it was my fault I was there in the first place. He was the one who insisted I drive him home. I did him a favor. "All you had to do was tell me you wanted to go to bed, and I would've been fine with that. Maybe I would've taken a nap too. It would've been better than sitting on your couch, staring at you with your eyes rolled back and your mouth hanging open."

He jerks his head back. "You watched me while I slept?"

Oh...nuts. "I—not for very long. There was nothing else to do."

"I see." He squints at me as if gauging the honesty of my response—which, I have to admit, was a little muddy. "I do feel bad about that text, Meg. Can we forgive and forget?"

I work my jaw back and forth, considering his words. "I guess I can forgive you for the text." Since I sent an almost identical one to Nora, I really have no reason not to. "And I'm sorry I held it against you."

His lips are pressed together firmly as he inhales and exhales. "Okay, we're making some progress now. I accept your apology, and I would really like it if we could put this all behind us and be friends."

Friends? Friends is a big ask. I don't make it a habit to go out with a guy, get rejected, and then invite him the next day to make fondue. "Let's just consider ourselves acquaintances who share mutual friends."

"Really?" When I say nothing, he turns back to face the windshield, then shakes his head. "I don't know why you're making this so difficult."

Because that's what I do. I make everything difficult. Braxton can attest to that.

Maybe if I were brave, I would tell Garrett the entire truth—that I actually started to like him last night, that I allowed myself to picture a second date with him, and that, even now, I find him frustratingly attractive. But because I know that attraction and those feelings are one-sided, I feel like the biggest fool on the face of the earth.

In my limited experience, when a guy gets close enough to see who I really am deep down inside, he realizes he

84

doesn't like me that much after all. So instead of sharing what's on my heart, I say nothing and come off looking like a first-rate jerk.

A moment later, Nora returns to the car. She climbs in, and a wave of freesia-scented air floats past my nose. "Sorry, guys. Milo had something he wanted to talk about quick."

That's code for: Milo wanted a good-bye kiss.

She starts the engine and looks at Garrett. "So, are you two all made up now?" She cranes her neck to look at me, her expression hopeful.

I glance over to Garrett's seat. "We're just fine, Nora. Don't worry about us."

Garrett stares straight ahead, his countenance hard as igneous rock. "Yeah, we're just super."

She scoffs. "Really, you guys? I thought if you had some alone time, you'd warm up to each other."

Yeah. Alone time. Good idea. Me alone in my apartment, and him alone in his hotel room. Our two paths never crossing again as long as we live. That sounds just about perfect.

ten

FOR THE DURATION of the ten-minute drive to Garrett's hotel, the air inside Nora's car is so thick I'm surprised her windows aren't fogging up. Nora tries to engage us in small talk, but she doesn't get very far. I learn that Garrett is the master of one-word responses, and I have to give him props for that. It's a talent few possess, although men are better at it than women, so he does have that advantage over me.

I manage to put my wounded pride aside when it's time to help Garrett out of the car. I hold his crutches while Nora pulls on his arm to help him out of the bucket seat. We walk across the parking lot and ride the elevator in silence. When we get to his hotel suite, I hold the door.

Later that night, after I finish my devotions, I struggle to fall asleep. I have so many thoughts whirling around in my head. Have I truly forgiven Garrett for that text? If I have, shouldn't I feel less angry when I think about him? Is it vanity to reject his offer of friendship? Or maybe pride? Why does he have to be so stinking attractive? And what the heck is a mucous plug?

It's like one of those game shows where the contestant is trapped in a glass room with a ton of paper money, but then someone turns on a fan, and the money swirls up into the air, making it nearly impossible to grab.

That's what my thoughts are—hundred dollar bills. My brain is full of them, yet I can't capture a single one and focus on it. Well, maybe that isn't entirely true. There is one thought that I can't escape, like the fan has blown it directly into my face and it's stuck there, covering my eyes and blinding me from all the others: I owe Garrett a massive apology. Yes, another one. He asked if we could be friends, and without any conversation whatsoever, I shot him down. Of course, it was an act of self-preservation, but that doesn't make it right. Once he apologized and I forgave him, I should have nothing left to hold against him. Even if I still feel stupid around him, that's not his problem. It's mine.

If I want to have any hope of sleeping tonight, I have to let this go—even if it means humbling myself, which is often a struggle. But I know that Christ died to forgive my sins, every last one of them, even before I came to him in repentance. Garrett asked for my forgiveness, and I forgave him, so what right do I have to withhold kindness and friendship?

None.

I sit up in bed, close my eyes, and lower my head. "Lord, if there is still an ounce of forgiveness I'm withholding from Garrett, please help me to let go of it. Thank you for sending your son to die in my place, because we both know I don't deserve it. Because you've forgiven me for a lifetime of sins against you, I can certainly forgive Garrett for one thoughtless text."

~

After church on Sunday, I go to my parents' house for lunch and get caught up on the latest family news, aka gossip. I stay longer than usual to help my mom plan the menu for her annual Fourth of July picnic. It's the one day each year that she's overly hospitable. She invites the entire family to her house. Knowing how much it means to her—and how much she stresses out over it—I want to help her make sure it's perfect.

I don't see much of Nora until Monday after work when I meet her at the gym. By the time I arrive, she's already been there long enough that sweat is glistening on her forehead. No wonder. Her treadmill is set to seven miles per hour. She's full-on jogging. I never set mine over four, which is like taking a brisk walk.

"How was work?" Nora isn't even out of breath.

"Uneventful, as usual."

"Glad to hear it." Her cute pink-and-gray Brooks trainers pound the black treadmill belt. "Are we ever going to talk about the cookout?"

"You were there. What's there to talk about?"

"The fact that you avoided Garrett the entire night so you didn't have to talk to him. Aren't you embarrassed?"

Embarrassed? The entire reason I avoided him was so I wouldn't embarrass myself.

I reach for my water bottle and take a long swig. I've only begun my twenty minutes of fast-paced walking, and already my throat is parched. "There were a lot of other people there I needed to talk to."

Steadying herself with a hand to the metal frame, Nora turns to face me. "Really? So you'd rather humor Milo's neighbors and stare at a birdfeeder than talk to the handsome man who only came there to talk to you?"

I roll my eyes. "Garrett did *not* go to the cookout for me."

"Yes, he did. He wasn't planning on going because he thought it would be a hassle with his crutches. But when Milo mentioned you'd be there, Garrett changed his mind and asked if he could get a ride. He really wanted to apologize to you."

My heart thuds against the wall of my chest. "You probably misunderstood."

"I didn't."

"Oh." Guilt bubbles up inside my stomach. He went to the cookout just to talk to me? And I was so busy protecting my ego, I rejected his olive branch. No wonder I couldn't sleep last night. God has a lot of work to do in me.

I look up to the ceiling and sigh. "I was just so embarrassed. Garrett was the last person I wanted to see after our sad excuse for a date. I wasn't ready to deal with it."

"I get that," Nora says, bobbing her head. "He hurt your feelings."

My shoulders slump as I exhale, defeated. My feet feel like they're strapped to the belt as I force them to keep pace with the treadmill. "So what do I do now? How do I make this right?"

She wipes her forehead with the back of her wrist. "You should talk to him."

"Talking to him is what gets me into trouble. I'd rather try something that doesn't involve seeing him again. I could text my apology. Or send an e-card."

"Well, here's the thing..." Nora's words drop off, and I can tell by the way her throat tightens in a swallow that there's something she doesn't want to tell me. "You may have to get used to seeing him more regularly."

"Why?"

Her eyes are laser-focused on me. "Because last night, while you were getting a lesson in the fine art of backyard birding, Milo offered Garrett his spare bedroom. He's moving in."

"What?" My shoe snags on the treadmill's belt, causing me to stumble. I lose my balance and barely regain it before almost flying off the back of the stupid contraption. I grip the frame for support. "He's moving in with Milo?"

Nora nods. "Temporarily. There've been a few more delays with Garrett's apartment building, and he'd have to stay at the hotel for another month. Milo told Garrett he should save his money and move in with him while he waits. They'll be roommates, like us. Doesn't that sound fun?"

I don't know how many seconds pass before I blink, but my eyes begin to burn. Still, I can't help but stare. What did Nora just say? Garrett is moving in with Milo? So now, whenever I go to Milo's with Nora, Garrett will be there?

This definitely puts a major wrench in my plan to avoid him forever.

Historically speaking, whenever a first date doesn't end well, it's been my usual practice to avoid that particular man like I avoid excess carbs. Until now, that has worked well for me. Nate from the gym? No sweat avoiding him. He works out every morning at six, and that's why I go in the late afternoons. And because I have no desire to buy an aquarium, there's almost zero chance I'll ever run into Todd.

It takes a tiny life adjustment here and there to hide from

these guys, but it makes things easier, and my self-confidence stays intact. Not so with Garrett. It appears the biggest dating disaster of my entire life is moving into my inner circle—literally. I need to mend the rift between us or I won't see the inside of Milo's house for at least another month. And that is a problem because Nora spends a lot of time there. I'll be facing quite a few lonely nights if I avoid going to Milo's.

Nora pushes her treadmill's down button several times to begin her cooldown, then releases a long, steady breath. "So...you'll talk to Garrett?"

I shrug. "I'm still leaning towards the apology text."

Her eyes bulge. "Meg!"

"Okay, I'll talk to him." Having lost all enthusiasm for walking, I slow my pace to a near crawl.

When Nora's treadmill comes to a complete stop, she hops off, grabs a little white towel and a sanitizer bottle, and sprays and wipes her hand grips. Then she passes it to me. After we've cleaned our machines, we walk to the weight room. It's time for the part of our workout where Nora lays on the weight bench and presses a hundred pounds on a barbell over her head while I stand in front of the mirror with a pair of five-pound dumbbells and work on toning my upper arms.

"You should view Garrett moving in with Milo as a good thing," Nora says as she sits on the bench.

"And why is that?"

"Because now things will be even when we get together. It won't just be the three of us. You'll have a counterpart. A companion."

"I would love to not be the odd woman out, Nora. That's why you started trying to fix me up in the first place. But we've already established that Garrett isn't the man for me." And besides that, if all I truly need is companionship, I'll get a dog.

But I need more than that. I *want* more. I want love, a relationship, the promise of a lifetime of happiness—and to prove to Braxton that he isn't the only one who's capable of finding a partner. What I do *not* want is another man in my life who feels exactly the same way about me that Braxton does.

"I think that if you and Garrett spend more time together, you'll learn to like each other." Nora leans back against the bench and exhales, satisfied. The smile on her lips is a little too self-assured.

I set my dumbbells on the floor and walk toward her with my hands on my hips. "The more time we spend together, the better he'll get to know me, and the less he'll like me. It's already starting to happen. I can tell. So please, Nora, forget about him. Cross him off your list with permanent red marker and help me find someone else to bring to Braxton's wedding. That's what I'm paying you for, after all."

"What?" Nora's brows scrunch on her forehead.

Okay, so I'm not paying her a dime. But she has a lot to gain from me finding true love and happiness—mainly, more Meg-free time with Milo—so in a way, she would profit from it. We both would. She'd have her man to herself, and I wouldn't have to lie awake every night, wondering if I'm actually incapable of finding someone to love me.

eleven

SIX DAYS HAVE PASSED since the cookout, and I haven't spoken a word to Garrett. I heard from Nora that he's already moved into Milo's place. I didn't help him with that, mainly because I wasn't needed. He doesn't have a lot of belongings since most of his furniture is locked up in a storage facility, and Milo told him to keep it there until his apartment is ready.

I realize I should've apologized to him by now, but I keep chickening out. Not only am I scared of rejection, but I also don't know how to go about delivering my apology. I can't just stop by his office in the middle of the day and interrupt his work. Then I'll have two things to apologize for. And Nora has flat-out forbidden me from doing it over the phone.

And now, thanks to Nora, I only have an hour until I have to see Garrett again. With him living at Milo's, Nora thought it'd be fun to have a little party for him—kind of a welcome-to-the-household party. It'll be just the four of us. We'll have dinner, play a few games, maybe watch a movie.

But all that will be incredibly uncomfortable if Garrett and I aren't on speaking terms. So I have to apologize for acting like a child, and I have to do it soon so we can all move on and spend tonight playing *Codenames* and *Apples to Apples* instead of avoiding eye contact and giving each other the silent treatment.

I check the clock on the microwave. It's almost five, which means I've been pacing the living room floor for an hour. I'm about to rehearse my apology speech to Garrett for the sixteenth time when Nora bursts into our apartment. She kicks her shoes across the floor and starts pulling her hair band out, releasing her ponytail.

"Change of plans." She hurries past me on her way down the hall. "Milo has this client, Bryce, who just opened his own restaurant. Milo's been helping him work out some issues with the budget." She vanishes into her room and then returns to the hallway thirty seconds later wearing a completely different shirt. She pulls a brush through her long, dark brown hair. "Milo met with him today, and he invited us to come to his restaurant tonight. He said we could bring friends along, and he'd cover the tab." She reaches out and shakes my shoulders. "Free food, Meg. You love food."

"Why bring me along? Why not go out with Milo and have a romantic night, just the two of you?"

"I haven't told you the best part—Bryce is single. He made a comment to Milo about how hard it's been to meet the right woman because he's been so busy."

"That's the kind of stuff people talk about with their accountants?"

"You're missing the point!" Nora throws her head back and groans. Then she reaches for my hand and squeezes, securing my attention. "Since you haven't been impressed by any of the guys I've introduced you to, I thought you could meet this one first. Then you can decide if you even want me to set you up or not. With Milo's help, it would be easy."

"Hmm." I mash my lips together. This is definitely a different approach from the one Nora has been taking, which hasn't been very successful. Part of me is intrigued, but a bigger part of me is skeptical. "What else do you know about this guy?"

"From what Milo said, he's driven, successful, creative —he could teach you how to cook. And he's got to be adventurous if he took the risk of opening his own place. He sounds like someone you would really like, only I don't know what he looks like. Does that matter? We could look him up online if you want. If only I could remember his last name."

"No need." I hold up my hands, palms out. "Looks aren't that important. He sounds promising, and I would like to meet him."

"Great. I'll text Milo, make sure Garrett is okay with the change of plans—"

"Wait." My body freezes in place. "Why would we bring Garrett?"

Nora scoffs. "The four of us already have plans to hang out tonight, so we can't really leave him behind."

"So...you want me to go to a restaurant to scope out a guy while it looks like I'm on a double date with someone else?"

"How would it look if you tagged along with Milo and me?" Nora asks.

"I'd rather tag along than have Garrett sitting beside me the entire night."

"You think being the third wheel would make a better first impression?"

I cringe. I have heard the term *third wheel* enough in the last few months to claim it as my legal name and put it on my driver's license. I exhale, long and loud. "Maybe not."

Her expression softens. "Don't worry about Garrett. It's pretty safe to say the two of you won't look like you're interested in each other."

That's the understatement of the century. "Okay. But we can't tell Garrett that we're there to check out Bryce. I'll feel dumb enough without him knowing what I'm up to."

"No problem," Nora says. "Just be yourself and try to relax. Pretend Garrett isn't there. All you're doing is getting a glimpse of a man you may or may not be interested in. No pressure."

I sigh, relieved. "Okay. I think I can handle that."

Nora rubs her hands together, clearly excited. "If you and Bryce have chemistry, I'll have Milo drop a few not-so-subtle hints to him next week letting him know you're single and interested. Who knows? Maybe he'll ask you out."

Wow. That would be amazing, although highly improbable. That's just not how my life usually works. But still, I can't stop myself from smiling. For the first time in several days, I have something to look forward to. A little. Without getting my hopes up too high.

Yet, even with all the excitement and promise this evening holds, I still won't feel right until I make peace with Garrett.

～

I'm sitting in the passenger seat of Nora's sporty Nissan as she drives us to the Mill District in Minneapolis. My stomach is filled with butterflies. I'm about to meet a man who might be my date to Braxton's wedding. Is that why I'm so nervous? Or is it because Garrett will be there when it happens, sitting at the table with me?

We slowly pass the historic brick building in search of a parking spot, and I catch a glimpse of Garrett and Milo standing on the sidewalk. Immediately I have my answer to my nervousness question. It's Garrett. Just one look at him and my sweat glands kick into overdrive. I try telling myself it's not him causing this reaction but the thought of apologizing to him.

Yes, that has to be it. I hate confrontation. I avoid it at all costs—and that's often difficult because my unfiltered, runaway mouth lands me in the middle of so many confrontations. So obviously, the thought of apologizing to Garrett *again* is causing my heart rate to accelerate. It has absolutely nothing to do with the fact that he's six foot three and has a jawline that can cut glass.

I take a deep breath, willing myself to calm down. I can do this. I can act like a normal person who has never been slighted by the very handsome man standing outside the restaurant. I can apologize for letting my temper get the best of me at the cookout, and for shooting him down when all he wanted was to call a truce and be friends.

Man, I've messed up a lot in a short amount of time.

Nora parks in a two-hour parking spot and pays the meter, and we cross the street to meet the guys. The closer I get to Garrett, the more I doubt my outfit selection. The cropped jeans, heeled sandals, and loose-fitting blouse I borrowed from Nora make me feel like an imposter. These clothes aren't my style. My style says "comfort," while this outfit screams "high maintenance." Will Garrett sense that I'm trying to impress someone? Hopefully he won't think I'm trying to impress him.

I push all self-conscious thoughts aside and follow Nora to where the men stand outside the restaurant's entrance.

Like the hostess of a gameshow showing off a collection of *fabulous* prizes, Nora holds her hands out to one side and wiggles her fingers. "So, what do you think of this place? Isn't it the coolest building ever?"

I gaze up at the tan-colored brick with its black iron hardware accents and farmhouse-style lights. "It's nice. I love the architecture in this part of the city." The painted wooden sign above the door reads *Crop and Herd*. This is likely one of those farm-to-table restaurants that have become so popular. How contemporary. Bryce is earning points already, and I haven't even met him.

Milo gently nudges my lower back. "We're not here to admire the building. Let's eat." He holds the large glass door while we enter.

Inside, my gaze wanders up the walls to the two-story-high ceiling, then to the exposed iron beams and ductwork that has been painted black. Tall, floor-to-ceiling windows grace the front, giving guests views of the bordering Mississippi River and the iconic Stone Arch Bridge.

Milo walks up to the hostess stand to give his name, and Nora follows. I have to talk to Garrett and clear the air before we sit down, or I won't be able to focus on the issue at hand—making a good first impression on Bryce.

I pull on Garrett's arm, keeping him from following Nora. "I need to talk to you."

He stops and bends his head toward me, raising his eyebrows. "I'm all ears."

My palms are sweaty. I'm so bad at apologies, mostly

because I hate admitting when I'm wrong. Doesn't everyone? I swallow, then clear my throat. "I didn't know you came to the cookout last weekend just to talk to me. I wish you'd told me."

He scoffs. "Does it matter why I came? When I tried to talk to you, you blew me off. Then you ignored me."

The heat of shame creeps up my neck. As hard as it is for me, I make a point of looking him in the eyes, forcing my gaze not to drift. "I'm sorry. I let my temper get the best of me, and I ended up making things worse than they'd been before. I hope we can put it behind us—along with our entire date night, if that's possible—and try to be friends."

"Are you sure this time? You really want to be friends, not just *acquaintances with mutual friends*?"

I don't miss the way he flings my own words back at me in a sarcastic tone. I inhale, long and deep. I can handle being friends with him. Never mind the fact that I obviously annoy him, and that we'll likely get into another argument before the night is through. And who cares if he's hotter than an asphalt parking lot in July? I have lots of guy friends who are way hotter than Garrett.

I'm just having trouble recalling any of them at the moment.

I release my long-held breath, along with all my misgivings. "Yes. I want to be actual friends."

His smile is hesitant, but it seems genuine. "Okay, then. We'll be friends."

A few moments pass, and neither of us says anything. Out of the corner of my eye, I notice Nora waving at me. Only now do I realize I've been participating in an unofficial staring contest with Garrett since I first pulled him aside. I looked at him so long I'm tempted to swipe the back of my hand across my chin in case there's a stream of drool running down.

"Our table's ready," Nora calls out.

Garrett holds out his hand in a gallant gesture. "After you."

I blink, then offer him an awkward smile. "Thank you," I say as I pass him.

The hostess seats us in a far corner instead of by a window, and I sigh with relief. At least here in the shadows I can hide the way my face has flushed. What is my problem? Do I have to break out in a rash every time Garrett so much as looks at me? I'm here to check out a potential wedding date prospect, not stare googly-eyed at someone I've already crossed off my list.

I scoot my chair closer to the table, and then the hostess returns with a carafe of water to fill each of our glasses. She leaves it at the table and tells us our server will be with us shortly.

I thank her, then pick up my menu and lift it high, covering my face so no one can read my lips as I whisper to Nora. "When do we meet the chef?"

Her hesitant gaze flits to Milo, then Garrett, and then back to me before she lifts her menu as well. "He'll probably come out after the meal. I'm sure he's busy with the dinner rush, but Milo assured me he would check on us at some point in the evening."

"Okay, good. That gives me more time to prepare my opening line." I lower my menu and smile at the guys, as if I wasn't just whispering behind my menu. Like a third grader.

Garrett stares at me beneath a raised brow, which isn't unusual for him. Or for anyone. I get that look a lot, and at this point in my life, it doesn't faze me.

I pick up my menu again, this time to actually read it. My sole purpose in coming here is to meet a man who has made a career out of cooking, so I figure I should put some thought into my meal selection and give him a chance to show off his skills a little. I skim past the appetizers and move over to the entrée section. Should I try the Bison Tartare? That sounds a little risky. The salmon burger is more my style. I settle on that, along with a side of beet hummus, and put my menu down.

The server returns to our table to take our orders, and I nervously watch the back of the dining room while Nora converses with Garrett and Milo. I only half-listen. My eyes are trained on the kitchen doors, hoping they'll swing open and a handsome man in a chef's coat and hat will step out and walk toward us.

I catch bits and pieces of the table talk around me. Nora asks Garrett how he's settling in at Milo's place, and he answers that everything's going smoothly. Then she asks about his ankle, and he says it's feeling much better. I assumed as much when he showed up without crutches.

Then the kitchen doors open. My breath hitches—but the only person who exits is a server carrying a large round tray. I sigh and wilt into my chair. I pick up my cloth napkin and start folding it like a limp fan.

"So Garrett," Nora says, "the Fourth of July is only a couple of weeks away. Do you have plans for the holiday? Does your family live nearby?"

My hand flattens against the table, squashing my fan as I sit up. I shift my gaze to Garrett, who is nodding.

"My parents live in southern Minnesota," he says, "but they'll be at my brother's in Iowa visiting his family. It's a five-hour drive from here, so I'll probably just stay at home —er, Milo's."

Nora draws in a sharp, excited breath. "Well, now that you're temporary roomies, you'll have to come with Milo and me to Meg's parents' picnic. They live on Lake Minnetonka. It's the ideal spot to spend the Fourth."

I clench my jaw and turn to her with wide eyes. What is she doing inviting him to my parents' house?

"There's always a ton of food," she continues, ignoring my stare. "Plus, at the end of the night, you can sit on the hill in their backyard and watch the fireworks from Excelsior."

Garrett's lips form a rather mechanical smile. "It does sound fun, but I wouldn't want to intrude."

"You wouldn't be intruding. You'd be Meg's guest."

I let my arm fall to my side, then drill my index finger hard into Nora's thigh beneath the table. She turns to me, all smiles, as if she's in no pain at all. "Your parents won't mind one more person at their picnic, right, Meg?"

I push harder, but Nora doesn't flinch. "Well, my mom is kind of particular," I say through gritted teeth. After that, I blink twice—that's Morse code for: *Don't you dare invite him to my parents' picnic!*

Actually, I think I blinked the letter *I*, but Nora doesn't know Morse code anyway. When I don't give in to her request, she kicks my Achilles tendon. *Ouch!* I glare at her. She stares back, her eyes wide and imploring, but I won't back down. Garrett cannot come to my parents' picnic. How would I explain him to my family? *"Oh, Mom and Dad, this is my new, single, male friend Garrett."*

Yeah, they'd let that one go without issue. The comments would be unending. My mom would tell me how gorgeous he is, and that I'm crazy for not dating him. My dad would probably invite Garrett to join his golf club.

They'd introduce him to my nosey Aunt Emily, and

she'd make a fool of me while Garrett stands there, watching. She'd pull all her old tricks—the sad look, the head shake, the shoulder shrug—all while saying, "Oh, Meg, you're still single?" No thank you. No one needs to see that.

"So then, it's all arranged." Nora's voice breaks into my daytime nightmare.

"Huh?" I shake myself from my trance, turn to Garrett, then back to Nora. They both watch me like they're waiting for a response. "What's been arranged?"

"Garrett will ride with us to the picnic. We'll be there around noon."

No words form. I just stare with my mouth hanging open like a carp.

Nora clears her throat. "Meg."

"Um..." I know inviting him is the right thing to do. No one should be alone on a holiday, but this is Garrett we're talking about. What is it about him that makes me want to hide in my closet with a paper bag over my head?

I clench my fists, praying for control over my emotions. Garrett is just a man. A man who is not interested in me. And since that could easily describe 99 percent of all the men I've ever met, Garrett is not unique in any way. I can survive an entire day with him. At my childhood home. With my entire family there, witnessing me fluster in his presence and flub up every attempt at conversation.

I swallow, then nod. "Yes, that's a great idea. I wish I'd thought of it."

"I'm...really looking forward to it." Garrett's face is bright red. Does he even want to go to my parents' picnic? It sure doesn't look like it to me. I'll bet he feels as forced into this as I do.

I'll pull him aside after dinner and talk to him. Together, we can find a way out of this predicament. Maybe he'll find a different picnic to attend, and then Nora won't feel obligated to drag him along with us. But I can't deal with that now. I'm waiting to meet Bryce, the chef. The man who might be my date to Braxton's wedding, and after that, who knows?

I have a feeling that tonight anything is possible.

twelve

BRYCE HAS NOT EMERGED from the kitchen. I realize it's the dinner rush and he's likely swamped, but it's nearing seven thirty. We've been here for an hour and a half, and we're done with our meals. I ate my beet hummus one mashed chickpea at a time, hoping to make it last as long as possible so we didn't leave before Bryce came out to see us. But now Nora is getting fidgety, and Garrett and Milo have run out of things to talk about. For Milo, that has to be a first. From across the table, I see him take a deep breath, and I'm afraid he's going to say it's time to leave.

But then the kitchen doors swing open, and I inhale a quick breath, causing Milo to turn his head. A man—I assume it's Bryce, based on his attire—walks toward our table.

Finally.

I hold my breath. My fists clench and unclench in my lap as he approaches. This is the moment I've waited all evening for, the scene I've envisioned probably a dozen times, but when it happens, I feel...underwhelmed. I don't know what I expected to feel. Fireworks, maybe? A force like a magnet drawing the two of us together? Or maybe something physical, like heart palpitations or a fainting spell. I don't experience any of those things. It's not that Bryce isn't attractive—it's just not love at first sight. But there's always love at second sight, or even third. I'm not worried.

Bryce's black hat covers his hair, but I can see from his exposed sideburns and the hair at the nape of his neck that he's a redhead. Red hair isn't a deal breaker for me, but my hair is auburn. If I marry Bryce, our kids won't stand a chance.

From what I can tell in the dim light, Bryce's eyes are sort of a hazel-brown color, not shockingly blue like *some* people's. Garrett's eyes make me want to jump in and swim a few laps, which could be considered a liability. I've caught myself staring into them more than a few times, and that makes it very hard to appear unaffected. Bryce's eyes remind of the breading on fried chicken. Sure, fried chicken is good, but I don't want to swim in it, and I can't imagine staring at it for hours on end without getting bored.

Bryce stands just between Milo and Garrett and clasps his hands together. "I'm glad you guys could make it," he says. "Sorry it's taken me so long to sneak away from the kitchen. We've been swamped tonight."

He has a nice voice. Masculine, but not too deep. I give him two points for that.

Milo scoots from the table and stands to introduce Bryce to the rest of us. "You've met Garrett," he says, nodding to his right. "And this is my girlfriend, Nora, and her roommate, Meg."

Bryce smiles at each of us in turn. "It's nice to meet you both."

"It's nice to finally meet you too," Nora says, smiling up at him. Beneath the table, she knocks her knee into mine.

I jump. "Um, yes. Congratulations on opening your own restaurant. I hear the reviews have been good. I was so excited to come here and try it for myself." I can't help smiling at the way I flawlessly executed my opening line.

Bryce beams at me. "I'm so glad to hear that. What did you order?"

I gesture proudly toward my empty plate. "I had the salmon burger and the beet hummus. Everything was excellent."

He nods in approval. "That's wonderful."

"And I had the butternut gazpacho," Nora adds. "It was delicious. So refreshing."

Is there really any other way to describe cold squash soup other than "refreshing"? Not really.

Bryce nods. "I'm glad you liked it." He angles his head toward Garrett. "And how was the dry-aged duck breast? I've heard mixed reviews."

A moment passes, and then Garrett clears his throat. He looks down at his plate, where half of his meal still remains. "It was, um..." He presses his lips together and squints his eyes like he's in pain. "Different."

Different? Oh no. How could Garrett say something like that? If he didn't like his food, he should keep it to himself. Not that I'm surprised he didn't like it. It has to be hard for a picky eater like him to find anything appetizing at a place like this, with such an unusual and limited menu. Even I was a bit hesitant, and I'm willing to try almost anything. Except raw bison meat.

Nerves buzz in my chest. I hope Bryce's feelings aren't hurt. If he only knew about Garrett's selective eating habits, it might've softened the blow.

Someone should let him know. *I* will let him know. As his possible future girlfriend, I feel obligated to protect

Bryce's ego. "I think Garrett has a freakish aversion to wild game," I say, looking up at Bryce and then back to Garrett.

Garrett scowls at me. "That's not true. I knew it was duck when I ordered it."

I lean forward and speak in a slightly hushed tone. "If you're not averse to it, then why didn't you finish it?"

He follows my line of sight to his plate, then splays his hands. "I did."

"No, you left a third of your meal untouched." As I point to the food in question, I feel worse and worse for Bryce. He probably pours his heart and soul into his recipes, and here comes Garrett, squashing Bryce's heart and soul right before my eyes. I stare at Garrett and narrow my gaze.

Garrett stares back, his cheeks flaming red. "I'm full, Meg. That's all."

"I'm sure a few more bites won't cause indigestion." I smile up at Bryce, but am discouraged to see he is not smiling back. He actually looks embarrassed. With his pale skin, it's easy to see the blush covering his cheeks. But why? I'm standing up for him, taking his side. That should make him feel good, right?

Beside me, Nora forces a laugh. "Don't worry about it, Garrett. Meg is just having fun with you." She turns to me, her wide, penetrating gaze on me. "Tell him you're just having fun with him, Meg."

"But I'm not," I say. "He's being wasteful, and honestly, a little rude."

I didn't think Nora's eyes could open any wider, but she proves me wrong.

Bryce shifts his weight from one leg to the other. With a small wave, he takes a step back from the table. "I'm glad you all enjoyed your meals...for the most part. I really should get back to the kitchen now." He nods to me and

Nora. "It was a pleasure meeting you." His lack of a smile makes me doubt the sincerity of his words.

As he stalks back toward the kitchen, my heart sinks. As far as first impressions go, I doubt I've made the best one on Bryce. I dare to sneak a peek at Garrett, who is still staring at me. He's gnawing on one corner of his lower lip when he leans forward, pressing into the table.

"What was that all about?" He practically growls at me. "Why did you make such a big fuss over my food?"

I can't tell him the truth. How pathetic would I look? I hesitate, hoping Nora will jump in and rescue me from humiliation, but she doesn't. Apparently, she's done stepping in to save me from myself. So I come up with an answer that I hope will satisfy Garrett while technically still being true. "The chef is one of your firm's clients. He gave us this meal for free. Don't you think it was insulting to him that you didn't eat it?"

"I was trying *not* to insult him," Garrett says. "To be honest, it was a little dry."

"It's called dry-aged duck breast. What did you expect?"

His fists clench on the tabletop. "Dry-aging meat is supposed to make it more tender, but this meat was the opposite of tender. I had to drink an entire glass of water to wash it down. I wasn't about to tell Bryce that to his face."

"So to protect his ego, you called it *different*? How is that better than saying it was dry?"

He throws his hands in the air. "What else was I supposed to say? He probably wouldn't have made an issue of it if you hadn't put me on the spot."

I scoff. "You wouldn't have been put on the spot if you had just finished it in the first place. That's what I would've done."

He pushes the plate across the table. "Then why don't you? It's all yours."

I push the plate back. "I would, but I don't eat other people's food."

Just then, the server approaches our table. "Can I get you guys anything else?"

I point down at Garrett's plate. "He'd like a to-go box, please."

The server's brow rises. "Okay. I'll be right back with that." Then she turns and leaves the table.

Garrett spins around in his chair and calls out after her. "Really, it's not necessary..." But she's already out of earshot. He turns back to me. "You did not just request a take-out container for something I don't plan to eat."

I lift my chin. "Yes, I did. I'd like you to give it another try. Tomorrow you can reheat it, but try adding a little water in a cup beside it in the microwave. Maybe it'll moisten up."

"I'm not going to reheat it tomorrow." His hands are spread flat against the tabletop. For the first time that evening, I notice a rather enlarged vein pulsating on his forehead, right between his eyes. "Why can't you leave it alone?"

"I'm just trying to salvage what's left of an evening that you ruined by being picky."

"Please stop calling me picky." His voice is stern.

"Why? You're one of the pickiest people I've ever met."

"Clearly, I'm not picky enough when it comes to who I go out with."

He did not. Just. Say that. The sting of tears burns my eyes, but I fight back the emotions raging inside me. "Let me rectify that situation for you immediately." I rise from my seat and throw my napkin down as hard as I can.

Man, I wish the napkin were made of porcelain instead of nylon so it would shatter into a hundred pieces. No, a thousand. As it is, it only makes a quiet thump. Not enough to turn any heads, and not enough to make the grand exit that I desire. But hopefully Garrett takes notice.

I turn from the table and storm out of the restaurant. Once I'm outside, I hear the sound of Nora's heels clip-clopping behind me, following me down the sidewalk. "Meg, wait up."

"I can't. I'm going home," I call over my shoulder.

"You're walking home?"

"Yes." Okay, maybe I live fifteen miles away. So what? And maybe Minneapolis isn't the safest place to be at night, but I don't care.

"Meg, please. Stop."

"Fine." I stop and turn, my face still burning with anger and embarrassment. "I am *so* mad at Garrett. Why did he have to come tonight? He ruined everything."

She places her hand on my upper arm. "You know we had to include him tonight. But if it's any consolation, I don't think he likes himself all that much right now either."

Silly, unwanted tears sting my eyes, but I won't let them fall. I blink rapidly. "Why would he say that? That he should be pickier about who he goes out with?"

"I think you pushed him to the edge. You tend to do that, especially with him."

I run my index fingers beneath my eyes, trying to not smudge my makeup. "Garrett and I will never be friends. I'm never going over to Milo's house again."

Nora shakes her head as she exhales. "Sure you will. Just give him time to calm down, and then everything will go back to normal." She squeezes my arm. "An apology from you would go a long way toward making that happen."

"I feel like I'm always apologizing to him."

She chuckles. "You have to admit, you made an issue out of nothing. And in front of Bryce."

I groan as my shoulders slump. "I did, didn't I?" I squeeze my eyes shut as I rake my fingers through my hair. "He's not going to want to ask me out after tonight."

"Probably not. I'm sorry."

"Please tell Milo not to mention my name to Bryce. Ever. I'm crossing him off my list of potential wedding dates." And adding his restaurant to the ever-growing list of places I'll have to avoid for the rest of my life.

Just then, the door swings open, and Garrett hesitantly steps out onto the sidewalk, holding a small Styrofoam box. He looks at Nora first. "Do you mind if I talk to Meg?"

She gives me a reassuring smile then looks back at him. "Sure. I'll leave you two alone."

Please don't. I start walking toward home again, but Garrett only has to take a few quick strides to catch up to me. He puts a hand on my shoulder to stop me and turn me at the same time. "What was that all about?"

I keep my gaze aimed at my feet. I can't look at him. "You wouldn't understand."

"Well, I think I at least deserve an explanation. Why did you insult me like that? Why do you care what I eat or don't eat?"

My shoulders fall. "I was trying to spare Bryce's feelings."

"Why? I'm sure chefs are used to people not liking their food. It goes with the job. Why do you care so much what he thinks? Do you know him?"

If I could hang my head any lower, I would. "No, but...I

was here to meet him. Sort of. Nora thought I might hit it off with him."

"Wait." Garrett takes a step back. "This was some sort of setup? Like a blind date?"

I hate that he knows what I've tried all evening to keep from him. I lift my gaze to meet his, and then I wince. "It was more like a blind introduction that might lead to a date." Not that it would anymore.

"So back there," he says, pointing toward the restaurant's entrance, "that was you trying to impress a guy? By throwing me under the bus?"

When he puts it like that, I want to bury myself in a vat of beet hummus. "I didn't know whose side to be on."

Garrett scoffs. "There were no sides, Meg. I was asked my opinion and I gave it. You should've stayed out of it."

I feel so stupid. Garrett's right. When will I learn to keep my mouth shut? "Do you think there's any chance he'll ask me out?"

If Garrett's trying to stifle a laugh, he's failing miserably. "Do you really need to ask?"

"No. I'd rather he forgets I exist."

He stands there for a moment, shaking his head and staring at me like I make no sense at all. "Why didn't I know this was going on tonight? I assume Milo knew. Nora obviously knew. So why did no one tell me? I might've been more patient with you. Maybe I would've gone along with whatever crazy thing you said."

Why didn't I tell him? That's a good question, and one he deserves an answer to—if only that answer didn't make me feel like the world's biggest loser. I decide to go for the watered-down, share-no-details version. "I didn't want you to know."

"Why not?"

Ugh. Apparently Garrett is a man who requires details. I avert my gaze and speak in a voice that's barely audible. "I was nervous enough already."

"And my knowing would've made you more nervous?"

"Yes." My hands fall to my sides. "Don't you get it? Not only was I going to meet a guy I hoped would ask me out, but I had to do it in front of the last guy I went on a date with—who, by the way, did *not* ask me on a second date, which only proves that I'm terrible enough on blind dates without having witnesses."

He scratches the side of his head. "Wait. Did you want me to ask you out again?"

"That's not what this is about!" I exhale with force, and my shoulders slump. "And no, I didn't. I mean, I didn't expect you to. But that's all beside the point."

Garrett's expression softens. "I see. So my presence made things awkward—well, *more* awkward, if that's possible."

"Yes, that's the gist of it." A slight breeze blows and it makes me wish I'd worn more than this lightweight shirt of Nora's. It billows like a ship's sail, the wind going in one sleeve and out the other. I wrap my arms around my middle. "By the way, I'm sorry for embarrassing you. I see now that I should've left you out of it."

A smile parts his lips. "I appreciate that. And you're forgiven. I also owe you an apology for what I said about needing to be more picky about who I'm with. That was way out of line."

I lift my face to meet his. "I probably deserved it."

His eyebrows rise in a playful gesture. "Maybe a little."

Even though his comment stings a bit, a tiny laugh escapes my lips, followed by another. With the laughter comes relief.

Brick by brick, my walls of self-preservation are crumbling, and it feels so good to let go and let them fall. "I do feel bad for ruining a perfectly good evening. We were supposed to be celebrating the fact that you and Milo are roomies."

Garrett rolls his eyes. "It's really not that big of a deal. I think Nora just wanted an excuse to get together."

"Well, then, we shouldn't disappoint her. I know we just ate, but there's no way you're full. Should we pick up a pizza or two?"

He grins. "That sounds like a great idea." He glances at his watch. "It's not even eight o'clock. I know an amazing place not far from here. Milo and I could pick up a few on the way home."

I clasp my hands together. "That would be amazing. Nora and I will be there—I think. Let me ask her if she had something else planned." I turn to look for Nora behind me but find only empty sidewalk.

Garrett's head swivels toward the door. "Maybe she went back inside."

"Her car's gone. Did she abandon me?"

"I'd bet money that Milo went with her."

How did I not hear Nora's car pull away? I groan. "I guess I will be walking home after all."

With his arm extended, Garrett gestures toward his truck, parked just down the street. "Let me give you a ride. Unless you're intent on walking?"

I look down at my strappy heeled sandals. "I'd rather not."

"Good. I'd rather you didn't." He presses his hand against the small of my back and gives me a gentle push toward his truck. "We can pick up the pizzas on the way. You know what Nora likes, right?"

"Yes. Sausage, green peppers, and onions. And I like Hawaiian."

He makes a face. "Are you serious? Pineapple does not belong on pizza."

I chuckle. "That's exactly what a picky person would say."

When we get to his truck, I make a beeline for the driver's side. "Is your ankle strong enough to hold down the clutch? Because you know, I'm pretty good with a stick shift."

"Oh, no you don't." He lunges for the handle and blocks me with his right arm. "I don't care how much pain I'm in. You're never driving this truck again."

thirteen

I SPEND the next two-and-a-half hours playing games and eating pizza—which I have to admit *is* the best pizza I've ever had—while Milo and Garrett poke fun of my cringeworthy dinner behavior. By the time Nora and I leave, I'm feeling much better about how the evening went down. Bryce was a long shot, and I'm probably not losing out on my soulmate by making a scene at his restaurant. And I can live the rest of my life without eating beet hummus again.

When Nora and I arrive back at our apartment, I'm exhausted, still slightly embarrassed, and ready to go to bed. I shuffle toward my room but stop in the hallway to remove the earrings Nora lent to me. I hold them out to her as she passes. "Thanks for letting me wear these," I say. "And the clothes." Not that Bryce noticed my outfit. I could've been wearing a sequin prom dress tonight, and it still wouldn't have made me any more appealing. "I think I'll stick with my classic attire from now on—black and gray and stretchy—if I ever go on another date."

"You will." Nora clasps her fingers around the gold teardrop earrings. "I'm sorry things with Bryce didn't pan out. Maybe we could try again? You could wear sunglasses and a wig next time, use a fake name. Maybe he won't recognize you."

I roll my eyes. "Nah. I think it's best if I move on. There was no spark for me. I'm ready to meet the next person on your list."

Nora's face falls. "There is no next person, Meg. It's not like I have a little black book filled with endless names and numbers. Bryce was a surprise, one I was glad for."

"But you seemed so excited when I told you I needed you to resume your matchmaking efforts."

"I wanted you to meet Garrett, and when you fired me as your matchmaker, I thought I wouldn't get a chance to set you two up. But then I did, and we both know how that turned out. At this point, I'm out of ideas."

"But I need your help."

With a side nod of her head, Nora makes her way into my bedroom, and I reluctantly follow her. She sits at the foot of my bed and pats the comforter beside her. "I'm not giving up, but it might be wise to ask Garrett if he'd be willing to go to Braxton's wedding with you—just so you have someone lined up."

With a loud exhale, I plop down next to her. "I can't ask Garrett. The whole point of bringing a date to Braxton's wedding is to show him that I'm in love and happy with someone of my own."

"But you aren't."

"I will be...when I meet the right guy."

"I don't have anyone, Meg. I'm sorry."

She already said as much, but hearing the finality in her words is like pounding the last nail in the coffin that holds my deceased love life. The last petal has fallen from my enchanted rose. The sun has set on the third day. I've taken a bite of the poisoned apple, and I'm about to fall asleep for the rest of eternity...and now I think I've read too many fairy tales.

I fall backward on the mattress and stare up at my bedroom ceiling.

"I don't want you to go to Braxton's wedding alone," Nora says, concern softening her tone. "Please consider asking Garrett. I'm sure he'd go with you as a favor to Milo."

I groan and roll onto my side. "That's just what I need, someone going on a date with me as a favor to someone else. No thanks."

She leans back and props herself up with her elbow so we're at eye level. "You could always try online dating."

"No way."

"Why not?"

"Because I have no desire to be catfished, that's why. I don't want to fall in love with someone only to discover he's actually still in high school. Or in jail."

Nora's eyes roll up toward her eyebrows. "Come on, Meg. Not every person online is a predator or a scammer. Tons of people meet their spouses through dating sites. It's really common. There's nothing taboo about it."

"Maybe, but I'd prefer to meet someone naturally. Organically."

"That's not something you can force, especially with your timeline."

"It worked out for you. You met Milo the old-fashioned way."

A slight blush spreads across Nora's cheeks. "Yes I did, and I still view it as a minor miracle. Things like that don't happen every day. I'm afraid if we don't get you set up on a dating site, you'll miss out on a huge pool of possible matches."

119

"Then I guess that's my loss."

Nora pokes me in the side with her finger. "Don't be stubborn. It's getting a little late now, but I can help you create a profile in the morning. You might make a few matches, start up some conversations, and with any luck, you could have a date as soon as next weekend."

I sigh, extra loud for Nora's benefit. "Fine. I'll think about it."

"That's all I'm asking." My bedsprings squeak as she scoots to the edge and stands. "You'll be surprised by how well this is going to work."

After Nora leaves my room, I brush my teeth and scrub my face. Streams of black mascara run down the porcelain sink and into the drain—evidence that I tried way too hard to be someone else tonight. Wearing Nora's clothes, layering on the makeup—none of it helped. No amount of makeup in the world could cover up my *unique* personality.

I climb into bed and lay awake for a long time. My body feels tired, but my mind is in overdrive. I spend some time in prayer, asking God to forgive my rude behavior at dinner, and thanking him that I finally made peace with Garrett. It feels like it will stick this time.

I also pray that I can meet someone without having to resort to online dating—unless it's God's will that I meet someone that way. But why would it be? Maybe God wants me to step way outside my comfort zone, because online dating would certainly accomplish that. The whole idea of letting an algorithm find my perfect match intimidates me, not to mention the fact that some of the people I connect with could be total frauds. How will I know if the person I'm talking to is genuine and not just trying to take advantage of me? Even face-to-face, I'm not the best judge of character. But from behind a computer screen? Talk about an impossible task.

I end my prayer, snuggle down under my comforter, and close my eyes. Maybe I am being too stubborn about this online dating thing. If Nora thinks it might work, then I'll give it a try. It could be the only way I'll find someone who isn't completely annoyed by me, someone who loves me for who I am—and who *I* can tolerate in return.

Tomorrow, I will place my love life into the hands of the internet. Hopefully it will be safe there.

Unlike credit card numbers and personal information and passwords...

I groan and roll onto my other side. I squeeze my eyes shut and try not to think about what tomorrow will bring.

When I wake up, Nora already has her laptop set up on the kitchen table. I walk past her to make my breakfast. I'm in the middle of pouring milk on top of a bowl full of cereal flakes when I hear the irritating screech of metal scraping across linoleum. She's using her foot to push the chair across from her out from beneath the table.

"Stop stalling and come over here," she says to me. "I'm going to need a few really good pictures of you so I can finish setting up your profile."

I sit down and take in a spoonful of cereal, chewing it slowly and thoroughly. "First of all, eating breakfast is not stalling. And second, I don't take pictures of myself. Don't you have any on your phone?"

"Probably." She swipes a finger across her touchscreen. "We'll come back to that. Let's move on to the bio for now." She turns the laptop around until it faces me, then pushes it forward. "Try to describe yourself in a few sentences—your personality traits, your interests—and then say what you're looking for in a mate."

"Okay." I'm still not totally sure what I'm looking for. I know I want someone unlike me, someone much more interesting, with an exciting job and maybe a few hobbies. To be honest, I have a better grasp of what I do *not* want, so I go in that direction on my profile. I type, delete, and retype for about five minutes, then I spin the laptop around for Nora to see.

"That was fast," she says. "Let me see what you have." She adjusts the angle of the screen. Her eyes narrow, and her head jerks back as if she's staring at something vile, then her jaw drops. Apparently, I've gone too far. It's not the first time. She shakes her head, grimacing. "No. No, Meg, this is terrible." She pushes the laptop away from her body like it's contaminated.

I roll my eyes at her theatrics. "What's so bad about it? I told the truth. I was upfront."

"No man in his right mind would want to match with you."

"Then why are we wasting time with this?"

"It's not a waste of time. You can make your profile better. Talk about yourself more, but just give the barest of details. Leave a little to the imagination so guys are curious and want to learn more."

"I can do that," I say.

"And when you're describing your ideal guy, try wording it differently. Try to focus on the positives instead of what you don't like. The way you have it written limits your options so much that no one will meet the qualifications. You're not even giving people a chance before shutting them down."

"It's called vetting."

"Vetting? Is that why you added that bit at the end, the part that says 'no accountants'?"

I chuckle, a little embarrassed about that line but not enough to delete it. "That's for Garrett's benefit, just in case he's using this same site. I don't want to get matched up with him. We've already been down that road."

Nora levels me with a stern gaze, her lips pressed firmly together. She lowers the screen, then pushes her laptop toward me. "Start over, please. And this time try to make it sound like you actually want to meet someone."

I groan, and then start hitting the delete button.

We spend the next hour tweaking—and by tweaking I mean totally rewriting—my bio until it no longer sounds like me, but a rather sterilized, bleached, watered-down version of me. I'm generic.

But it's not all bad. Nora has found several photos to add to my profile, and I have to admit, they're pretty flattering. If I were a guy, I would want to get to know me.

Once we have everything looking and sounding the way Nora wants, I click the button that allows my profile to go live and let the algorithm do the work. After a few moments, my screen fills with suggestions of guys I'll supposedly like. So I guess that means there are guys out there who are now seeing my picture? I'm so nervous my stomach feels like a butterfly factory. One of these guys could be my future husband. Or at least my next boyfriend.

"Go ahead." Nora slides her chair from the table and stands. "Scroll through some profiles and see if any interest you." She puts away a carton of orange juice that's been sitting out. Then she closes the door and leans across the table. "If you're daring enough, you could even start messaging some of them." She winks at me. "Have fun."

She leaves the kitchen and heads to her room to change. She's spending the rest of the day at Milo's. As usual.

I spend the next half hour scrolling through picture after picture of guys. There are shirtless guys, guys with long hair, guys hugging their yellow labs, guys with their mouths hanging open as if they're laughing at something really clever—even though I know they probably sat posed that way for at least ten seconds while they tried to get the camera angled right. What a joke.

And man, what is it with everyone wearing aviator sunglasses? I want to see a guy's eyes, not a reflection of the phone he's holding out in front of himself.

I decide it's best for me to let the guys make the first move. I'm not putting myself out there and messaging first. No thank you. And knowing my luck, no guys will be interested in me, so maybe this was a huge waste of my morning. Only time will tell.

Right now I don't have time to sit and stare at a screen. I have plans to go out to coffee with my mom at eleven. If my profile sees any action in the next couple of hours, I'll be surprised.

fourteen

MY MOM and I go out for coffee once a month. Other than most Sundays when I eat dinner at my parents' house after church, it's the only time I really talk to her. My mom isn't much for phone conversations unless they're quick and to the point.

I suggested we meet at my favorite coffee shop in Excelsior. It's a nice halfway spot for both of us. When I arrive, Mom's already there. She's waiting for me at one of those tall café tables in the center of the dining area. When she sees me, she rises from her seat and joins me at the counter. She pats my shoulder a few times, which is about all she can offer as far as physical affection in a public place. She's never been one to give a really powerful hug or, heaven forbid, a kiss on the cheek.

We place our orders at the register. A few moments later, the barista sets two paper hot cups on the counter. "Janice," she calls out. We each grab our cups, then return to our table. I thank my mom for the coffee, but I don't think she hears me. She's too busy examining her beverage with a critical eye and a frown. Then she clucks her tongue and huffs. "Must they use two cups for one latté?"

"What?"

She grasps the plastic lid and tugs on the cup. I watch as one paper cup slides from beneath another one. "See? Two cups. What a waste of resources."

I shrug. "They probably don't want you to burn your hand. Or maybe two cups insulate the drink better, keeping it warmer longer."

"I didn't ask them to do that. It's already too hot to drink. I don't need it to stay that way for an hour. Besides, those cardboard sleeves are there for those who don't want to burn their hands. This is unacceptable."

She rises from her seat and takes up the issue with the teenage boy behind the cash register. I can only shake my head as the heat of embarrassment infuses my cheeks. Memories from my dinner the night before replay in my mind like a mini horror film. Did I really make that big a deal about a partially unfinished meal? I acted just like my mom is now, making a huge issue out of nothing. No wonder the vein in Garrett's forehead was pulsating.

After she talks to the manager, Mom walks back to our table. She rolls her eyes and sits down beside me. "They gave me a coupon for a free coffee, as if that fixes anything."

I know the rest of our coffee date is ruined. When Mom gets in one of her moods, there's no getting her out of it. I shake my head. "Was that really necessary? Maybe it's just their policy to double-cup certain beverages."

"If that is the case, then their policy needs adjusting. And how will they know that if I don't bring it to their attention?"

My shoulders drop with my exhaled breath. "If it were me, I would bring the extra cup home. You could use it sometime when you're taking coffee to go and don't want to hold on to your travel mug all day. And then you could simply throw it away when you're done."

It's an odd role reversal—me acting like the adult while Mom frowns like a spoiled child. I hate the fact that I sometimes see the worst parts of myself in my mother. I try several times to veer the conversation to the Fourth of July picnic. That topic always gets her talking. I also want to warn her that I might be bringing a friend this year—a *male* friend—and that although he's single and super good-looking, he's only a friend, and she has no reason to get excited and start planning my wedding.

But I don't get a chance to tell her about Garrett. My mom has a one-track mind, and once it settles on something—in this case, the wasteful double cups—it cannot be redirected. So I give up and listen to her go on and on for another few minutes before telling her that I need to go.

"That's fine," she says as we both rise from our seats. "I should go too. I have some shopping to do." Her hand flies to her chest. "That reminds me. Talia's bridal shower is next Saturday at eleven. I'm on my way to buy her something now. Should I put your name on the card? Make it a joint gift?"

Talia's having a shower? It's the first I've heard of it. "I don't plan on buying anything." And I'm not planning on attending any showers either. Especially showers I'm not invited to—not that I mind. "When did your invitation come?"

"There was no invitation," Mom says. "Deborah called me personally just a few days ago. With the wedding coming up so soon, I think she's throwing it together at the last minute for friends and family on Braxton's side. I told her you'd be coming with me. I knew you would want to."

My jaw drops. "What? You didn't think to tell me about the shower, yet you RSVP'd for me? Why on earth would I want to go? I've never even met Talia."

"Neither have I. But Deborah is a friend of mine, Braxton is her son, and I think we should show our support."

I'm showing my support by going to the wedding. Isn't that enough? Besides, Talia doesn't even know who I am. I doubt that Braxton has told her anything about me, since our relationship meant so little to him. But even so, what would I say to her? How would I introduce myself?

Hi, I'm Meg, one of Braxton's exes. We're barely friends now, but please accept these dish towels as my gift to you, along with my blessing.

"Meg?"

I shake myself from my musings. "Yes?"

"Please come to the shower with me. I can see you don't want to, but think of how odd it would be if I went alone."

"I'm sure you'd find someone to sit with."

Mom hangs her head in that over-dramatic way of hers.

"Fine," I say on an exhale. "I'll go. We can both feel out of place. But I'm not staying longer than one hour. And if anyone asks, I'm very much looking forward to the wedding and so is my plus-one."

Her eyes brighten. "Which plus-one would that be?"

"I haven't narrowed it down, but I can tell you, he's very excited."

After Mom leaves, I'm too keyed up to drive home. I have to walk for a bit to work off my anger. I'm so frustrated with my mother. How could she sign me up to go to Talia's shower without asking me?

I shouldn't be the least bit surprised though. She pulls stuff like this all the time.

A warm breeze blows, whipping my hair into my face. I tuck it behind my ear as I stroll down the sidewalk with no real destination in mind and look in the quaint shop windows. By the time I reach the end of one block, I feel much calmer. It's probably the lake-town atmosphere rubbing off on me. Excelsior has always been one of my favorite places. On the southern shore of Lake Minnetonka, it's close to Minneapolis, but far enough away that it maintains its unique, small-town charm.

I cross the street. At the end of another block of brick buildings, I pause in front of a bridal shop. I've always enjoyed looking at the mannequins in their satiny, pearl-studded dresses and flowing veils. They give me hope and cause a surge of expectancy to flow through my veins at the thought of wearing one of those dresses someday...of being like a princess with my prince waiting for me at the end of the aisle.

But this time it feels different, almost like the mannequins are mocking me. In their own frozen, expressionless way, they remind me that Braxton is getting married and I'm not. Talia will be the one wearing the white dress, and I will still be on the other side of this window, staring in, wondering when it will be my turn.

When I get home, Nora's already left for Milo's.

My stomach rumbles, reminding me that I've eaten nothing but cereal and coffee, and it's well past noon. I'm rummaging through the meat and crisper drawers in my fridge, searching for sandwich makings, when my phone dings.

I pull the phone from the countertop, swipe up to open

the screen, then peer down at it. At the top of my screen is a notification from my dating app. My heart rate accelerates. Do I have a match? I lower a shaky finger toward the screen, hesitating above the thin sheet of glass. With my luck, the app is simply reminding me to download an update or something.

But then—*ding*—I get another notification. I tap it, and the app opens. I have two new matches, and they've both messaged me.

My hand flies to cover my gaping mouth. Two matches. This is much more exciting than I thought it would be, but it's also terrifying. How do I make conversation with a man I've never met and know very little about? My palms feel sweaty as I open the first message. It's from a guy named David. If I remember correctly, he's a high school band director.

How's it going? I see you're a librarian. That's so cool. What's your favorite book?

Two points for David. He asked about books—my favorite topic. At least he read my bio. I take a moment to think about my answer, then reply.

Too many to list. I love anything by Jane Austen. You?

Within seconds, his response pops up.

I'm not much of a reader. I only asked because I thought you might be.

Oh. Well, that's disappointing. His response has left me with little to build on for my reply. I remember reading in several articles about online dating that the first few messages are key in keeping a guy's attention. I have to find a way to keep him engaged, or he'll move on to the next woman and forget I ever existed. I type back another reply while he's still interested.

That's ok. Not everyone likes books.

I lean against the counter and stare at my phone, trying to telepathically force David to write back. Seconds pass. Minutes. And still, there's nothing. I try another approach —the "annoying pest" approach, because I've had a lot of practice at that one.

You're a band director, right? What instruments do you play?

Nothing.

Are you a sports fan?

Silence.

Are you an animal lover? I am. Cats or dogs, which do you like better?

Someone please slap me in the face. I'm dying here. David isn't messaging me. I'm pretty sure I scared him away, and yet I can't stop texting. Why can't I stop?

Because I've never been good at patience, that's why. What I really need is to find a way to stand out despite all the competition. To be honest, standing out has never been a problem for me—it's just that I stand out for all the wrong reasons. I'd like to stand out while coming across as a regular, normal human being. In order to do that, I'll need help from someone who knows how to be normal.

I need Nora. Thankfully, I know right where to find her.

fifteen

I SEND Nora a quick text telling her I'm on my way over.

When I get to Milo's, I park along the curb behind Nora's car, then walk around to the back door and let myself in. I often take that liberty—not that Milo has ever said I can, but I figure if he's dating my roommate and monopolizing all of her time, I can enter his house without knocking.

"Nora?" I kick my shoes off on the entry mat. "I need your advice."

"She's not here," calls a masculine voice from the other room. It's not Milo, so that only leaves...Garrett.

My stomach clenches. A second later, Garrett waltzes into the kitchen, scratching the back of his head. I try to ignore the way his T-shirt lifts up, exposing his abs. They're nice. Of course they are. Why can't Garrett have a spare tire or a muffin top hanging over the elastic band of his pants? Or maybe just an obscene amount of hair on his stomach, something to make him less—

"Meg?"

My eyes dart up to meet his gaze, which is zeroed in on

my face and probably has been for a while. From the mischievous twinkle in his eyes, I can tell he caught me gawking. I cringe and turn away.

"Nora and Milo went out to lunch," he says with a chuckle. "They should be back within the hour. You can hang out here if you want."

Gah! An hour alone with Garrett? No way is that happening. "I should leave. You look...busy." Which, in the original Old English dialect, translates to: *You look way too good in those joggers.* "I'll come back later." I walk backward until my heel collides with my shoes, and I start to lose my balance. My arms flail as I try to maintain an upright position.

Garrett's brows rise in question—of my walking skills, no doubt. "You don't have to drive back. Just wait here. It won't be long."

"You just said it could be an hour."

He shrugs. "I was spitballing. Besides, it's Saturday. The library's closed, right? What else do you have going on today?"

I square my shoulders as my defenses rise. "A lot."

"Really?"

"Maybe. You can't assume I don't have any plans."

"Well, do you?" He folds his arms across his chest and leans against the counter in a nonverbal challenge.

"Um..." Unfortunately, the only plans I had for the entire day—coffee with my mom—I've already accomplished. I'm as free as a bird. I can do nothing but stare at Garrett.

"That's what I thought." He pushes away from the counter and heads toward the living room. "Just leave your shoes where they are and come hang out with me. I know how much you love nature shows, and there's a great one on right now about extreme weather."

I groan. Does it get any better than this? The last time I watched TV with Garrett was right before he sent a text begging Milo to pick me up. But since I've forgiven him for that, I have to stop dwelling on it. Eventually, my blood pressure will stop spiking every time I think about it.

I let my hands fall to my sides and follow Garrett into the living room. He drops onto the couch, and I look for anywhere else to sit. The recliner is the furthest seat from the couch, so I head there.

"So, Meg," Garrett says, leaning back into the cushions, "Did I hear you mention something about needing advice? Can I help?"

My pulse kicks into high gear. "Uh, no thanks."

"Why not?"

"It's somewhat personal."

He bobs his head. "Oh, I see. Feminine issues."

"What? No!" My cheeks burn. "I have some relationship questions for Nora, that's all."

When he says nothing more, I sit back in the recliner and try to relax a little. Eventually, Garrett gets completely sucked into what he's watching on TV.

I have to admit, weather is far more fascinating than giant reptiles who live in the Amazon. It isn't long until I, too, am totally engrossed in the story of an Oklahoma family who lost their home in an F-5 tornado. After ten minutes, there's a teaser for the upcoming segment on deadly volcanoes.

I don't know if my brain can handle learning any more about the unpredictable violence of nature. I'd rather live in ignorance and think of Yellowstone National Park as a great place to go hiking and see bison, not a supervolcano that has the potential to wipe out the entire continent of North America.

During the endless string of commercials, my gaze wanders over to the couch and the frustrating yet handsome man sitting there. While I try not to stare at him, I can't help but appreciate his most obvious physical attribute—his *maleness*. There is a living, breathing resource sitting right in front of me, one who could help me get inside the minds of other members of his species, and I'm not taking advantage of it. If I leave out the details, maybe he could help me find ways to snag a guy's attention without knowing that he's helping me.

I pull the TV remote from the coffee table and turn the volume way down. Garrett looks at me, eyes wide. I clear my throat and smile. "Can I ask you something?"

He drapes his arms across the back of the couch. "Sure."

"I don't want you to read into this, and please don't ask any questions, okay?"

"I'll try."

"What kinds of qualities do you look for in the women you date?"

He scoffs, then shifts in his seat. "Wow. That was direct."

My cheeks warm with embarrassment. "I'm not asking about you specifically, but men in general. Try to answer on behalf of *all* guys. What traits do most men like in the women they date?"

His brows knit together. "Can I at least know why you're asking me this?"

"No." I waggle my finger at him. "I said no questions. Just answer."

He runs a hand through his wavy hair. "I don't feel comfortable having this conversation with you."

I roll my eyes as I push against the fuzzy armrests of the recliner, preparing to stand. "You said you wanted to help. I should've left when I had the chance."

"Wait." Garrett leans forward and reaches his hand out toward me, stopping me. "I'm sorry. You're right. I did tell you I'd try to help, so I'll do my best."

"Thank you." I let my shoulders relax as I ease back into my seat. "I'll try to narrow the field of questions to make it easier. Let's say you're getting to know someone new, possibly through...correspondence. What kinds of things might a woman ask you that would make you interested in her?"

One side of his top lip hikes up, Elvis-style. "What do you mean by correspondence? Do you mean letters? Why would I write letters to a woman rather than talking to her in person?"

I dig my fingernails into my thighs, frustrated. "It doesn't have to be letters. There are other types of correspondence, like email, for example. Or texting."

At first Garrett's brows are drawn down over his eyes. But a moment later, they hike upward. "Are you talking about online dating?" He claps his hands against his knees. "Are you using one of those dating sites to meet guys?"

My hands ball into fists. "No."

"Yes, you are. Otherwise you wouldn't be getting so upset right now."

I exhale through my nose and stare him down. "I am not. Getting. Upset."

He snort-laughs. "Yes, you are." He falls back against the cushions. "This is awesome."

Every muscle in my body contracts. Why did I think I could ask Garrett about this? I launch myself from the recliner and stand. "Forget I said anything, okay? Tell Nora I stopped by. Actually, don't. Don't talk about me ever again with anyone." I stomp toward the kitchen, ready to slip my shoes on and get out of here.

But Garrett follows me. "Meg, wait." He jogs over and places his hand on my shoulder. "I'm sorry. I shouldn't tease you, but I can't help it."

I huff a breath. "Because you're a bully."

He lowers his chin to his chest and looks down at me. "No, because you make it so easy. You get all worked up over the littlest things."

"Only when you're around. You irritate me like no one else can." Well, there's my mom, but that's different. Years of never being quite good enough eventually take a toll on a person.

Garrett rocks back on his heels. "Let me make it up to you. What are you doing right now, other than waiting for Nora?"

My arms fall to my sides. "Nothing. We've already established that."

"Good. I want you to come with me. It's a nice day, and we shouldn't be wasting it inside watching TV."

Nervous energy fills my chest. I can't leave with him. I don't even know where he's planning on taking me. "Nora should be back any time now. I don't want to miss her."

He swipes a baseball cap from the back of a kitchen chair and slips it on his head. "You won't. She'll be here when we get back. She's always here."

That's true. He's only lived with Milo a short while, but already Garrett has picked up on the fact that Nora and Milo spend every daylight hour together during the weekends.

"Fine," I say. "But you have to promise I'll make it back alive."

He pulls his truck keys from a wooden hook by the door. "I promise you will live to see another day."

∼

Curiosity nags at me as we drive south of the city, but eventually we turn onto a familiar tree-lined boulevard, and I realize we've reached Lake Harriet.

Garrett pulls up alongside the curb next to a park where kids are running around screaming and climbing on a jungle gym that looks like a giant pyramid made of rope. "Here we are," he says. "Are you ready to walk?"

I side-eye him. "That depends." If we're only walking around Lake Harriet, it will take an hour. I've done this trail before, and it's almost three miles. Very doable. But there's a longer trail that connects to another lake which is six miles long. If he plans on walking that loop, he brought the wrong partner. "How many miles are we walking, and do you plan on getting back before tomorrow morning?"

He laughs. "We'll only go a few miles. You'll be fine. I was on crutches not too long ago, so if I can handle it, you can too. We can turn around whenever you're getting tired. Just remember we have to walk back as far as we came." He steps out of his truck and comes around to my side to open my door. "I was hoping we'd walk as far as my favorite food truck though. I didn't eat lunch, and I'm starving."

I clap my hands. "Ooh, me too." Talk of food reminds me that I started making a sandwich earlier, but when my dating app distracted me, I forgot all about it. Now I'm so hungry, my stomach is eating itself to stay alive. Feeling more motivated than before, I start walking and pumping my arms for extra speed. I call back over my shoulder to Garrett, "Let's see you try to keep up, gimpy."

I guess I forgot that Garrett's legs are over a foot longer than mine. He catches up to me in seconds and has no trouble matching my pace.

"Do you really want to walk this fast the entire way?" he asks. "We have all afternoon. I wouldn't want you getting a cramp before we get to the food truck."

I'm actually starting to feel a twinge of pain in my side, so I slow my pace and take a deep breath. "Okay, if it's too fast for you, we can slow down."

He laughs. "I think it might be easier to talk if we're not winded. You wanted my help snagging a guy, right?"

"I do." But I'm a little worried I'll get made fun of again. "Are you sure this isn't going to be awkward for you? Because I understand that the fact that we went out makes you uncomfortable."

He snorts. "We went out one time, Meg. That's not why I was uncomfortable with the conversation."

"It's not?"

"No. I just don't like talking about my dating life. It's personal."

"Oh." I exhale and hope my disappointment doesn't show. "Fine, then it's not awkward." At least not for him, which proves how much our date meant to him—nothing. He's already over it. Way over it. Just like I am.

I feel the need to explain why I'm trying online dating in the first place, but then I'd have to tell Garrett about Braxton, and that's not something I want him to know. He'll probably assume I'm doing it because I'm one of those women who has to have a boyfriend in order to be happy— and I guess that's better than telling him that my ex-boyfriend is getting married to someone else because I wasn't the sort of woman he wanted to be with. Appearing needy is the lesser of two evils.

"For reasons I don't care to divulge," I say, "I have set up an online dating profile. I have two matches already, and I've started messaging one of them, but it's not going very well. Actually, I think I killed our conversation by being too demanding. What I need is a way to grab a guy's attention, make me stand out above the other women he's talking to."

"If you want to stand out, then just be yourself," Garrett says. "You want to find someone who likes you for who you are, right? Don't try to play it cool with catchy one-liners or make a bunch of flirty comments. That's not you. The right guy will appreciate you for who you are."

"Do you think so?" I look up to read his expression.

Garrett nods. "I guarantee none of those guys has ever met anyone quite like you."

"That's exactly my problem. I don't want to annoy anyone."

"Then you're not being genuine."

My shoes skid across the concrete as I halt my steps. "What? Are you calling me annoying?"

He lets his head fall back as he stops. He turns to me and places both hands on my shoulders. "No, I'm not calling you annoying. Well, maybe I am. Anyway, I think you're putting way too much pressure on yourself. You don't have to do anything at all, and you'll stand out. Believe me."

"How can you be so sure?"

"Because I've experienced it. Do you remember the crazy get-to-know-you questions you asked me?"

My cheeks immediately warm. "Yes, and you thought they were too personal."

"A little. But how much second-guessing did you do before you asked them? How much did you doubt yourself?"

I raise my shoulders in a half-shrug. "Not much."

"Right. And after the first few strained moments, we ended up having a good conversation."

"We did." A nervous laugh escapes my lips. "I remember you asked me about my hobbies."

"And you said you had none."

"Not true." I hold up my index finger. "I said I liked reading."

"Oh, that's right." He bobs his head. "And I said you needed to get out more."

"Yes, you did. And I think I'm still mad at you for that." A smile spreads across my face as I remember that part of our date, the part when it seemed like Garrett and I actually liked each other. "You said if you hadn't sprained your ankle, you'd take me somewhere the next day. But then—" My breath hitches as I catch myself almost mentioning the ill-fated text, which I promised I wouldn't dwell on anymore. I swallow, because my throat is feeling very dry all of a sudden. And now I can't look at Garrett anymore because the regret is almost too much to bear. So instead of looking at him, I start walking again. He eventually catches up to me.

"In case you're wondering," he says once he's beside me again, "if I hadn't been laid up with a sprained ankle, I really was thinking of bringing you here to Lake Harriet."

Something ricochets inside my chest cavity. Is it my heart? Did I just have a heart attack? If I did, it was mild, because I'm still breathing, still walking. I clear my throat. "What?"

"For our next date. I was planning to bring you here. I also thought about a couple of state parks that have nice trails."

Did he just say "our next date"?

Just keep walking. One foot, then the other. And try not to trip.

When I finally feel like I can speak without sounding like Homey the bullfrog, I turn my head and look up at him. "You were planning on taking me out again? Even after everything that happened that night?" I know I'm squinting at him, because the sun is behind his head, but he must think I'm giving him some kind of evil glare. He kind of flinches, then starts waving his hands in front of him.

"Yeah, but—that was before." He shakes his head. "Before the text, before the cookout...before Bryce."

"Ah." Now that makes more sense. "Before you knew better."

"No, that's not what I mean. It's just that by now we've had time to figure out what we probably would've learned on a second date."

"Which is?"

He briefly removes his hat to run a hand through his hair as a swath of red covers his cheeks. "Listen, Meg, I know full well how you feel about me. And it's totally cool because I think we're on the same page now."

"We are?"

"Sure. I get why you were so reluctant to be friends with me at first. We drive each other crazy. Sometimes you make me so angry, and I don't understand that because I normally don't have a temper." He shrugs. "Well, not much of one. But whatever I say, you almost always say the opposite."

"That's not true."

He raises a brow.

"Okay, maybe, but only when I know I'm right."

Garrett chuckles. "You just proved my point. Being friends is hard enough for us. We don't need to press our luck by trying to be more." He narrows his gaze. "Or...do you feel differently?"

I stare up at him for a moment, trying to interpret the look in his eyes. Does he want me to feel differently? Or is he hoping I don't? I can't tell. "Well, no. I mean, yes." I shake my head. "I feel the same way as you. For once, you and I actually agree on something."

"Great. So let's forget I said anything, okay? The whole point of this outing is to help you find someone who's right for you."

I offer him an exaggerated nod. "I won't bring it up again. Consider the subject dealt with. And thanks for being so cool about everything."

"No problem."

As we continue our walk in silence, I can't ignore the pang of regret that builds in my chest. Garrett wanted to ask me out? Does that mean he liked me? It must've been a fleeting thought, because he certainly didn't make it obvious. But maybe he's like me in that way. Maybe he isn't one to put himself out there and let his feelings show in case he gets hurt. Did I hurt him? I was so busy dwelling on the fact that he had hurt me, I didn't even stop to think about him.

But none of that matters now, because it sounds like Garrett has moved on. Like he said, we're not right for each other. At least that's what he thinks. And that's good, because I feel the same way. Obviously I do, or I wouldn't be here asking Garrett for pointers on how to lure another guy into a relationship. I wouldn't need to do any of this if he were the guy I wanted to be with.

And he's not.

So it's all good.

sixteen

IT TURNS out the food truck is only about a mile and a half from where we parked. The savory scents of oregano and cumin reach my nose even before we round the corner and the colorful Mexican restaurant on wheels comes into view.

I clasp my hands together. I've never been so excited to see a food truck. Not only am I starving, but eating will also give my mouth a much needed break from talking. My conversations with Garrett have been ping-ponging between *too embarrassing* and *too personal* all afternoon. I need to stuff a taco in my face before I say something I'll regret.

We grab two orders of street tacos with chicken and eat them as we continue around the lake.

"What do you think?" Garrett asks between bites. "It's good, right?"

"So far, this is the best food I've ever had in my life." I wipe my mouth with my tiny white napkin and then take another huge bite. "It's even better than the duck breast at Crop and Herd." I can't help the jab.

He responds with a snarky smile. "That's the under-statement of the century." Garrett finishes his tacos, then tosses his wrappers in the next trash can we pass. "So are you feeling a little better about your chances of snagging a man now that you've gotten my expert advice?"

It takes all my willpower not to roll my eyes. "I'm not trying to snag a man—yet. Right now I'm just trying not to ruin another conversation after the opening line. If I can do that, then I'll work on the snagging part. But yes, I feel pretty hopeful that it will work out. Thanks for your help."

He stuffs his hands into his pockets. "Any time."

"And if you're interested, I'd be glad to return the favor. Anytime you need insight into the female psyche, you know where to find me."

He scoffs. "Thanks, but I don't need your help."

"What?" A flash of aggravation rises up inside me, warming my cheeks. "Why don't you want my help? You're not in a relationship."

"That doesn't mean I need help finding someone."

"But you went out with me on a blind date. Why would you bother putting yourself through that if you weren't looking for someone?"

He shakes his head. "I wasn't looking."

"But you went."

"So?"

"So? Why did you go?" I want to stomp my feet and throw a tantrum, but I manage to refrain. "Were you just looking for a good time? Were you bored?" I stop walking, hoping he'll do the same, but he doesn't. For several seconds I stand there, staring open-mouthed at his retreating back. "What, so you're not going to answer me?"

He splays his hands and keeps walking.

"You're just going to leave me hanging?" I wait five

more seconds, then I dash ahead to catch up with him. I'm a little out of breath when I try to speak again. "Okay," I say, "we don't have to talk about your love life."

"Thank you."

"But I do think it's a little unfair that you know every detail about my romantic pursuits and I know nothing about yours."

"There's nothing to know about my love life, Meg. If there ever is, you'll be the first one I tell."

"Fair enough." I think. Or maybe it would be better if I didn't know. If Garrett were to go on a date with someone else, I don't think I'd like to hear the details. So never mind. I'd rather be left in the dark.

When Garrett and I arrive back at Milo's, I find Nora nestled against the couch's armrest watching a home renovation show. Milo is in the kitchen creating something that smells like pineapple mixed with chili powder. Is he grilling again tonight?

When Nora sees me, she sits up, looking ready to pounce. "Finally you're here. I wondered where you'd gone. Your text said you were coming over, and your car was here but you weren't. I texted you back, by the way."

"Yeah, sorry," I say as I plop onto the couch beside her. "I couldn't reply. I had street taco juice all over my hands."

"Street taco juice?" She eyes me suspiciously, then turns her head in time to catch Garrett entering the kitchen. "Were you two out together?" Her gaze returns to me, but now her eyes are wide.

I put my hand on her knee. "Don't read anything into it. I came here to ask you for help responding to these guys who I matched with online, but you were gone. Garrett helped me instead."

"You've been messaging with guys already?"

"I've only responded to one so far, and I totally botched it up."

"It can't be that bad," she says. "Let me see." Nora holds out her hand.

I open up the dating app and place my phone in her open palm.

Nora swipes the screen a few times, and then rolls her eyes. "Oh, girl. This is bad."

"I know."

"You practically attacked him with all these questions. If a guy doesn't respond, just let it go. Move on."

I nod, taking my phone back. "I'm planning to do that next time. I have to learn to be chill." Obviously something that will require lots of practice.

Garrett emerges from the kitchen with an ice pack and a towel. He sits beside me on the couch and props his foot up on the coffee table. "I think it was too soon to take such a long walk." He drapes the ice pack over his ankle and wraps the towel around it to keep it in place.

I whip around to face him. "Why didn't you tell me your ankle was bothering you?"

He waves a hand through the air. "It's not a big deal."

Another ding sounds from my phone, stealing my attention from Garrett. I glance at Nora. "That's my dating app. I have a new message."

She scoots closer, and we both stare down at my phone. "Well?" she says. "Open it."

I have the strangest feeling that I shouldn't be reading messages from other men when Garrett is around. I don't know why, but it makes me uneasy. Or maybe it just seems rude. I look over at him and raise my eyebrows. "Would that be okay?"

He scoffs. "Of course. Why wouldn't it be?"

Exactly. Why wouldn't it be okay? Because as Garrett pointed out earlier, he and I are lucky to be friends. And since friends only want the best for each other, I have no reason to feel guilty for reading a message from some other guy when Garrett is sitting beside me. "Okay, then, I'll see who it's from." I hit the screen to open the message. It's from Erik. He's a dental assistant. I read his message out loud. "All he says is, 'Hey, how's it going?'"

Nora shakes her head. "Oh, no. First rule of online dating—you do not lead with a line like that. He put absolutely no thought into it. Pass on him, Meg. Trust me."

All the breath leaves my lungs in one huge sigh. "What if I never hear from anyone else? I ruined my first match, and this could be my last. I should give him one more chance." I type my reply back to him.

Good.

Nora covers her face with her hands for a moment before looking over at me. "Really? You're just as bad as he is. You've basically just killed this conversation."

"Maybe not. Guys don't like chatty women. At least that's what I've heard." I can't help looking at Garrett for his reaction. Maybe he'll back me up on this one. But his face looks like he's in pain, like he's just stepped on shards of glass in bare feet.

"Sorry, Meg," he says. "I have to agree with Nora on this one." He pats me on the back and offers me a smile that doesn't look very enthusiastic. "I'm sure you'll get better with practice." He leans forward, lowers his foot to the ground, then pulls off the towel and ice pack. "This is all way too intense for me." He stands with a grunt. "I'm gonna check and see how Milo's marinade is coming along."

I watch him amble into the kitchen before I turn back to Nora. "Wow. I'm even too boring for Garrett, and he's an accountant. Do you think I'll be able to keep a conversation alive for more than two messages?"

Nora shrugs. "Hopefully. What did Garrett tell you to do?"

"He said to be myself, which basically means to be weird. He thinks it'll make me stand out." I purse my lips. "I'm not so sure about that tactic because I've been practicing it my whole life and I think that's why I'm still single."

"Just try it. Be yourself, like Garrett said. You have nothing to lose."

I sigh and turn my attention back to my phone. Nora's right. I have nothing to lose. I've made zero progress, and you can't go backward from the starting line. If I continue to fall flat on my face in the online dating arena, I will have maintained the status quo.

All I have to do is get really good at sending messages to men who probably won't like me. It's just like eighth grade when I walked up to Ben Talbot's locker and handed him a note, asking him to the end-of-the-year formal. He read the message, looked back at me, and laughed in my face.

Yeah, I'm no stranger to rejection. It only took me five years to be able to look Ben in the eyes again, and by then I was out of high school. Compared to that, this will be a breeze.

seventeen

AFTER A FEW INITIAL SETBACKS, I gained
enough confidence to message guys without scaring them
away. I started using weird, random facts in my opening
lines, and some guys actually took the bait. I figured if a guy
didn't like weird, random facts, he wasn't for me.

I even managed to line up a date with Paul, a mechanical engineer. He seemed a little nerdy, but his job actually
sounds kind of exciting. He designs high-tech medical
equipment like pacemakers and insulin pumps. That's real
lifesaving stuff, so in a way he's a hero.

We messaged back and forth for a few days. Finally he
asked me to meet him at a deli tonight for supper. It's
Friday and I know the place will be busy. I've been there
before and the food is great, but I'm not sure a crowded
restaurant is the ideal place to meet someone for the first
time.

I remember how uncomfortable I felt when I got all
gussied up to meet Bryce, so this time I take my own advice
and dress more casually. Only I don't have many clean
clothes. I want to wear leggings and a stretchy top, but I

wore my favorite black leggings to the gym and they smell like sweat and rubber. I don't want to show up smelling like a gym mat.

I text Nora, who is out with Milo, of course, and ask her if I can borrow a pair of her leggings. She has at least ten pairs of black ones. I also take the liberty of borrowing a really cute cropped top that is a bit bold for me—if I raise my hands in the air, my belly button will show—so I'm just going to make sure I don't raise my hands. Future crisis averted.

I arrive at Uncle Sammy's Deli a few minutes early. Through the window, I notice it's quite busy, so instead of waiting for Paul outside, I decide to snag a table and wait for him there. I don't have to wait long. I've only begun to look over the menu when the door jingles. I know it's him the second he walks in. He looks just like his pictures. I wave at him to catch his eye, and he smiles and makes his way toward me.

When he arrives at the table, he says, "Meg, right? I knew it was you when I saw your auburn hair. I like it." He smooths his hand down the front of his shirt. "You remind me of a Scottish princess."

"Um, okay. I actually do have Scottish genes on my dad's side. My last name is Rowland, but I think the original family name was *Rolland,* like Holland. The spelling was changed somewhere down the line."

Oh my. Am I putting out nerd vibes too early on in the date? If I am, Paul doesn't seem bothered.

"My mom's family is Scottish," he says. "I think that's why I noticed your hair."

"Wow, that's crazy. I thought most people in Minnesota were Scandinavian. Well, my mom is, so I guess I'm part Swedish."

151

"I am too. Finnish, that is."

Now that we know each other's genealogies, we seem to have hit a lull, and we're just staring at each other. I realize he's still standing, so I motion to the chair across from me. "Sit down. I'm so nervous, but excited at the same time." I hold out my hand. "I'm even shaking a little."

Paul pulls the seat from beneath the table, and after he sits, he takes my hand and gently squeezes my fingers until they grow still. "Don't be nervous. I feel like I already know you so well after all the messages."

"Me too!" Well, that was a little loud. I wince and shrink in my seat a little. "Sorry. I should let you look at the menu. I already know what I'm getting."

"Really?" His brows rise. "Have you been here before?"

"Yes, and I always get the Italian hero sandwich. I've never tried anything else."

"I think you should stretch yourself," he says. "Try being daring and order something you've never had."

"Um..." I scrunch my nose. Will he understand that I've made it a rule never to mess with a good thing when it comes to menu selections? Most people don't, so I won't bring it up. "Maybe another time. I'm eating out with someone I met online. I think I've stretched myself enough for one night."

He laughs at that. "I guess you have."

Once we order, our food comes quickly. We don't run out of interesting things to talk about, like how cool the artwork is on postage stamps these days and the increasing popularity of succulents.

From what I can tell, Paul is a genuinely nice guy. He's not the type of guy I would normally consider my type, but I'm beginning to wonder if I ever had a type to begin with. Maybe my type was all wrong for me and that's why dating has never gone well. So far, I can't find anything wrong with him. No deal breakers have reared their ugly heads. I'm comfortable around Paul, and I've discovered we have several things in common, like our love of raspberry iced tea. Speaking of which, I've had one glass too many, and my bladder is crying out for relief.

"Excuse me for one minute," I say. "I have to run to the restroom."

"Go ahead. I'll order you another tea if you'd like."

I stifle a groan. "Sure, that sounds great." I make a beeline for the restroom. As I pass by the other tables, several people give me weird looks. One woman looks pointedly down at my rear, slants her brows, then looks back up at me. It gives me a funny feeling, like when someone passes gas in a room and you know it wasn't you, but everyone thinks it was, and then you start wondering if maybe it was you.

I run into the bathroom and hurry over to the mirror. What is wrong with my backside? Is something on my pants? Did I sit in mustard? Maybe I have cherry cheesecake smashed all over the back of my—I mean Nora's—leggings. I turn around and crane my neck to view my backside, and that's when I see it.

My leggings. Nora's leggings. They're completely see-through, which means that maybe they aren't leggings at all, but footless tights. I can see my bikini-cut underwear plain as day and the stupid words written across the back in bright block letters that say, "Good Times." At least I didn't wear the pair that says, "Sizzle." That sends the wrong message.

Not that "Good Times" is any better.

I groan, lean my head as far back as it will go, and close my eyes. Of course I had to wear a cropped shirt too. It doesn't even come close to covering up anything, and I can't pull it down.

And here I thought showing my belly button would be the worst thing that could happen.

I feel exposed. And humiliated. I also feel like I can never leave this bathroom. But I have to or pretty soon Paul is going to wonder what's taking me so long. I hope he didn't notice my underwear when I left the table. He probably didn't because his seat is facing away from the bathroom, thank goodness. I'll just have to walk back to our table with my backside to the wall for as long as possible.

Once I've used the facilities and washed my hands, I give myself a two-second pep talk—*You can do this, Meg*—then I exit the restroom with my hands casually folded behind my back like I'm on a stroll through the park. Most of the people I pass, including the stern-looking woman who gave me the judgmental look earlier, have already seen everything there is to see, so I'm not too concerned with them, but there is still a chance I can save face in front of Paul.

When I get to our table, I turn and walk backward the rest of the way to my seat.

Paul smiles at me as I sit. "Your drink came while you were gone."

"Oh, goody." I take a sip, but I can't risk drinking too much, or I'll have to go to the bathroom again—and no way am I doing that. I set my glass down and try desperately to regain the easy rapport we had before. Our free-flowing conversation, the lighthearted mood—things were going so well, but I can't get back to that place. I can't stop thinking about my underwear and what I'm going to do when it's time to leave.

"After this, if you want, I thought we could get a coffee

and maybe go for a walk down by the river. Mill Ruins Park is one of my favorite places. Are you a coffee person?"

I nod, but I'm only more disappointed now that he's suggested coffee. Of course he would have a wonderful idea like that. I love Mill Ruins Park. And walking there along the river sounds so romantic—and disastrous. All of the joggers and bikers and dog walkers who pass by will see the back of me. I can't risk the humiliation.

I could just tell Paul the truth. I could have him wait for me to go home and change, and then we could go on our walk. But I barely know him. I certainly don't know him well enough to ask him to act as my body shield while we walk out of this place. It's way too personal and embarrassing for a first date.

Another problem is that I'm just like my mom sometimes—which I'm not proud of, by the way—and I have a one-track mind. Once something goes wrong, the whole night might as well be over. In the same way that one extra paper cup could ruin an entire coffee date for my mom, my see-through leggings have ruined my mood this evening. Now I just want to go home.

I place a hand to my chest and clear my throat. "Um, do you mind if we take a rain check on that walk? It sounds like a really fun idea, but I'm getting kind of tired."

Paul's eyes widen. "Really? It's not even seven."

"I know, but I have a bridal shower to get ready for tomorrow, which reminds me, I need to call my mother. I'd better do that now. It could take a while, because that's how it always goes with my mother, so feel free to take off. I'll get the check. I had a really good time tonight. Thank you."

Paul stares at me for a beat, his brow furrowed, but then he scoots his chair from the table and stands. He lays down a ten-dollar bill for his part of the check, which is rather thoughtful, since I said I'd get it. "Okay." He still looks dismayed. "I had a good time. Um, I'll catch up with you later, I guess."

"All right. We'll talk soon." Only, we probably won't. I'm sure Paul is just being polite and has no intention of catching up with me later. Why would he want to? I acted like a lunatic and I couldn't tell him why.

My shoulders drop as I exhale. I should have just been honest. I'll message him later and explain everything. It'll be easier when we're not in the moment. He's a nice guy. Maybe he'll understand and give me another chance.

But for right now, I need to figure out a strategy for escaping this crowded deli without getting called out for indecent exposure.

I go straight home instead of stopping by Milo's to talk to Nora about my date. I'll fill her in later when she gets home. I'd rather sit in my own apartment and sulk in solitude than spill the details of my evening to Nora with Garrett in the next room. Plus, I really need to get out of these leggings. Tights. Whatever they are.

I no sooner close my bedroom door than I hear my apartment entry door close, followed by the sound of keys being tossed against the counter. "Meg?"

It's Nora. Why is she here?

I step into the hall, still clad in my outfit of shame, and Nora meets me on her way to her room. "What are you doing here?" she asks. "I thought you had a date."

"I did. It's over."

"But it's only a little after seven."

"It's a long story. What are you doing here? I thought you were at Milo's."

"I was. We were just on our way to a movie when I realized I have a gift card for the theater. Milo said we could swing by and pick it up."

The door opens again, and this time the sound of loud clomping shoes echoes from the entryway. "Are you almost ready?" It's Milo. "The movie starts in fifteen minutes."

"I'll be right there," Nora says, calling over her shoulder. Then she grabs my hand and tugs me into her room. "Okay. Tell me what happened. Didn't you like Paul? He seemed like a nice guy."

"I did like him. But I borrowed your leggings and look what happened." I turn around and bend over. I only have to wait about two seconds before I hear the sound of smothered laughter coming from behind me.

"Oh, Meg. What on earth...why would you wear those tights with that underwear? You had to have known the words would show through."

I straighten my spine and whip around to face her. "You would think. Had I remembered my underwear said *Good Times* on the back, and had I known the leggings were not leggings, but in fact, tights—see-through, footless tights— I would have chosen a different outfit. But none of that occurred to me when I dressed myself this afternoon."

"I'm so sorry, Meg," Nora says. And she really looks like she means it, even though there's still a hint of a smirk on her face.

I sigh. "It's not your fault."

"Do you want to come to the movie with us?"

"No, that's okay. I'm just going to chill here for the rest of the night. Maybe I'll work up the nerve to send Paul a message explaining what happened."

"I think you should." Nora walks over to her dresser where she rummages through her top drawer and eventually pulls out an envelope. "Aha! I knew I had a gift card." She looks back at me and smiles. "I'll see you when I get home."

"Okay. Have fun." I'm right on her heels as she exits, but I quickly dash across the hall to my own room so I can swap these faux leggings for a pair of flannel boxers. If I'm going to spend the evening wallowing in self-pity, I might as well be comfortable. Not that the leggings aren't comfortable— there are just too many bad feelings attached to them now. They're tainted.

I wait in my room until I hear the door click shut, alerting me that Milo and Nora are gone. I heave a giant sigh, and then amble down the hall toward the living room. When I round the corner, I stop dead in my tracks. Garrett is here. In my apartment. He's sitting on my couch with his feet propped up on my coffee table.

Well, isn't this right on cue? Because obviously since I've just lived through one of the most embarrassing experiences of my dating life, *someone* should be here to rub salt in my wounds—and why shouldn't that someone be Garrett? He's so good at it. And it would be far too easy to just be left alone after suffering from the humiliation of wearing see-through pants to a public place. As I've realized these last few months, nothing is easy for me when it comes to dating.

This is so typical of how my life works these days. Pretty much nothing surprises me anymore.

eighteen

I PROP my hands on my hips and stare at Garrett, waiting for him to explain himself, but he just stares down at his phone. I don't know if he doesn't realize I'm here, or if he does and chooses to ignore me. I clear my throat, and he finally looks up.

"Oh, hey, Meg," he says, smiling.

Hey, Meg? I fling my hands toward him. "What are you doing here? In my apartment?" Suddenly realizing I'm still wearing Nora's cropped shirt, I tug it downward, trying to pull it over the elastic waistband of my flannel boxers. I am unsuccessful.

Garrett sets his phone down, drops his feet to the floor and sits up straight. "I came in with Milo."

Oh, well that explains it.

"I didn't hear you come in." As if that somehow proves he did not, in fact, come in. "You didn't say anything."

"Should I have announced myself?"

"Milo did."

"No, he called for Nora to hurry up, and I didn't think I

needed to do the same. But maybe next time I will. She'll love having two men pester her to move faster."

I groan. "Fine. That's not even the issue. The real issue is why are you still here? Milo and Nora left. Didn't you want to go to the movie?"

He leans forward, resting his elbows on his knees. "I was going to, but I got the impression that your date didn't go so well. I thought maybe you'd want someone to talk to. Nora left, so I decided to stay."

I narrow my gaze at him. "Wait. How did you know my date didn't go well? Did you hear what Nora and I were talking about?" My heart races as I replay that conversation in my head. Did I say anything incriminating to Nora or did I just show her the evidence? I remember bending over.

"Um..." He swallows. "Your voices were pretty muffled coming from the bedroom."

I nod. "Oh. Okay, then."

He clears his throat. "Also, it's not even seven thirty, and you're already back."

"That is true."

Garrett pats the couch cushion beside him. "So, do you want to talk about it?"

I press my lips together for a moment, like I'm really giving the idea some thought, even though it requires zero consideration whatsoever. "Sorry, Garrett, but I don't feel like talking about what happened. It's nothing personal, it's just...well, it is kind of personal. For me."

He shrugs. "Okay, I won't push. But since I'm here and now I'm stranded because my ride left me, what do you want to do? We could watch TV."

"Yeah, I guess we could spend a couple hours together." I plop myself down beside Garrett. I sit facing him, with my knees pulled up to my chest and my arms wrapped around my legs. "I'll bet you're just dying to check out the latest nature documentary on public television," I say. "But since we're at my place, I think you should have to watch what I choose." I drum my fingers against my shin bone.

He rubs the stubble growing on his chin. "Or, we could make a compromise. We can watch a movie—but no chick flicks."

"No action films either," I say. "No suspense, no horror, no mystery."

"Fine. How about a comedy?"

"I can do comedy." I try to flatten my smile as I snatch my remote off the coffee table then settle in against the couch cushions. Garrett stretches out his long, lean body, getting comfortable. We scroll through the offerings of three different streaming services until we settle on something we both want to see.

"Popcorn?" I ask.

"Sure. Popcorn sounds great."

I head to the kitchen, toss a bag of popcorn in the microwave, and set the timer. While it's popping, I return to the living room and stand beside the couch. As the opening credits play on the TV, I look over at Garrett and can't help but smile. I may have wanted to spend tonight alone, but maybe this will be better. "Thanks for giving up your movie. I think it'll be fun to hang out, just you and me."

"Really? Do you think we'll have...*good times?*" He winks at me.

My gut clenches as the heat of embarrassment climbs up my neck and spreads out over my cheeks. I can feel my blood pressure spike. "You said you didn't hear!"

"I may have heard bits and pieces."

I need something to throw. Thankfully Nora has a thing

for decorative pillows. I reach for the first one I see and chuck it at Garrett's head.

"Hey." He raises his arms to shield his face.

"You said you only heard muffled voices."

"I did." His eyes are wide, like he's trying to convince me. "But there were one or two words that came through pretty clear."

I clench my jaw and reach for another pillow. Garrett lunges forward and clamps his hands on my wrists before I can grab anything. "No more pillow throwing," he says as he forces me to sit down.

"But you lied."

"I didn't—okay, maybe I lied a little, but I didn't want you to be embarrassed."

"And then you suddenly changed your mind and decided it was okay to embarrass me? If you knew what happened, you should've kept it to yourself. I never would've found out."

Garrett stares into my eyes and I stare back. After a few long seconds, I realize he's still got ahold of my wrists. He must realize it too because he lets go and scoots back about a foot. I run my suddenly sweaty palms across my flannel shorts.

"I'm sorry," Garrett says. "I couldn't help it. I don't know why I like to tease you, but I do." He shrugs. "I hope in time you'll be able to laugh at yourself. We all do embarrassing things from time to time."

I turn my head. I can't look at him. "I do embarrassing things all the time."

He chuckles. "I know. It's one of my favorite things about you."

"Um, thank you. I think." The timer on the microwave goes off. "Popcorn's done." I pop off the couch and dash to the kitchen, grateful for a distraction. I shake the contents of the bag into two bowls before returning to the couch. This time when I sit down, I give Garrett a lot of space. I'm feeling a little too exposed to sit close to him. He knows too much. That, and my body can't seem to handle being close to him without going into spasms.

I am vaguely aware that Nora's calling my name. Why is she in my room? I sit up and lift my head from the hard pillow I've been resting against. My ear is throbbing. With the heel of my hand, I massage it to alleviate the pain caused by— oh. Not a pillow, but Garrett's shoulder. I must've fallen asleep during the movie. And apparently, when the movie ended, Garrett didn't bother waking me up. He just switched the channel and started watching a nature documentary. Go figure.

In the glow of the TV screen I can see him look casually at me. I slide away from him, but then I start to feel chilly. Is it wrong that I felt comfy and cozy pressed up against his side? It was kind of nice. And he obviously didn't mind or he would have said something or at least pushed me the other way so I could lay against the armrest.

Behind me, Nora clears her throat. She enters the living room and stops beside the couch. I look up at her and my gaze collides with hers. She makes a point of looking from me to Garrett and then back again. "You two look cozy."

Great. I glance again at Garrett, who's as relaxed as a cat in a sunny window. Looks like I'll have to get out of this one on my own. "You left Garrett here. He didn't have a ride home."

"You could've given him a ride home," Nora says.

"I could have, but I fell asleep."

"Clearly." Nora rolls her eyes at me, then looks at Garrett. "Milo is parked outside. He's waiting for you."

"All right. I'd better go." He stands and stretches, and then walks toward our front door.

All I can do is watch him, trying to gauge where his head is at. Did I seriously just fall asleep on him? That sends so many mixed messages. Do I need to do damage control?

Probably.

I spring from my seat and scamper after him. "Hey, Garrett, thanks for the big-brotherly time-spending thing you did with me tonight. That was really cool of you."

He leans against the wall while he slips a shoe on. One of his brows hikes up. "Big brotherly? Is that what we're calling it?"

I shrug, because I'm so unaffected by him. So very, very unaffected. "Yeah, I mean, not that I know from experience, since I don't have brothers, but if I did, I would hope they'd let me fall asleep on them. From time to time." Oh, for crying out loud. I'm muddling this up, as usual. "Anyway, I...appreciate how you wanted to cheer me up after my date. You turned my frown upside down."

And now I just want to slap myself.

He pushes away from the wall and smiles at me. "Great. I'm glad I was so helpful. Have a good night, Meg." He opens the door, then walks out.

"Thanks, you too," I call after him.

Once the door closes, I head back toward the living room and turn off the TV. Now it's off to bed. Well, almost. Nora's waiting for me in the arched doorway that leads to the hall, and she's got her arms folded across her chest. She's also kind of glaring at me.

"What?"

"What was that?" she asks.

"I told you, we were watching a movie."

"Not that, the whole brotherly love speech. What was the point of that?"

I fling my hands out. "I'm not sure. I just wanted him to know what it meant to me."

"No, you wanted him to know what it *didn't* mean."

"Well, yeah, there's that."

"What would have been so bad if there was something more behind it? What if you watched a movie together and had fun, then you fell asleep on him and realized that you actually like him? What would be wrong with that?"

I exhale, and my shoulders fall. "Everything would be wrong with that. I can't let myself have feelings for Garrett. He's made it clear that we're not right for each other."

"He has? Or you have?"

"It's kind of a little bit of both, actually. We've come to an understanding. We both feel the same way—that we're not a good match. I'm done trying to change myself to fit someone else's image of the perfect woman. I tried to be that for Braxton, and he saw right through me. Eventually. If Garrett doesn't think I'm right for him, I'm not going out of my way to convince him otherwise. He knows what he's looking for, and it's obviously not me."

From the look on Nora's face, she doesn't quite believe me, but she doesn't press the issue either. "So you were just hanging out."

"Yep."

"And there's nothing between you two? You want me to believe that?"

"I'm afraid you'll have to."

She sighs and turns toward her bedroom. "Whatever.

Just remember, when you and Garrett finally admit that you love each other, I have the right to say I told you so."

"Noted." I flip off the hall light as I pass by. "I have to be up early tomorrow so I can get ready to go to Talia's bridal shower. With my mom."

"Lucky you." Nora smiles as she steps into the bathroom.

Yes. Lucky me. My life is just one recipe for disaster after another.

When I finally climb into bed, I decide to send Paul a quick message to tell him in as little detail as possible what happened. He deserves to know it wasn't anything he did. I'm beginning to think I was too rash—I could've tried to explain my predicament. I'm sure he would've understood. We might just be getting back from an incredible riverfront walk right now if I'd only been honest.

If I apologize for letting my self-consciousness control my actions, maybe we can reschedule that walk...and the coffee too. I was so looking forward to those.

I open my app and swipe the screen a few times to open up our chat. But I can't find it. His profile is gone, too, and there is no evidence that we'd ever messaged each other.

Wait. Does that mean we're not matched anymore? Did he unmatch me?

I toss my phone toward the foot of my bed and throw my head back against the pillow. Ugh. So much for second chances.

Well, I guess I did act pretty weird during the second half of our date. I really can't blame him, can I? Looks like I'm back to square one, relying on my magnificent conversation-starting skills to snag a guy's attention. What could be better?

I can think of one thing that isn't better—going to my ex-boyfriend's fiancée's bridal shower. This weekend is going down the tubes, and it's not even halfway through.

nineteen

MY MOM PICKS me up at quarter to eleven on Saturday morning and drives me to the White Pines Community Church for Talia's bridal shower. She parks in the front row because she doesn't like to walk...or consider others who are less mobile. I grab the gift from the back seat, and the two of us walk into the church in silence. I'm not in much of a mood to talk since I'm still reeling from everything that happened last night.

Inside the foyer, a sign on a brass easel directs us to turn left toward the fellowship hall. The sound of women chattering grows louder the closer we get. When we pass through the balloon arch and into the lavishly decorated room, I have to take a moment. It's like a bomb went off beneath a botanical garden and tossed leaves and rose petals all over everything. There are flower garlands running down the centers of each table and vases of roses stationed every three feet. There are even loose petals scattered across the floor. That part is a bit much. Someone could slip, for crying out loud.

"Talia must love flowers," I say.

"Apparently." My mom's brows are lifted high as she takes in her surroundings.

I take our gift to the gift table and place the pink package in among the others. To the right is the dessert table, and when I see the sheet cake I stop cold. Braxton and Talia's engagement photo has been printed on edible sugar paper and covers the entire surface of the cake. It's the same picture that I saw on social media, the one that forced me to try and find a wedding date in the first place.

I will not be eating a piece of that cake.

I turn to rejoin my mother, but she's no longer alone. She's talking to Braxton's mom, Deborah. Talia is standing right next to them. She looks even better when she's not made out of frosting.

I had hoped I could put off meeting her until I adjust to the fact that I'm actually here. But no. I'm not afforded the luxury of time.

"Meg Rowland." Braxton's mom holds out her arms and waits for me to step into them.

I oblige. I lightly wrap my arms around her and pat her on the back. "Mrs. Hughes. How are you?"

She steps back, her gaze taking me in from head to toe before finally settling on my face. "I'm wonderful. And you're looking...very lovely as always."

I resist the urge to roll my eyes. "Thank you." The woman has never called me *lovely*, not even while Braxton and I were dating. She'll probably always remember me as the gangly, glasses-wearing spelling bee champion of the eighth grade. Though that reputation was hard won, it has been hard to shake as well. I've tried for years.

"Let me introduce you both to my future daughter-in-law." She steps back and places a hand on the shoulder of the tall, radiant blonde beside her. "This is Talia. Talia, this is Janice and Megan Rowland, old friends of our family."

Talia smiles and extends her hand, first to my mother, and then to me. She has a firm grip—more firm than Garrett's, actually. I have to give her points for that. "It's nice to meet you both," she says. "I'm meeting so many new people today. It's good to know that Braxton has so many friends."

"Yes," I say. "He is a friendly guy." I allow my gaze to drop to our joined hands and the mammoth-sized ring on her fourth finger. I stare. I can't help it. How much did Braxton shell out for that thing? Way more than I currently have in my bank account, no doubt.

I force my gaze back up to Talia's face and release my grip on her hand.

"Meg." Mrs. Hughes cuts in. "I noticed on your RSVP that you're bringing a guest. Might there be a wedding in your future as well?"

My stomach clenches. "I...well...there *might* be. But not in the near future. The guest I'm bringing is, um, it's a rather recent development. To be honest, I haven't even asked him to go to the wedding with me." Because I haven't met him yet. "But I will. And I'm sure he'll say yes."

My mom looks at me, her brows arched high. "It must be recent," she says. "Last we talked, you were still narrowing down your options." Great. Now she's offended that I didn't keep her updated on my love life. But how could I when there's nothing to tell?

"Well, I'm looking forward to meeting...whatever his name is." Mrs. Hughes smiles, then places her hand on Talia's arm. "If you'll excuse us, we should be moving along. I have a few more people to introduce Talia to, and then it will be time for games."

Yay. Shower games. Who doesn't love those? I smile once more before turning away and tugging on my mom's elbow. "Can we go now?"

"Of course not. I'm going to get some punch, and then you're going to tell me all about this young man whom you've failed to mention until just now."

I clench my teeth and try to speak through them. "Mom, there is no young man."

"Then why would you RSVP for two? That sounds awfully optimistic."

"Thanks a lot." My voice comes out more like a growl than a whisper. "I am hoping I'll have a guy lined up in time. I've been getting to know a few people, and I expect to have a date lined up for this weekend."

"Let's pray it goes well. I'm not getting any younger, and you're my only hope for grandchildren."

There are so many things I want to say in response— but I keep my mouth shut. I'm only twenty-five and I don't even have a boyfriend, yet I'm being pressured to procreate. This is why I don't like attending bridal showers, weddings, or baby showers with my mother.

After two shower games, where we're tested on how well we know the happy couple, we're treated to a light lunch of sandwiches, Caesar salad, and fresh fruit. After that, Talia opens her gifts. I check my watch and realize we've over-stayed the hour I've committed to, so I gently elbow my mom. "We should go. It's almost twelve thirty."

Mom huffs a breath, then slips her purse strap over her shoulder. "All right. Let me tell Deborah we're leaving." She walks to where Braxton's mom is packing gifts into plastic totes. A few moments later, they both walk toward me.

Mrs. Hughes smiles at me and clasps her hands in front of her chest. "Thanks again for coming, Meg. It's been too long since I've seen you."

"I agree," my mom, says. "We should really get together more often." And then her eyes grow big. She has an idea, which is almost never a good thing. "You should come to our Fourth of July picnic! You and Davis. Invite Braxton and Talia too."

"No!" I shout.

Mom turns to me, scowling. "Meg, what on earth?"

"Sorry. I meant to say *oh* no, you beat me to it. So unfair. I wanted to extend the invitation to the picnic myself. How could you, Mom?"

She narrows her gaze. She doesn't believe me one bit. "I'm sorry," she says, "but it's my picnic. I usually take care of the invitations."

"It sounds wonderful," says Mrs. Hughes, "but we already have plans for the Fourth. We're spending the entire weekend in Wisconsin with Talia's family. We haven't even met them yet, if you can believe that."

"I can totally believe it." I press my lips together, but it's too late. I've already spoken. Next time I have to remember to clamp my mouth shut *before* I speak.

My mom shoots me a stern look before aiming a super-polite smile at Mrs. Hughes. "Well, I hope you have a wonderful holiday with them, but we'll miss you at our picnic. Maybe next year."

My jaw clenches as another retort threatens to burst forth from my lips. Why must my mother encourage situations where I'm likely to run into my ex-boyfriend? At least

I'm safe here at the bridal shower, where only women are invited.

Just then, the front doors bust open and a decidedly *non*-female person enters the hall. "Hello, did someone request a pickup truck?"

Oh no. *No, no, no.* At the sound of the very familiar male voice, I instantly drop to the floor and crouch-walk over to the nearest table to hide behind it.

It's Braxton. Braxton is here. Why is he here? Doesn't he know he's not allowed?

Women only, Braxton!

I know I must look like an idiot down here, but I'm not in any way prepared to see him. I have seven weeks until his wedding, and I need every last one of those weeks to make my life seem as settled and impressive as his. I can't talk to him now when my world is just one big question mark. So to justify my position down here on the ground, I pretend I'm looking for something on the floor. I must've dropped a contact lens. Yep. I was just standing here taking it out of my eye for some reason and it fell onto the floor.

Darn contact lenses. They're so slippery and so practically invisible.

I hear footsteps approach. They sound too loud and *click-clacky* to be men's sneakers, so I know I'm safe for now. I peer up from my hunched-over position and catch my mom staring down at me with a look of annoyance. I shake my head and try to communicate with her using only my facial expressions. I widen my eyes and make a kind of scared face like I've just seen a huge spider. I'm telling her to ignore me, and not to let on that I'm down here, but the *V* of her brow just keeps getting deeper and deeper. She crosses her arms. She's mad—or embarrassed. Probably both.

But imagine how embarrassed I'll be if Braxton sees me, especially now that I'm on the floor.

"Meg, what on earth are you doing?" she asks.

"I dropped my contact," I say, loud enough that hopefully Mrs. Hughes will hear, but not loud enough to draw Braxton's attention.

Mom rolls her eyes. "You don't wear contacts. Now stand up. You look ridiculous."

"I can't," I whisper-shout up at her.

A series of hand claps snags our attention. "Okay, everyone," Mrs. Hughes says in her too-sweet voice, "now that Braxton is here to pick up the gifts, we should have the happy couple pose for a few photos. Talia, why don't you go over and stand next to Braxton beneath the balloon arch. That will make a gorgeous backdrop."

From the happy chatter that fills the air, I can tell everyone thinks that's a great idea. And it's actually a really good distraction while I make my escape. Now to formulate a plan. I could run to the bathroom, but I'd eventually have to come out, and who knows how long Braxton is planning to stay. My head turns on a swivel. I notice a side door. I don't know where it leads, but anywhere is better than here. I'll take my chances.

I look up at my mom and say, "I'm leaving. Now. Meet me at the car." I spin myself around then creep, bent over, to the end of the long row of tables until I'm only a few feet from the door. That's when I make a run for it. Well, sort of a run. It's more of a duck-waddle, but whatever. I don't look back. When I get to the door, I reach up for the knob, twist it—it's unlocked! *Thank you, Lord*—and fling the door open. Once I'm outside I stand up and run around the building toward the parking lot and my mom's car. I have to get inside it before Braxton comes out with his first load of gifts.

I pull open the passenger door, duck inside and shut myself in. Whew. Thank goodness for tinted windows and reclining seats. I'm safe here. I'm pretty sure I made it out of the building unseen, at least by Braxton. Anyone else can think what they want. They probably already think I'm weird, so I have nothing to lose.

My heart is pounding and I'm breathing hard. I feel like I've just finished a marathon. And in a way, I have. I would rather run twenty-six miles than sit at a flower-covered table with my mother, drinking punch and watching my ex-boyfriend's fiancée open beautifully wrapped presents while talking about how happy they are together. But that's exactly what I did today, and if that doesn't make me a champion, I don't know what will.

twenty

THROUGHOUT THE NEXT WEEK, I spend most of my non-working hours on the dating app attempting to strike up conversations with as many guys as possible. Unfortunately, I've only managed to hold the interest of two. One is a guy named Adrian, a travel writer. He really intrigues me. We've been messaging each other every day and I'm always impressed by the interesting tidbits of information he shares with me about the places he's been. We've even taken the all-important step of giving each other our real phone numbers. He's not always in places that have Wi-Fi or good cell service, so texting is easier.

I feel like I've known Adrian for longer than a week because I already know so much about him. I know that he grew up in Michigan and that he graduated from Auburn. I know the name of his quirky youth pastor who led him to the Lord when he was fourteen, and I know that his sister is expecting her first child—his first niece or nephew—in a matter of weeks. I can't wait to meet him in person, but he's away on an assignment and can't take me out this weekend. With Saturday being the Fourth, I have to take that night off from dating anyway. I've got plenty to keep me occupied.

I've also been talking to this guy named Tony, but I'm not exactly clear on what he does for a living. His profile just says "computer geek," so I'm not sure if he's a software developer, programmer, or in sales. I do know he's Italian, he loves Italian food, and actually we're going out on Friday night for what he promises is the best Italian food in the Twin Cities. He assures me I will not leave hungry.

When Friday night arrives, I'm a bundle of nerves. I'm meeting Tony at the place he suggested, which is in Roseville. I feel like it might be fancy, so I'm wearing a simple black dress. It's definitely my color, but it's a little shorter than I normally wear. It's Nora's. Yeah, I know I should've learned my lesson about borrowing clothes from her by now, but my wardrobe is sorely lacking.

Tony didn't give me the name of the restaurant, just an address. So when I pull up to a house in a residential neighborhood, I'm confused. This can't be right. Unless...maybe he's cooking for me? That's kind of romantic, even if it is a little bold for a first date. This house is really nice. No wonder he was vague about what he does for a living. He's probably made quite a bit of money in the software business, and he's too humble to talk about it. I can appreciate that quality in a guy. Tony gets two points for humility.

I walk up the front steps and knock on the door. Moments later, Tony greets me with a huge smile, and I'm reminded how much I like his dimples. He looks just like his profile picture, which is a relief, because when I pulled up to this house I started to wonder if maybe he gave me a fake address. It almost seemed too good to be true. But so far, real-life Tony is everything he appeared to be online.

"Meg, welcome." He opens his arms wide, and I hesitate a second before stepping into them for an awkward—my trademark style—hug. I'm not used to hugging someone I've just met, but Tony is Italian, so I have to adjust to his cultural expectations.

"Come on in to the dining room," he says, holding his hand out to show me the way. "Mom should be right out with the salads. I've also requested garlic bread. She makes the best Italian bread—from scratch."

"Oh?" My ears perk up not at the words *from scratch*, but at the word *Mom*. I take my seat, and Tony sits across the table from me. "So you asked your mom to come over and make dinner for us?" I hope that's what's going on here.

He gives a noncommittal half-shrug. "Well, it really wasn't much to ask. She makes all my meals."

"She does? So she comes here every night to cook for you?"

He laughs. "Of course not. She lives here."

I clear my throat. "And where do you live?"

"In the basement."

And now online Tony is disappearing before my eyes. "So...this isn't your house?"

"Oh, it is," he assures me. "I've lived here my entire life."

"Huh. How nice." I take a sip of water. "So, Tony, what exactly do you do?"

"Do you mean for a job?"

I nod. "Yes, we've never really talked about it. You mentioned computers."

"Yeah, I don't have a job at the moment. I'm just really into computers."

"Oh, that's..." That's what? I don't even know how to finish that sentence, so instead I drain my water glass.

All I know is this better be the best Italian food I've ever eaten because that's all I'm going to get out of this date.

After dinner, which I ate with Tony *and* his mother, I offer up an excuse to leave early. "Tomorrow is the Fourth." That's all I say. I figure leaving it vague allows them to fill in the blanks however they choose. Maybe I have a lot to do to get ready for a picnic I'm hosting, or maybe I'm getting up really early to go to a parade that's several hours away. They can assume what they want, and I don't have to hurt anyone's feelings with the truth—that Tony is not what I'm looking for. Yes, his mom is an amazing cook, but all the delicious Italian food in the world is not enough if it comes with the caveat of living in the woman's basement with her man-child of a son for the rest of my life. The minute I get into my car, I open my phone to the dating app. Tony and I are officially unmatched.

As I drive home, I check the clock on my car's dash and groan. Two Fridays in a row, my date has ended before seven p.m. How pathetic is that? Last weekend I tried to hide the fact by going to my own apartment, and look what good that did me. My friends showed up and eventually found out about my wardrobe malfunction.

This time I'm not even going to try and hide my failure. I'm bad at dating. There, I said it. Everyone knows it, so I might as well make the best of what's left of this Friday night and spend it with people I actually enjoy being with.

I swallow my pride, along with the piece of gum I've been chewing to get rid of the garlic taste in my mouth, and take the exit that leads to Milo's house.

When I get out of my car, I can hear voices in Milo's

backyard, so I head toward the gate and let myself through. Sure enough, Milo and Garrett are involved in what looks like a rather intense game of cornhole, and Nora is stretched out on a chaise lounge playing referee. When she sees me coming, she launches herself off the chaise and runs toward me.

"Oh, no, Meg," she says. "You're back early again." Her bottom lip protrudes as she pouts.

I sigh. "No need to point out the obvious. Is it all right if I hang here with you guys? I don't feel like going home yet."

"Of course." She walks back to the elongated chair and sits on the edge, making room for me to sit beside her. "Did you at least eat dinner? I have leftovers inside if you're hungry."

I shake my head. "I'm stuffed. That's the one thing Tony was honest about—his mother's cooking is excellent. He neglected to mention that he still lives with her. In her basement."

Nora shrugs. "There are worse things. A lot of people our age live at home. There's a housing shortage, you know. And rent is expensive."

"I got the feeling Tony has no desire to go anywhere anytime soon. Not when he has everything he needs at home."

A loud cheer draws my attention to the cornhole game, which Milo just won if his fist-pumping is any indication.

"That's twenty-one, Atkinson. Should we go again?"

Garrett looks at me before answering, his expression hesitant. "Um, I think I'll sit this one out." He nods toward Nora. "Do you think you can take on your boyfriend? He plays by his own set of rules."

"I'm well aware of his rules," Nora says. "But I have a

few of my own." She takes Garrett's place across the yard from Milo while Garrett saunters over to where I'm sitting.

He motions to the folding chair beside me. "Do you mind?"

"Go ahead." I scoot back on the chaise lounge and stretch out now that I have it to myself.

We sit in silence for a while, watching the bean bags fly and listening to Nora and Milo argue over how the game should be scored. Then Garrett turns to me. "So your date turned out to be a mama's boy, huh?"

I scoff. "I don't remember telling you that."

He scratches the back of his head and laughs quietly. "I couldn't help but overhear."

"You were eavesdropping like last time." When I catch sight of the repentant look on his face, I heave a sigh. "Don't worry, I'm not too broken up about it. Even if Tony didn't live in his mom's basement, things wouldn't have worked out with us. He's an only child."

Garrett gives me one of those *you've got to be kidding* looks that he's so good at. "A guy can't help how many kids his parents had."

"No, he can't, but *I* can help falling for a guy with no siblings. I'm an only child. If I marry an only child, my kids will have no aunts or uncles, and therefore no cousins. And if we decide not to have any kids of our own, both our family lines will die off."

He stares at me for a good minute before speaking. "Wow. You're thinking way too far into the future for a first date."

I fold my arms. "I don't think I am. I want my kids to have a bigger family than I have." Which reminds me, I don't know a whole lot about Garrett's family. "You have one brother, right? I remember you saying your parents were headed to Iowa to visit him."

"I do." He nods. "But I also have a sister who's younger than me. She lives in California. She goes to school out there, and this summer she's working and taking some classes."

"Wow, I didn't know you had two siblings."

"You never asked."

His words hit me like a blow to the chest. He's right. I never did ask about his family, but not because I didn't want to know. We've spent most of our time together talking about me. Come to think of it, I talk about me with most of the people I'm with. I think that's the thing I struggle with most, being an only child—self-focus. It's something I'm trying to be more aware of, but I'm obviously not doing a good enough job of it.

"What's it like being an only child?" Garrett breaks the silence. "It must've been lonely growing up."

I shrug. "I never felt lonely, probably because I didn't know any better. I had a few school friends, and of course my parents were always around. Then there were my cousins, my aunts and uncles—" I sit up and inhale a quick breath. "Wait. Tomorrow's the picnic. You'll be at my parents' house, and you'll meet all of these people, and I haven't prepared you."

He laughs. "What's there to prepare for? Is your family involved in some kind of illegal activity? Are they members of an underground crime ring or something?"

"My Aunt Emily is scary enough to be a mafia boss. You'd be better off avoiding her."

His brow furrows. "You want me to avoid your family members? Do you still want me to come? I don't have to if it's going to be hard for you."

"No." I wave a hand in front of me. "I mean, yes, I do want you to come. But if I could give you a few pointers, it might help you get through the day." I tell Garrett all about my mom's sister Emily and their sibling rivalry when it comes to their children's success, which, in my mom's case, all centers around me. That means I also have to confess that I'm not living up to my mom's high expectations for me, which makes me sound pathetic, but that's probably not news to Garrett.

"Now don't be too surprised if my mom stares at you like you're from outer space," I say. "I may have forgotten to tell her you're coming, and I don't make a habit of bringing guys to family events, so she'll probably be pretty shocked."

"You could tell her now," he says. "Just call her."

I shake my head. "I'm a little scared to, so I think I'll just spring it on her tomorrow." I'd rather not listen to my mom scream into the phone, *Why didn't you tell me sooner? You've had two weeks!* So I'm just not going to tell her at all. Being a rational person, I realize that one unexpected guest isn't going to throw off the brat-and-bun count enough to matter, but my mom might not understand that. By keeping this information to myself, I'm actually being nice, saving her from a late-night run to the grocery store for an extra jar of pickles.

Garrett leans back and steeples his fingers. "I think this is going to be very entertaining. What time do you want me there tomorrow?"

"*Entertaining* is not the word. Regardless, the picnic starts at noon. I'm planning on getting there around ten to help my parents get ready."

"Why don't I go early too? I could help."

"You don't have to do that."

"I want to," he says. "I have nothing else going on. Milo

and Nora are going to a parade. I have to admit, I'm not big on parades. They're long and hot, and I'd rather go where I can actually do something useful."

I smile. "Okay, that sounds great. I'm sure my dad will appreciate the help setting up tables and yard games."

"Can you text me the address? Or do you want to ride together?"

I imagine Garrett arriving before me, wandering around my parents' yard looking handsome and unmarried while fielding questions from my mom about his identity and our relationship.

"I'll pick you up at nine forty-five."

twenty-one

GARRETT AND I REACH MY PARENTS' house just before ten on the Fourth. The neighborhood streets are lined with cars. Apparently we aren't the only family having a large gathering.

My dad is in the front yard placing little American flags in the grass along each side of the driveway. When Garrett and I step out of my car and approach the house, a feeling of nervousness fills my chest at the thought of introducing them, though I'm not sure why. It's probably because Garrett is a guy, although he's not *my* guy. So why is my gut all knotted up like that pair of mittens I attempted to knit last week?

My dad looks up, looks at me, then at Garrett, and back at me. His brows hike up. "Hello, Meg. I see you brought a guest."

Leave it to my dad to state the obvious. I choose my words carefully, as if I'm offering a treat to a dog I don't know. He might be friendly, but he also might bite off my hand. My dad doesn't have a history of biting, but I don't have a history of bringing strange men home, so I'm not

185

sure what to expect. "This is my friend Garrett," I say. "He's also friends with Milo and Nora, not just me, so there's no reason to get excited."

My dad side-eyes me, then smiles at Garrett and offers his hand. "Nice to meet you. I'm Glenn Rowland." As the two of them shake, I pray that Garrett gives this handshake a little more effort than the one he gave me when we first met. My dad puts more stock in a good handshake than I do, and that's saying something.

I hold out my bag, showing Dad what I brought. "Mom asked me to bring extra sprinkles and some dessert napkins."

"She's in the kitchen."

I wave Garrett toward the house. "Come on. Let's go inside and get a few more awkward introductions over with."

Garrett starts to follow, but then my dad clears his throat. "Or," Dad says, "you could put that off for a bit. I could use some help setting up the volleyball net and the tables and chairs."

"Good thinking, Dad." I turn to Garrett. "Will you be okay if I go inside and leave you here with my dad? I think you'll be safer with him."

Garrett waves off my concern. "Of course. I'd rather be outside than in the kitchen anyway."

"Great. I'll come out and find you in a little while."

At that, he turns and follows my dad around the house to the backyard.

After they disappear around the corner, I take the sidewalk up to the front porch and open the door. As soon as I step into the foyer, I'm audibly assaulted by "The Washington Post March." Playing holiday-inspired music is my mom's way of getting into the spirit. On Christmas, it's a welcoming, pleasant sound comprised of carols and bells. Choirs, harps, and Bing Crosby. But on the Fourth of July, it's a bit harsh. Trumpets blasting. Cymbals clashing.

I follow the rhythmic beat into the kitchen where I discover Mom and Aunt Emily with their backs turned to me, busily decorating everything under the sun with red-white-and-blue sprinkles. Cupcakes, Rice Krispie treats, brownies—if sprinkles can stick to the surface of any particular food, it will be sprinkled. I wouldn't be surprised if the potato salad has sprinkles on top of it this year.

"Mom," I call out. No response. I drop my bag on the countertop and tap her on the shoulder. "Mom, I'm here."

She starts, her hand flying to her chest as she turns around. "Goodness, Meg. You don't need to shout." She looks me up and down, then frowns. "Shoes, Meg. This isn't a barn."

"Oh, right. Sorry." I shuffle to the back door and kick off my sandals, then push them off to the side so no one trips over them.

Thankfully, Mom turns down the music. "How do you like my new playlist?"

"It's very patriotic."

"I thought so. And with the new Bluetooth speaker system your father installed, I can play it throughout the entire house."

"Wow. That is so..." I want to say "patriotic" again, but I already used that one, and there's really no other way to describe what I hear other than "loud" or "obnoxious." Since I don't want to make her mad, I just stop talking.

At that moment, as if suddenly aware of my arrival, Aunt Emily turns away from the counter where she's been assembling a fruit salad. "Meg, you're here." She holds her hands out in greeting. It's not really an invitation to hug her, not like it would be for most people gesturing that way. Aunt Emily just likes to hold her hands out for show. She's dramatic like that.

She was smiling at first, but then as she steps closer, she angles her head to the side and gives me that concerned, sympathetic look of hers that I hate. "Meg. How *are* you?"

Why does she always have to say it like that—how *are* you—like we're at a funeral instead of a picnic? No one has died. I'm simply single, as I've always been. Maybe to her, that is a fate worse than death. Or maybe now that Braxton's engaged, my singleness is more of an issue. Did Mom tell Aunt Emily about his upcoming wedding?

If she did, we will have words. Later. In the meantime, I give my aunt the same answer I've been giving her for years. "I'm excellent. Thanks for asking."

To avoid any further questioning, I think it's best to go outside and find Garrett. Hopefully my dad isn't probing him about the balance of his 401(k). Just as I'm about to excuse myself, Garrett slides open the back door, walks into the kitchen, and stands beside me.

"Sorry to interrupt," he says, "but your dad wants to know where the croquet mallets are."

Aunt Emily freezes, and my mother is her mirror image. They're both staring with wide eyes. No one speaks for at least ten seconds. Ten very long, very awkward seconds.

Finally, my mom breaks the silence. "Megan? Are you going to introduce us to your guest?"

"Um..." I swallow. "Yes. Mom, this is Garrett."

I motion to my mother, and then to my aunt. "This is my mom and my Aunt Emily."

Garrett smiles at the two women standing across from us. "Nice to meet you both." He is blissfully unaware of the fact that at this very moment, my mom is creating our wedding guest list in her head. Soon she'll be calculating how much it will cost to feed two hundred and fifty people their choice of either beef or chicken.

"So, Garrett," Mom says, "you must be the mysterious plus-one Meg's been hinting at. She's been very skimpy with the details when it comes to your identity."

Garrett looks at me, confused. "Plus-one?"

I force a laugh. "Oh, she's talking about the, uh, dating app I'm using. She refers to every guy as a plus-one." I turn to my mom while nudging Garrett back the way he came. "No, Mom, Garrett is not my plus-one. He's a friend of Milo's from work."

Through the glass of the back door, I catch sight of my dad. He has found the croquet set. *Way to go, Dad!* I tug on Garrett's arm. "Look, you can go back outside now." I practically shove him toward the exit. He looks back at me with a puzzled expression. I know I'm being pushy and I feel sort of bad about it, but I'll apologize later. When the danger has passed.

"So I'll see you outside in a little bit?" Garrett ducks his head as he backs through the doorway.

"Yes, I'll be right there. Just a few more things to take care of here."

With that he nods, then makes his way down the steps and across the yard toward my dad.

I turn back toward my mom and aunt, only to catch their eyes following Garrett's departing form.

My mom folds her hands in front of her. "If Garrett's not your plus-one, does that mean you still don't have one?"

My cheeks suddenly feel hot. "Like I've told you, I have several options, and I'm trying to narrow it down."

"You should bring Garrett. He's very handsome."

"I'm not bringing Garrett to Braxton's wedding, Mom. He and I are just friends."

"Really? You brought him along to a family gathering, so he must be more than *just* a friend."

"Today is different. He had nowhere else to go, and it's a holiday. No one should be alone on a holiday."

"I see." She turns to my aunt. "Emily, do you believe any of this nonsense?"

"Not a word," Aunt Emily replies, shaking her head.

"All right." I offer my mom and aunt a sugar-coated smile. "I'm going outside. You two have fun creating wild fantasies about my life, but I assure you, the truth isn't half as exciting." I pull two plastic bottles of sprinkles from my bag. "Go crazy star-spangling everything in sight."

Since they're so eager to use their imaginations to color my love life, I can't wait to see what they do to the food.

twenty-two

IT TURNS out I had no reason to worry about leaving Garrett alone with my dad. I should've known they'd hit it off—they're so similar, they're practically the same person. I wonder why I didn't notice it before.

By the time I join them outside, they're talking and laughing like old pals. They've already finished setting up all nine croquet wickets in a perfect double-diamond pattern and have moved on to setting up the volleyball net. These are the things I usually help my dad with since I can only stand to be in the kitchen with my mom and aunt for so long before I feel like ripping out my hair.

Watching them, I feel a little useless. I walk up to one of the net poles they've just sunk into the ground and give it a good shake. Nice and secure. Dad is on his hands and knees, unrolling the net.

"Wow, you guys are making great progress," I say. "What do you need me to do?"

Dad sits back against his heels, then scans the yard, his lips pursed. "You could assemble the screen tent for Grandma. I set it over there, under that tree." He points across the yard to the leafy maple that still supports my old tire swing from its thickest branch.

"Sure. I can put together a simple tent." In fact, I've done it so many times it's become routine. Only each of those times my dad helped me. But that's okay. I can do this by myself. It'll just take a little longer, that's all.

Ten minutes later, the men have the volleyball net set up, the cornhole boards are placed the perfect distance apart, and the ladder ball game is assembled—and I'm tangled up in ten yards of green nylon and screen material, with about three hundred feet of aluminum tent poles attached end-to-end lying on the ground beside me. I have no idea where the top of the tent is, where the zippers are, or where to insert the poles. It's hot, and sweat is running down the sides of my face.

Suddenly, someone pulls on one end of the tent, sliding the material across my head and taking most of my hair with it. I lift my arms, and eventually Garrett's face comes into view. He pulls the remainder of the tent off of me, then stands there with a smirk on his face.

"What?"

"You look like you just got electrocuted."

Frantically, I pat the top of my head, then run my hands down the length of my hair, smoothing it back into place. "It's called static electricity, and it's your fault for pulling the tent across my head."

"Sorry, but you looked like you were struggling under there."

I huff. "Please. I would've figured it out."

Garrett chuckles, then bends to retrieve one end of a tent pole. "Here, let me help you." He points to the shapeless heap on the ground. "Try to find the loops to run this through, and I'll help you guide it in."

We work on the tent for another ten minutes and get it put together. "What is this thing for anyway?" Garrett asks.

"My grandma likes to sit in shade, but she also hates mosquitoes and flies, so sitting under a tree isn't enough. We put this tent together for her every year."

"I'm sure she appreciates it."

"I know she does. Once she gets inside it, she never leaves."

After setting up the tent, Dad asks Garrett and me to place lawn chairs in clusters around the yard. I'm glad Garrett came early to help, especially when he volunteers us to make the ice run for the beverage coolers. Already I feel like I need to get away from the house, and the picnic hasn't even started.

The morning flies by. At noon, the guests start to arrive. My grandparents are the first, as usual, followed by several of my aunts and uncles, and a slew of cousins. I introduce Garrett to my grandpa and suggest that they play each other in a round of cornhole—just in case Garrett needs a warm-up for our match against Nora and Milo later on.

A little after noon, I spot the happy couple rounding the corner into the backyard. Milo spots Garrett instantly and joins him and my grandpa. I recruit Nora to help my mom and me carry out platters and bowls of food.

Once the feast is set up, my dad calls everyone together to say grace. He prays, thanking God for the food and for the beautiful weather. Then he claps his hands together and says, "Dig in."

I stand back and observe, watching as a line forms beside the grill. Garrett and Milo hang back to allow the

193

older folks and families with young kids to go first before joining the end of the line. Nora finds them and sidles up to Milo, looping her arm around his as they stand side by side.

I watch them for a while, but eventually my gaze wanders over to Garrett. My eyes must like the view because I can't seem to get them to look at anything else. He's not looking at me, so it doesn't hurt to stare. But then a Frisbee whizzes by, just inches from my face, and my ten-year-old cousin Parker slams into me while trying to catch it. He nearly knocks me over. By some miracle, I manage to stay upright.

Parker looks up at me, terror-stricken. "Uh, sorry about that."

What does he think I'm going to do, yell at him? "You're fine. Just watch where you're going next time."

I clear my throat and glance around. Hopefully no one saw that little incident. I could've ended up flat on my back. It would've served me right, too, for standing there gawking at Garrett and drooling like I'd just eaten a pound of sour gummy bears.

I give myself a mental dressing down. Yes, Garrett is attractive. So what? Lots of people are. But looks aren't everything. I chance another quick glance in his direction, but this time he's looking right at me, and he has a sneaky little smile on his face. How long has he been watching me? Did he see my cousin nearly plow me over? Does he know I've been ogling him from a distance?

It takes enormous effort to smile back and try to appear nonchalant like I wasn't just imagining what he'd look like in one of those black-and-white men's fragrance ads.

What is wrong with me? It's got to be the heat. I'm delusional from heatstroke.

I march to the end of the food line, chastising myself for

acting so silly. When it's finally my turn to dish up, I pile my plate full of salads and Jell-O, then stop by the grill to get a brat from my dad, who's cooking with his old gas grill because he still hasn't figured out how to use the egg-shaped one. In no hurry to sit down, I meander through the crowd, saying hello to people I only see once a year, smiling at relatives who probably don't even know my name, until I eventually make my way to the picnic table where Garrett, Milo, and Nora have taken a seat. The only available spot happens to be beside Garrett, so I sit there. No big deal. I set my plate down and swing one leg over the bench, then the other, and give him a polite smile. "Are you enjoying your-self so far?"

He finishes chewing, then wipes the corner of his mouth with his wrist. "I am. How about you? I saw you playing Frisbee with that little boy. You really need to work on your catching technique."

Heat infuses my cheeks. "Actually, I was practicing a defensive block. The objective is to stop the other player from catching the Frisbee."

He offers me an exaggerated nod. "I see. You'll have to teach me that move sometime."

"I would be happy to."

Only when I do, I will be the one to plow into him and knock him to the ground. Then we'll see if he still feels like smiling.

By late afternoon, the temperature rises to about eighty-five degrees. My dad takes the boat out and hooks up the tube so he can give rides to the kids. Nora, Milo, Garrett, and I are going to take out the Jet Skis. My parents have two of them. Milo and Nora climb onto one, and I get to ride with Garrett on the other. I stand on the dock, staring at the Jet Ski that's bobbing in the water, tethered to a dock pole, and tell myself how it's really not going to be that big of a deal to sit so close to Garrett with my arms wrapped around his torso. Yes, he's in his swim trunks, and it's the first time I've seen him without a shirt, but that's nothing special. My dad is also in swim trunks and is also without a shirt. So whenever my thoughts start straying toward Garrett and his well-toned chest, I just look over at my dad and his slightly rounded belly.

My dad may have been well-toned when he was younger, much like Garrett, but he isn't anymore, and someday Garrett will have a dad-bod just like every other middle-aged man I know. So I just have to picture Garrett in his fifties with his dad-bod, balding head, and overgrown toenails, and then I can put my arms around him and ride behind him, and everything is fine and totally above board.

Suddenly a life vest goes sailing through the air and lands on the dock beside my feet. "Don't forget these," my dad says before tossing another one out of the boat.

"Oh, yes!" I shout. "Thanks, Dad, you saved the day." I hand the larger one to Garrett and take the smaller one for myself. My dad is a genius. He was probably thinking about the vests keeping us afloat should we fly off. But with a vest on, I can hold on to Garrett without pressing up against his bare back.

Because, let's be honest, I can say what I want about dad-bods, but Garrett does not have one, and I don't think he's going to have one for a very long time. And if I'm going to ride behind him and try to keep my thoughts about him on the "friendly" side, he needs to cover up that not-so-dad-bod. Otherwise, I might start to question why I haven't asked him to be my date to Braxton's wedding.

Wait, what?

There goes that stinking heatstroke again. It's affecting my ability to reason. Of course I'm not going to ask Garrett to go to the wedding with me. He's my friend. He's made that very clear.

Crystal clear.

"Are you ready?" Garrett breaks into my thoughts. He's climbing onto the Jet Ski, life vest securely fastened, and I'm standing here on the dock like an idiot.

"Uh, yep. Just buckling up." *And trying to picture you in unflattering ways.*

I hop on behind Garrett, clasp my arms around him, and he takes off. I scream as the force pulls me backward, making me latch on tighter. We glide across the water, just a little ways behind Milo and Nora. When Milo makes a sudden, sharp turn, the spray from his Jet Ski hits me in the face. I duck behind Garrett's back to avoid further assault. It takes me a few minutes to adjust to the fact that I'm wrapped around Garrett like a starfish, but eventually it feels totally normal, and I begin to relax. The wind blows through my hair and a fine mist of lake water sprinkles my skin, and I'm having so much fun it makes me wonder why I haven't done this more often. I grew up on this lake. I've had plenty of opportunities to participate in water activities—tubing, waterskiing, Jet Skiing—but I almost never did. I preferred to sit on the dock and read. Was I that much of a bore? Or did I just not have the right person in my life to do it with?

A speedboat crosses several dozen yards in front of us, and Garrett accelerates over its wake and launches us into the air. We come down hard, hitting the water with a crash.

My chin smashes into Garrett's shoulder, and the force knocks my head back. If it weren't for the death grip I have on his ribcage, I might've fallen into the water.

He turns his head to the side and leans back into me. "You all right?"

I give him a thumbs-up, still too dazed from the impact to speak. If I'd known Garrett was so fearless when it comes to operating personal watercraft, I might not have gotten on this thing with him. But since I'm already stuck here, I'm not going to complain too much because it's the most fun I've had in months, maybe even years. Although, if I'm going to spend my last moments on earth pressed up against the back of an incredibly handsome, yet reckless man, I probably should've opted for a much thinner life vest.

twenty-three

WE SPEND the remainder of the afternoon out on the water, exploring the many bays of Lake Minnetonka. We only come in for gas and supper, not because we're hungry, but because the evening hot dog roast over the fire pit is one of my favorite things about summertime on the lake. After we eat, we finally take on Nora and Milo in that corn-hole match. For the first time ever, I'm on the winning team —not because Garrett and I are amazing at cornhole, but because Milo's house rules do not apply at the Rowland home.

The sun begins to set around nine, and those who have stayed to watch the fireworks gather on my parents' lawn. Their sloping backyard hill has an amazing view looking out over the lake. Nora and Milo spread out a large quilt and lie side by side, gazing up at the darkening sky.

Garrett stands a ways behind them, hands in his shorts pockets. After getting a blanket of my own from the house, I walk up to him and stop. "You don't have to stand for the entire fireworks display, you know. I have a blanket. You're welcome to share it with me, unless you want to grab one of my parents' plastic chairs."

When he looks over at me, I notice the way his hair has dried, all shaggy and windblown. It looks good on him.

He offers a hesitant smile. "I'm fine sitting on the blanket, if that's okay with you."

I can't help but laugh. "I think I'll survive. Here, let's spread it out." I hand him one edge of the blanket, and together we unfold it, lay it down, and get comfortable. Garrett reclines with his arms folded behind his head like a pillow. I sit up, leaning back on my arms for support. I don't want us to appear too cozy, like our neighbors on the next blanket. I can hear them giggling and whispering, and it's all I can do not to rip out a handful of grass and throw it at them.

The sky grows darker, but the fireworks haven't started yet. It's only going to be a matter of minutes, but in the meantime there's nothing to do but talk. After spending the afternoon smashed up against Garrett's back and liking it way too much, I really don't know what to say to him. He seems equally tongue-tied, although I don't know his reasons.

Eventually he reaches across the blanket to tap me on the elbow. "Hey, do you remember when we went on that walk around Lake Harriet?"

I chuckle. "Of course." I'm not sure where he's going with this, but he's clearly got something on his mind.

"Remember when I told you I wasn't looking for a relationship, and you asked me why I went out with you?"

"Yes, and I also remember you refused to answer that question."

He tilts his head up toward me and then, using his elbows, he thrusts himself upright. Just like that, we're sitting side by side. His arm brushes against mine, and my skin tingles.

He looks into my eyes and opens his mouth like he's about to respond—and then he shuts it. His shoulders drop as he expels the breath from his lungs. "That first date...that was a really confusing time for me," he says. "I had just started a new job, moved to a new area. Dating wasn't even on my radar. Nora had been coming by the office a lot to visit Milo, and every time she saw me, she'd make some comment or other about how I had to meet her roommate —you, obviously—and that she knew we'd hit it off. At first I was reluctant, because, like I said, I wasn't looking. But then I started wondering what would happen if I didn't go. What if you were perfect for me, and because of my stubbornness, I missed out on the person God had for me?" He stops, his eyes searching mine.

I stare back at him, caught in his gaze, waiting for him to say something more. Is that the end? Is he done explaining himself? Was I the person God had for him and he didn't tell me? Or, like I've been led to believe these past few weeks, was the date in fact a total disaster and Garrett and I are lucky to be on speaking terms?

After several moments pass and Garrett still doesn't say anything more, I shake my head. "Why are you telling me this?"

He shrugs. "Because you asked, and I just wanted you to know."

"Umm...okay?" What does he want me to say? I don't know if he's testing the waters, trying to gauge where I'm at, or if he's just trying to make me feel better, knowing that so far, my online dating experiment isn't going so well.

I take the cautious approach, because I don't want to open up too much just to get my heart stomped on. I take a deep breath and blow it out between pursed lips. "I feel really bad that you went on that date with me expecting great things, and it ended up being such a letdown. Looking back, I'm sure you wish you'd stayed at home."

He looks baffled. "Meg, of course that's not what I wish. If I hadn't gone, I wouldn't have someone in my life who's becoming...a really good friend."

There's that word again—*friend*.

With my knees hugged to my chest and my arms wrapped around them, I'm a mountain of disappointment. I don't know why I'm surprised that he pulled the friend card again. He's always very careful to let me know where we stand. I force myself to smile and swallow down the lump of emotion that's clogging my throat. "Thank you for finally answering my question."

"It's only fair, since you were so open with me about your dating struggles. Sometimes it's harder for me to talk about certain things."

"I understand. Thanks."

He just smiles back at me. For some reason, I have the feeling that he wasn't being completely honest with me. But of course, that could just be wishful thinking on my part. Since lately I've been having all these weird feelings toward Garrett, I would've been over the moon to hear him say that while we weren't a love match on our first date, he had come to develop feelings for me over time—kind of like the feelings I seem to have developed for him. But he didn't. He had the perfect opportunity, and he didn't use it. So maybe there is nothing there for him where I'm concerned.

Or maybe he's scared.

Maybe I could be the one to take that first step, make my feelings known, and then he can do what he wants with that knowledge. Yeah, he'll probably flat-out reject me, but at least he'll know how I feel and I won't have any regrets. It'll hurt like heck, but maybe it's just time to rip the Band-Aid off.

I take a deep breath to calm my nerves, then clear my throat. I lean in. "Garrett, I've been thinking—"

Just then, an earth-rumbling boom hits my ears. A blaze of pink shoots up from across the lake, a straight line heading right for the heavens. The fireworks show is starting. I smile at Garrett, hoping we can put a pin in our conversation and come back to it later. If I ever get the courage back.

The sky lights up in a sea of twinkling, shimmering lights—gold, green, and white. They cascade in serene silence until another one goes off. It looks like a battle of colors and lights, each trying to be bigger and louder than the one before it.

The fireworks show lights up the night for the next forty-five minutes. Every once in a while I sneak a peek at Garrett, and I catch him glancing at me.

My cousin's four-year-old son keeps running in circles around our blanket until he eventually trips over Garrett's shoe and lands facedown on the ground. He only cries for a few seconds before Garrett flips him over and tickles him. He curls into a ball of giggles and rolls around in the grass, eventually rolling himself to someone else's blanket. He's cute, and his antics are a nice diversion from the awkward tension between Garrett and me. But my unvoiced question still lingers on the tip of my tongue and begs for release. If only the fireworks weren't so loud.

When the show is over, everyone claps, then stands, gathering their blankets and folding them up.

Garrett takes the blanket from me. "That was awesome.

This whole day has been incredible. Thanks for bringing me."

"You're welcome. I'm glad you came."

We stand there for a moment, silent. Our unfinished conversation hangs between us in the humid air. I clear my throat. "Garrett, I am glad we're friends, but sometimes—"

Nora nudges me with her arm on her way past. "Hey, guys, that was pretty great, huh?"

I give a nervous laugh, then nod. "Yeah, it gets better every year."

"Milo's ready to go, Garrett. He'll give you a ride. Meg, I'll ride with you if you don't mind." She takes one step, then stops and turns back to me. "Unless you want us to go and you can take Garrett home?" She looks over at Garrett.

I also look at Garrett. "I'll do whatever works best for you. Do you want to ride with Milo?"

He scratches his neck. "Um, I don't mind either way."

Great. Leave it to Nora to create an awkward situation. How would it look if I say I want to give Garrett a ride? He and Milo are going to the same place, so he should go back with him. That makes the most sense. "Um, since it's getting late, I think we should ride home with the people we live with, not the people we came with."

Nora shrugs. "Okay. I'll see you later, Garrett." She walks over to Milo and gives him a kiss on the cheek.

"Good night," he says. "Drive safe."

After she walks away, Garrett holds up my mom's blanket. "Should I take this back to the house?"

"Oh, yes. It goes in the living room. I'll walk with you."

Inside, my family members are packaging leftovers in the kitchen. Garrett says goodbye to my parents. He shakes my dad's hand and thanks my mom for all of the food. She graciously accepts. I give a little wave and turn to follow

Garrett out the door, but before I can go two steps, my mom grabs my upper arm and pulls me to the side. She waits until Garrett is out of earshot, and then she speaks in hushed tones. "I like him."

"Mom." I shake my head. "I already told you, he's just a friend." But for some reason, after the day we spent together and the conversations we had, my words don't ring true. I'm not being completely honest with my mom, or myself. "Actually, we did go on one date. Okay, maybe two if you count double dates. But nothing has come of it and I doubt anything ever will, so please don't make a big deal out of this, okay?"

She releases her grip on my arm and smiles. "All I said was I like him. No matter if you're just friends. I can still like him, can't I?"

"Yes." I take a deep breath through my nose and release it slowly. "Yes, you can like him." I do too. Maybe a little more than I'm willing to admit.

twenty-four

TWO WEEKS HAVE PASSED since the Fourth of July. I haven't gotten the courage to bring up the subject of our friendship status with Garrett again. The mood is never going to be what it was on that blanket, staring up at the stars from my parents' lawn. We've only seen each other a handful of times—usually after I've returned home from a date with someone else—and Milo and Nora are always around. And trying to circle back to a weighty conversation like that out of nowhere is much too awkward.

Now the month is half over, Braxton gets married in four weeks, and I'm no closer to securing a date to his wedding than I was when I started this whole blind date initiative. But it's not for lack of trying. I've been on seven dates already, including three new guys since the Fourth, and none of them have shown any potential. Several times I've considered deleting my online dating profile, but then I think of Braxton's smiling face as he watches Talia walk down the aisle, and I soldier on. I will not be left in his dust. I will be happy even if I have to force myself to fall for a ridiculously unsuitable man.

The night after my parents' picnic, I went out with Kurt, a painfully shy investment broker. I think he may have said a total of four words on our entire date. I've talked more during a root canal than I did with him. But because I promised Nora I wouldn't give up on a date too early on, I endured an entire dinner with him in silence, hoping that he'd eventually warm up to me and start talking.

He never did.

The next Friday, I went to a movie with a guy named Jacob, who couldn't pronounce his *R*s correctly. In the past, that would've been a deal breaker for me, but for the sake of finding true love, I looked beyond the speech impediment and tried to focus on his more attractive qualities. Unfortunately, I didn't get a chance to discover much else about Jacob, because he'd obviously never learned the phrase: "Keep your hands to yourself." Well he knows it now, and so does everyone else who was at the theater that night when I got up and walked out fifteen minutes into the movie.

Then there was Rob, who, in between bites of butterfly shrimp, which he stole from my plate—a punishable offense—peppered me with questions about my cooking ability, how many children I wanted, and whether I planned to breastfeed or bottle-feed.

Then he wanted to know if I was crafty. "Do you sew?" he asked. "I want my wife to be able to sew." I didn't dare tell him about my knitting aspirations because I didn't want to encourage him.

But thankfully, I still have Adrian. He and I have texted and called each other when he's not on some assignment somewhere, and our conversations have been good. Amazing, actually. We can talk about anything. His weekends have been busy up till now, but he finally carved out some time for an actual in-person date. It's tonight, and I'm nervously hoping nothing goes wrong.

He suggested we meet at a coffee shop near his office. He said they have the greatest nitro cold brew coffee, and that's my absolute favorite—which he knows because we've been messaging so much, and the topic of coffee has come up several times.

I told him how I never get to order a nitro cold brew when I'm out with my mom because she's convinced the nitrogen gas used to make the coffee is a health hazard. So I'm excited about this date for more reasons than one. There's the coffee, yes, but there's Adrian too. Talking to him has been effortless from the very start. It's almost like he and I share a brain.

I arrive at the coffee shop at six and check my reflection in the glass door before walking in. As soon as I enter, a man in the corner pops out of his seat and gives me a hesitant look. I look back at him, trying to match him with the pictures on Adrian's profile. He has the same blond hair and the same square-rimmed glasses. Yes, I think it's him.

He walks toward me. "Meg?"

I smile. "Yes, it's me. Hi, Adrian."

He smiles, too, then reaches out and moves to hug me, but then steps back and extends his hand. "Sorry, maybe it's too soon to hug on the first date."

I chuckle. "I don't mind. I'm not sure what the proper protocol is. You'd think I would by now, after going on so many of these blind dates, but—" I clamp my mouth shut. Maybe it's best *not* to come across as a serial dater. Keeping the rest of my words inside my mouth where they belong, I take his hand and give it a shake. I'm pleased with the amount of pressure I feel when he squeezes. His grip isn't like a vice, but he's also not afraid he's going to break me.

"Do you want to order and then we can sit down?" he asks.

"Yes, that would be great."

We both order cold brews, and they're ready within minutes. I follow him to the corner table where he was when I first entered, and we sit across from one another.

"So," I say, much more confident than I usually am on a first date, "do you do this a lot? Meeting women online?"

He shakes his head. "No, I've only just started using the app, and you're the only one I've really connected with. I haven't even been on any other dates."

I feel special, knowing that in all the time that we've been messaging, he hasn't been seeing other people. Of course, with his schedule, I don't know how he could have. I wish I could say the same about myself. "I'm surprised you haven't made dozens of matches already. You're so easy to talk to."

He laughs. "Really? I don't think I'm anything special."

"Oh, but you are. For one thing, you're so normal."

His brow wrinkles. "Thank you, I think. I'm a little scared to ask what kind of other guys you've met if you think I'm normal."

"You have no idea." I tell him all about Tony, the mama's boy, and Jacob with the wandering hands. I even describe a few of the winners from my pre-online-dating days, like Todd with the aquariums and frog-voice Jason. Man, if Adrian is anything like I think he is, then I guess all of those failed dates will not have been in vain. They've been good practice, and they've helped me recognize the kind of guy I'm looking for.

Adrian and I sip our coffees and talk for another hour. He tells me all about his recent travels and where his job is sending him next.

"You might find this a bit weird," I say, "but I've been reading through the archives on your travel blog."

"Why would I think that's weird?" he asks.

"Well, it is borderline cyberstalking, isn't it?"

He waves a hand. "No, not at all. That's why the blog is online, so people will read it. What did you think of it?"

I clap my hands. "I think it's fascinating. You've been to so many places. What's been your favorite spot so far?"

"Oh, that's a hard one. Each place is special and unique. I'd have to say I love Europe, especially the Alps. Have you been to Austria?"

I shake my head. "I've got a travel bucket list a mile long, but I've only ever been to Canada. Austria sounds amazing."

"It is. My favorite town by far is called Hallstatt. It's located in the mountains about an hour from Salzburg. It's exactly what you'd picture if you were thinking of an Alpine village. The houses have flower boxes beneath the windows and everything. It's really beautiful."

"It sounds that way."

"Would you like to see pictures? I have some on my phone."

I nod. "Definitely."

"Great." Adrian pulls up the pictures on his phone, and then holds it out to me. "There it is." He points to the screen and I have to lean closer to see. We're so close that our heads almost touch. But I don't mind. He shows me a picture of a riverfront village with mountains in the background and houses climbing up the hillside. It looks vaguely familiar to me.

"I've seen this place before," I say.

"I wouldn't doubt it. It's photographed a lot. You may have seen posters of it in your doctor's office waiting room.

You know the kind of poster with a beautiful picture and just one inspirational word at the bottom in all capital letters?"

"Like *Strength*."

"Right." He smiles. "Or *Fearless*."

I bounce in my seat. "*Courage*."

"Good one."

We both laugh. It's the most meaningless conversation —about posters, for crying out loud—but we're on the same wavelength. Having a conversation about nothing with someone makes it feel like we're old friends. As long as it's fun, does it matter what we talk about?

"I found a blog post I did a few years back about Portugal," Adrian says. "Did you read that one?"

I try to recall, but nothing pops into my head. "I don't think so."

He sighs wistfully. "I take up a few paragraphs alone talking only about the coffee they drink there. It's called Galão. Since we're at a coffee shop, I thought it'd be an interesting read."

"I would love to read that."

He smiles. "I thought you might."

When I finally climb into my car at the end of the night, I'm shocked to see how late it is. It's almost ten, and while that might not seem late, it's three hours later than my first-date average.

I must've lost track of time after the first hour spent sitting at that coffee shop. That never happens to me. I'm always so conscious of the day and the time and my schedule, but when I was with Adrian today, everything else just slipped my mind.

Now I'm on my way home, and I'm not sure what to do. It's become my habit to stop by Milo's and spill my guts about how terrible my dates have been, because that's usually how it goes. I cry on Nora's shoulder or, more often than not, she's not there and I end up giving a play-by-play retelling to Garrett, who seems to love listening to me relive my nightmarish dates. It's like he revels in my misery.

At least somebody does.

But this time it's different. This time, I don't have a sob story to share. I have good news. Exciting news! And the last person on earth I want to talk to about it is Garrett. I can't bring myself to tell him that I've actually found a guy I like.

And I'm afraid to admit to myself why that is.

Maybe I don't have to worry about telling Garrett anything. It's ten o'clock, so I should probably just go straight home and go to bed. I can put off telling anyone about my date until tomorrow. Except I really want to tell Nora because I had such an amazing time.

I speak into the air and instruct my phone to call Nora, just to see where she is. She picks up the call on the third ring.

"Hey, Meg, where are you? We've been waiting to hear how your date went."

"You have? As in *all* of you have been waiting? Or just you and Milo?"

I can hear Nora scoff. "We've *aaallll* been waiting." She draws out the word for emphasis. "We're at Garrett's new apartment. I thought you'd want to see it. If you hurry up, I'll still be here when you get here."

What? *Oh, no!*

I can't believe I forgot tonight was moving night. I told Garrett I would help if I could, and it completely slipped my mind. Now it's past ten, and the majority of the work is probably done. Garrett didn't have much of his stuff at Milo's house to move, but I'm sure he unlocked his storage unit and brought things over from there.

I feel like a jerk. I'm a jerk who wouldn't have been able to lift the heavy boxes, but a jerk nonetheless.

I'm pretty sure I remember where his new apartment is. He had told me once before, and I remember seeing the building when it was going up and commenting about how modern it looked.

When I pull up to where I think it is, I see Garrett's truck parked in the newly tarred parking lot, so I know I've got the right place. I hop out of my car and send Nora a quick text.

Which apartment number?

Her reply comes back in seconds.

6A. First floor.

First floor? Impressive. I'm happy for Garrett, although it is going to be weird not seeing him every time I go to Milo's, which is a lot. It makes me wonder if I'll go as often, knowing Garrett won't be there. And that makes me wonder why I'm even wondering. I had a great date with Adrian. Adrian is all I can think about.

I can only think about Adrian and the fact that my date with him made me miss moving night with Garrett.

twenty-five

I WALK UP to Garrett's door and knock. A few seconds later, the door swings open and Garrett appears in front of me, looking slightly exhausted but still smiling.

"Meg. You're a little late."

I wince. "I know. I'm so sorry. I had a date, and it lasted past seven. For once. Can I still come in and see your apartment?"

"Sure." He pulls the door open, and I step inside. "It's still kind of a mess. I haven't unpacked anything. We just hauled the boxes in and set them down. I do have a table though. And chairs. You can take a seat if you want."

"Sure." I make my way into the kitchen and find Nora and Milo sitting at the table playing cribbage and eating... barbecued chicken wings? From my favorite take-out place? They ordered take-out without me?

"Hey, you," Nora says when she sees me. "How do you like this apartment? It's pretty nice, isn't it?"

I make a show of looking around the kitchen. "From what I've seen so far, yes. It's really nice."

Garrett walks up from somewhere behind me. "I can

214

give you a tour, but there's not much to see other than boxes. If you come back in a few days, I'll have more to show you."

I look up at him. "Sure. I could help you put things away if you'd like."

He smirks at me. "You don't have to do that. I don't have much."

Nora clears her throat. "Meg, tell us about the date. I assume it's good news?"

My heart ping-pongs inside my chest. "Um…"

Garrett stares down at me. His expression looks to me to be half-dread, half-hope—but I don't know what he's hoping. Or dreading. Does he want to hear that my date went well? Or does he secretly hope it was disastrous?

I shift my weight from one foot to the other. "I-I had a really good time with him."

Nora claps her hands. "I knew you would, given the way you and Adrian stay up so late in the night texting. Obviously you have a lot to talk about."

"You guys text late at night?"

All eyes turn to Garrett.

"I mean…" He scratches the side of his jaw. His cheeks are bright red. "I guess I didn't know there was actually something going on with you two—or with any of these guys."

Nora glances up at him, a knowing expression on her face. "That's because you've only heard about the dates that don't work out. But they can't all be failures. Eventually Meg's going to find the right person, and I think that person is Adrian." She leans back in her chair. "You know, you should try online dating, Garrett. You'd be able to find someone in no time."

I prop my hands on my hips. "What is that supposed to

mean? Why would he find someone in no time while it's taken me weeks?"

"Just look at him." Nora gestures toward Garrett's long, lean body—which is currently clad in jeans and a plain gray T-shirt and looks so good it kind of makes me wish I'd stayed here tonight instead of going out.

Nora's not wrong. Garrett is a catch.

He lowers himself onto a stool beside the counter. "I'm not in the market for anyone right now."

"Why not?" Nora asks.

"Because he doesn't need to be," Milo says from across the table.

"Why not?" Nora and I say at the same time.

Garrett shoots a wide-eyed look at Milo, but Milo shrugs it off, ignoring him. "There's a woman who works at the consignment shop next to our office, and she has a thing for Garrett. She comes in at least twice a week to talk to him."

I briefly suffer a mild heart attack, then force myself to smile at Garrett. "Is that so? Well, you should ask her out. If she likes you, and if...if you like her, I say go for it."

Garrett's gaze swings to me. "Really? Is that what you think I should do?" His words come across more like a dare than a simple question.

"Yes." My voice quavers a little, and I swallow.

"So you *want* me to go out with her?" He quirks a brow, as if he's calling my bluff. "That would make you happy?"

I clench and unclench my fists, which are firmly stationed at my sides. "Of course it would. Why wouldn't it? I've finally met someone I like, and I'm happy, so you should be too." He just stares at me, and it's making me all kinds of self-conscious. "Don't you want to go out with her?" I ask. "Don't you like her?"

He shrugs. "She's fine."

"She's more than fine," Milo says. "She's hot. Garrett thinks so too. He just doesn't want to say it in front of you."

An invisible fist punches me in the stomach. I scrunch my brow at Garrett. "You can say whatever you want to me. About anyone."

"Okay, but do I have to? Or can we just stop talking about this now? Please?" He scoots his stool back as he stands, then swipes his cola from the counter and heads for the back door.

"What's up with him?" Nora asks.

"Don't worry about him," Milo says. "He's conflicted."

"Conflicted? How so?" she says.

Milo looks at me, raises one eyebrow, and then returns his attention to the cards in his hand. "Don't worry. He'll figure it out."

I peer through the glass door where I can see Garrett sitting down in a folding chair. I bite my bottom lip. "I'm gonna go talk to him," I say. "I'll be back in a few minutes."

Nora and Milo calmly resume their cribbage match.

I ease open the back door and step out onto a small slab of concrete. Garrett looks up at me. "Welcome to my patio."

I smile at him. "It's nice. Do you mind if I sit out here with you?"

"Go ahead."

I sit in the only other chair, which is about six inches from Garrett's, and lean my head back. I wait a minute or so before reaching over and lightly touching his arm. "I'm not exactly sure what I said in there that made you mad, but I can tell you're upset. Whatever it was, I'm sorry."

He meets my gaze. "I'm not mad."

"But something's bothering you. You're not as good at hiding your feelings as you think."

He bends to set his cola can on the ground. When he straightens, he angles his body toward me. Only now, because his legs are so long and our chairs are so close together, his knee brushes against mine. But he doesn't move away, and neither do I. I clench my teeth hard to keep from saying something idiotic like, "In case you didn't know, our knees are touching."

I swallow, my throat growing thick with an emotion that's becoming all too familiar when I'm with Garrett. "So what's really bothering you? I hope you know you can tell me anything."

"You're right. I can. So please don't be offended when I tell you that I think you're acting weird. I don't understand why you're pushing me to ask Julia out."

A prickling heat climbs up my neck. "I wasn't trying to push. You can do whatever you want to do in that arena. I just don't like seeing you lonely."

"Who says I'm lonely?"

"Well, aren't you? Now that you're living alone in this big, practically empty apartment?"

His brow arches high over his eyes. "Meg, I haven't even spent one night here. And every weekend up until tonight, after you go out with one guy after another, you come back and tell me how horrible it was. I spend every Friday night, and quite a few Saturdays, with you. How could I be lonely?"

"But we're just friends. Don't you want something more?"

"With you?"

I feel the blood drain from my face. "No," I say, placing my hand to my chest after suffering a mini-stroke. "Not with me. Obviously."

"Right. Obviously." He reaches up and smooths his hair

all the way from his forehead to the nape of his neck. "To tell you the truth, watching you suffer through date after failed date, I don't think I have the energy to get to know someone new."

"But when you meet the right one, it's worth the effort."

"Is it? You sound like you're speaking from experience. Do you really think this Adrian is the one? You've gone on one date."

"But we've also been talking for several weeks. And we have another date planned for next Friday."

He nods. "That's great. I hope everything works out the way you want it to. Just promise me you won't settle. Make sure that if you choose a guy, he appreciates every single thing about you—all of your quirky, perfect-for-you imperfections."

"I will." Maybe Garrett does understand me. I never realized it until now.

After another moment passes in silence, I force myself to stand, breaking eye contact with him. "I should get going." I turn toward the door.

"Yeah, I should probably head to bed soon." Garrett rises from his chair and comes to stand behind me as I place my hand on the doorknob.

But before I step inside, he stops me with a hand to my shoulder. "Meg."

I don't turn, but I can feel the heat of his body just inches from mine. "Yes?"

"I just..." There's a long pause. Then he heaves a breath, and whatever he was about to say evaporates into the night air. "Never mind. It's nothing."

My heart is a blob of melted butter sliding all the way down to my toes. I'm sure what Garrett wants to say isn't *nothing.* He clearly has something on his mind and he's holding back. My mind formulates several possibilities.

Meg, forget Adrian. I want you to pick me.

Meg, just say the word, and I will tell Julia to take a hike.

Meg, I think I'm in love with you.

Okay, it's probably not any of those things, but I'll never know.

In the kitchen, Milo and Nora are putting away the leftover chicken wings and crumpling paper plates and tossing them into a black trash bag. It's time for all of us to go home and go to bed.

I'll have no trouble climbing into my bed and resting my head against my pillow, but I have a feeling there won't be any actual sleeping taking place. Not for a long, long time.

twenty-six

I DON'T SEE Garrett much over the next week, and I feel his absence like a missing jacket on a cold winter day. When he lived at Milo's, I could at least count on a few short encounters with him throughout the week. Today is Friday, and I can't help wondering if Garrett is going to keep up with the Friday hang-out tradition and head over to Milo's for the evening. I'm seeing Adrian for the second time tonight. Will Garrett be waiting for me when I get back?

I shouldn't care one way or the other because I'm going out with Adrian, and I like Adrian. A lot. Maybe I'm just a little apprehensive about tonight. He's taking me to a jazz club downtown which is *way* out of my comfort zone. I don't do clubs, and I don't do dancing. But Adrian has assured me that I'll love it if I just give it a chance. I expect to get home pretty late. I'll probably get home so late that even if Garrett does stop by Milo's, he will have already gone back to his apartment. Heck, it'll be so late that even Nora won't be there anymore. I won't need to stop at Milo's at all.

How weird will that be? And why does the thought of it make me sad?

I get to the club just before seven. It's downtown, and I really don't like driving downtown at night and parking along the street. It's dark and it's a little chilly, and I wish Adrian had picked me up, but he's coming straight from work and it's much more direct for him to come here.

I hesitantly pull open the heavy metal door and walk inside the dark building, its neon signs casting rays of color on my clothing and my skin, and I'm greeted with the sound of jazz music. The syncopated rhythms, the heavy bass, the steady clang of cymbals—they make me realize why Adrian likes this place. The music alone takes me back to a time that I never even lived through, yet when I'm here, I feel like I have. It's an odd mixture of familiarity and discovery. I feel romantic and classy—and way under-dressed. Everyone here is wearing swanky clothes. Why didn't Adrian tell me there was a dress code?

Speaking of Adrian, where is he? We had agreed to meet at the entrance, but I don't see him anywhere. I feel a little on display standing right in front of the door, so I grab a seat at the closest table and wait for him there. He'll be able to see me when he walks in.

An hour passes. An entire hour, and there's no sign of Adrian. I text him a few times, and after my texts go unan-swered, I call him. But the call goes straight to voicemail without ringing. Have I been ghosted?

No. Adrian wouldn't do that. We had such a great time on our first date. And even last night we talked on the phone and everything seemed fine. He was so excited about tonight.

I've been texting Nora updates for the last hour. She's worried about me being here alone, and even offered to come and sit with me, but I told her not to bother. I can leave any time I want. Listening to the music helps pass the time.

Every time the door opens, I glance up, hoping to see Adrian walk through. And every time it's not him, my shoulders sag. They sag a little lower with each disappointment. Except when the door opens and Garrett walks in.

My breath hitches. "Garrett!" As his gaze collides with mine, I'm overcome with relief, and at the same time, embarrassment. I watch him make his way to my table and sit across from me. "How did you know I was here?"

"I've been listening to Nora read your texts to Milo for over an hour. I couldn't take another minute. I wanted to make sure you were okay."

I prop both elbows on the table and lean forward, cradling my chin in my open palms. "I'm fine. Just disappointed."

"Has he called you yet? Explained why he hasn't shown?"

I shake my head. "Still no response. I think it's safe to say I've been stood up."

His lips twist to one side as he considers my statement. "It's possible. Unless he's been in a terrible car accident, or he dropped his phone in a lake and then dove in after it, and he's still out there treading water..." He nudges my foot with his.

Guilt bubbles in my chest. "If either of those scenarios ends up being true, I'll forgive him. If not, I'm un-matching him and blocking his number." Since it appears he's already blocked mine, I doubt he'll notice.

"He doesn't deserve you."

"Thanks. But I still feel incredibly stupid."

"Why?"

I sigh. "Because I really like him. Scratch that. *Liked* him."

Garrett leans across the table and pulls one of my hands out from beneath my chin. He squeezes it. "I know you liked him, but if he's going to treat you this way, you don't need him. I'm sure you'll find someone else."

"But I only have a few weeks left."

One of Garrett's brows hikes up. "A few weeks? Until what?"

Oh no. I hadn't planned on telling Garrett about the wedding. About Braxton. It will make me look pathetic. But since I'm pretty much the poster child for pathetic, sitting here in this jazz club after just being jilted, I don't have much to lose.

"My ex-boyfriend, Braxton, is getting married in three weeks. I've been trying to find someone to take to his wedding to show him that he didn't ruin my life when he dumped me. I want to prove to him that I can find someone and be happy too."

Garrett looks dumbfounded. "So this whole time, all of these dates you've gone on, it's all been about finding a date to a wedding?"

"Basically, yes."

"Even when you went out with me?"

I wince. "Yes. But if it makes you feel better, Nora wanted to fix me up with you even before I knew about Braxton's engagement."

He releases a loud sigh, almost a groan, then rubs a hand down the lower half of his face. For a long moment he just watches me, his gaze narrowed. Finally, after an agonizing wait, he scoffs. "That's interesting."

"What?" I ask. "How is that interesting?"

He presses his lips together and peers at me beneath a

rumpled brow. "It just makes me wonder, given the amount of time we've been spending together, why you didn't ask me to go to the wedding with you."

I force myself not to break away from his gaze, even though looking him in the eyes makes me feel exposed, vulnerable. "I have thought about asking you," I say. "Several times, in fact."

"But...?"

"But I'm not just looking for a date for one wedding, for one afternoon."

"And that's what I would be? Just a date? I thought we were better friends than that, Meg."

"We are." I give his hand a squeeze. "We're friends, and I'm so thankful for that. But I'm looking for what Braxton has. His getting married only reminds me that he didn't choose me. It's not that he wasn't ready for a serious commitment, he just didn't want it with me. And that hurts."

He bobs his head. "I get it. But why do you care what he thinks? Do you still have feelings for him?"

"Not anymore."

"So you just want to prove something to him. Or to yourself?"

I shrug. "Both, if that makes sense. Ever since I found out about his engagement, I've begun to doubt myself, who I am, whether any guy would ever like me."

Garrett releases my hand and leans back in his seat, still keeping his gaze trained on me. "Why would you doubt that?"

Does he even need to ask? I squint my eyes and lean in close. "Can I tell you a secret?" I say. "One I haven't told anyone before?"

"Of course."

"I'm not like most other people."

Garrett smothers a laugh with the back of his hand. "Do you think that's a secret? Because I hate to tell you this, but pretty much everyone knows."

My face flushes. "I realize that. I mean to say that as an only child in a small family, I wasn't raised around lots of kids my age. I hung out with mostly adults, my parents' friends, my aunts and uncles. I don't know how to talk to my peers. I work at the library because I love books, yes, but also because it's a solitary job, a quiet one. People don't stand around talking in the library. I like it that way. I like my alone time, and I sometimes think I like books better than people." I blow out a long breath. "So to find someone who wants to put up with all that—it's no wonder I'm still alone."

He nods once, absorbing everything I've just told him, then he scratches the back of his head. "Huh."

That's all he's got? That's his only response? I splay my hands at him. "What does that mean? *Huh?*"

"Nothing," he says. "I just don't get why you need to be in a relationship in order to feel loved. That's bogus. What about all the people in your life who show up for you when you need them? What about Nora, who's gone to great lengths to try and help you with this crazy matchmaking scheme? What about Milo, who lets you come in and out of his house whenever you want, just because you need someone to talk to? What about—" his next words freeze on his lips, and I notice his hand is flat against his chest. Following my gaze, he looks down, and his face falls. He quickly lowers his hand, then clears his throat. "What about...your parents? I've met your dad. He adores you. And your mom loves you too, though she may have an odd way

226

of showing it. You don't need a romantic relationship to prove anything to anyone."

I cross my arms. "I don't expect this to make sense to you. Sure my parents love me. They have to. And as far as friends go, I'm lucky to have Nora. She's the only friend who will ever be able to understand me."

"Not the only one."

I look away. "Right."

"I'm serious." He grips my chin with his thumb and forefinger and turns me to face him. "I've realized that sometimes it takes more than one date to really get to know someone. Maybe we didn't hit it off when we first met, but the more time I spend with you, the more I realize how special you are—even if you don't always like people." He winks at me, and it sends a tingling sensation up my arms.

"Thank you," I say.

"You're welcome."

We say nothing more—because really, what could either of us say to follow up after that?—and the air between us grows thick with tension. The band wraps up an up-tempo number and begins a new song, this one much slower. All around us, couples leave their seats and make their way to the small dance floor. Garrett looks at me, and there's a question in his eyes that causes my cheeks to flush. Is he going to ask me to dance?

Oh, heaven help me. I'm not a dancer. I never once attended a school dance in all my high school years, and although I've been known to do the Chicken Dance and Hokey Pokey at weddings, I don't think they count as actual dancing either.

Garrett scoots his chair back, stands, and holds out his hand to me. "We shouldn't let everyone else have all the fun," he says.

My pulse quickens. I shake my head vigorously. "I'm not very good at it."

He shrugs. "Neither am I, but who cares? It's dark in here. No one will notice us. Besides, I'm not going to let this night be a total bust. You need to have one good date, don't you think?"

One good date. My mouth goes dry. I slip my hand into Garrett's and allow him to pull me to my feet and lead me to the dance floor. It's like I've lost all willpower. I no longer have control of my limbs. Normally, if someone were leading me toward a dance floor, I'd be digging in my heels and yanking my hand free, but for some reason, I want to go with Garrett.

When he stops, he turns to face me. He stands about a foot away from me, looking down on me from his six-foot-three height. He's still holding my hand, but he lifts it up and I place it on his shoulder. I do the same with my other hand while he grips my waist.

I shiver, then look away. I'm not sure I can do this.

"Calm down, Meg," he says. "Take a deep breath."

With light pressure on my back, he pulls me toward him until my chest touches his rib cage. I try to match the movement of his feet. After we settle into a comfortable rhythm, I rest my cheek against his chest.

I've never been so close to Garrett before. Not without a life jacket on, at least. The musky scent emanating from his body—whether it's cologne, aftershave, deodorant, or a mixture of all three—makes my head swim. I feel sleepy and dreamy and dizzy all at the same time. What's in men's personal care products, and does it come in candle form? If so, I need one in my room to help me sleep at night.

When the song ends, another slow song begins. Garrett

steps back slightly and angles his head down toward mine. "Do you want to sit down? Or should we keep dancing?"

Keep dancing, I want to say. But I can't. I don't think my voice works anymore. Instead, I just look up at him and nod.

He smiles and pulls me against his chest again. He wraps his arms around my back and squeezes slightly before settling his hands on my hips once more. For someone who, five minutes earlier, was about to have a panic attack, I've never felt more relaxed. Garrett's heart beating against my ear is like the perfect metronome.

Garrett leans his head down until his forehead touches mine. My skin zings with electricity. "Meg." He murmurs my name, his voice thick and husky.

"Yes?"

"I've been thinking." He swallows.

"About what?" I ask.

A throat clears somewhere beside me. A familiar voice says, "Meg?" and my heart drops. The voice isn't Garrett's. I whip my head around to find Adrian standing about two feet away from us. I gasp, then push against Garrett's chest, step back, and rub my hands down the front of my shirt. "Um, Adrian, hi. What happened to you? I assumed you weren't coming."

I look over at Garrett, whose face is flushed. His jaw bulges, a telltale sign that he's frustrated.

Adrian looks from me to Garrett and back again. "Um, my sister went into labor a few hours ago. At least she thought she was in labor. It's a week early and her husband is out of town, so she called and asked me to take her to the hospital. I was so nervous I left my phone on top of my car and drove off. I have no idea where it is, and I don't have your number memorized, so I couldn't contact you."

I place my hand to my chest. "Wow, that's...incredible. How is your sister?"

He sighs. "The contractions have stopped. False labor. The doctor said she'll monitor her for a while but will probably send her home in a few hours. I felt terrible about abandoning you. I came here hoping you'd still be here, but not expecting you to be."

I laugh nervously. "Well, here I am." I gesture to Garrett. "This is my friend Garrett. He came to check on me."

Adrian's concerned gaze flits back to Garrett. "I can see that." He holds out his hand. "Thanks for taking care of her," he says.

Garrett shakes Adrian's hand, but he's not smiling. "Not a problem."

We stand there for a moment, no one speaking, in an awkward little love triangle of sorts. Finally Adrian gestures toward the bar. "If you want, I could grab us a few drinks. Water, if nothing else. I'm parched."

I nod. "Water would be great."

Adrian raises his eyebrows at Garrett. "Do you want anything?"

"No thanks. I'm good."

"All right. Be right back."

When Adrian walks to the bar, Garrett takes me by the elbow and leans down to speak into my ear. "What do you want to do?" he asks.

"What do you mean?"

"Well, you're not staying here, are you?"

I blink several times. "I probably should. Adrian left his sister to come here."

Garrett flings his hand toward the bar where Adrian stands. "I can tell him you're tired. You waited for him long enough, and it's late. He should understand."

I swallow and look around the club. It's really not that late, and there are plenty of people still dancing. It's not like the place is shutting down for the night. "I feel like I should stay. Adrian and I did have a date, and I'm sure he feels terrible for almost standing me up. I would hate to ditch him now, after all that."

Garrett's eyes narrow. "So what do you want me to do? Do you want me to go? Even though..." He scratches his head, leaving the rest of his sentence at the mercy of my imagination. What had he been about to say? Even though we danced? Even though his face was so close to mine I wondered if he might kiss me?

Ha, no. See, that's the problem with imaginations. They tend to run wild. Of course Garrett wasn't about to kiss me. Just minutes before Adrian showed up, Garrett had reiterated—once again—that we're friends.

And friends don't kiss.

He's still looking at me, and I realize I never did answer his question—probably because I don't want to. The truth is I don't want Garrett to go. But that's just being greedy. Adrian's here now, and I can't spend the evening with both of them. They were practically staring daggers at each other when Adrian showed up. I take a deep breath, then exhale, nodding. "You can go. It's okay."

"Are you sure you'll be all right here? With him?"

I smile, trying to reassure him. "I'll be fine." As I stare into Garrett's eyes, a million different questions run through my brain—the chief among them, what would've happened if Adrian hadn't shown up?

I'll never know the answer to that, because Adrian did come, as he should have. He and I have a date, and now I need to see it through. I have to find out if Adrian and I have a future, and I can't do that if Garrett is here.

"Thank you so much for coming to check on me," I say. "You have no idea how much it means."

Garrett bobs his head. "I think I do." He turns and walks away, and the air around me suddenly feels colder. My heart feels a little emptier. And I can't help but wonder if I've just made a colossal mistake.

twenty-seven

I WAKE up the next morning at ten. I never sleep this late, but I got home after midnight.

The rest of the evening at the club was...confusing. Adrian apologized over and over for not showing up on time, and he was so thankful that I'd waited. He didn't sound quite so thankful that Garrett had come to my rescue, but I managed to change the subject whenever Garrett's name came up.

We talked a lot, mostly about how excited he is about meeting his new niece or nephew, and how much of a letdown it was that his sister's labor had stalled. I assured him that it can't be much longer now, and that God's timing is perfect. He seemed to agree with that.

I don't expect to hear much from him today, since he needs to buy a new phone before he can call or text me, but he did say he'd log on to his laptop and maybe we could message or live chat later.

In a sleepy haze, I trudge to the kitchen to make my morning coffee, and I find Nora seated at the table, reading one of her home decorating magazines. She looks up when I enter. "Hey, sleepyhead," she says. "Nice of you to finally join the living."

"It's not that late." I pull the coffee pot from the machine and take it to the sink to fill it.

"What time did you come in? Your last text came through when Adrian showed up, and then I never heard another word. And what happened with Garrett? He never made it back to Milo's, so I assume he stayed with you?"

At the mention of Garrett's name, my heart rate accelerates. "He came to the club, but once Adrian got there, I told him he could go."

"It was nice of him to drive all the way over there," Nora says. "He was so agitated last night when I was reading your texts to Milo. He couldn't sit still and kept pacing the living room floor."

Once the coffeemaker starts percolating, I pull out the chair across the table from Nora and sit. I run my fingers through my hair, then I plop my elbows on the table and hold my head in my hands. My hair falls forward and covers my face like a dark orange curtain.

"Wow," Nora says. "This is not the look of someone who had a great date last night. Do you want to talk about it?"

I groan. "Something crazy is happening, and I don't know what to do about it."

"What's crazy? Is it Adrian?"

I lift my head and shake it slowly, my hair swishing back and forth. "I've been having weird, confusing thoughts about Garrett."

"What? I thought you liked Adrian."

"I do. At least I thought I did. But last night, when Garrett came to get me at the jazz club, he held my hand.

And then we danced. We danced really slow and really close, kind of like a long hug, but with movement."

Nora's left eyebrow quirks upward. "Go on."

"He's constantly saying we're friends, so that's how I try to think of him, but the thing is, friends don't usually hug for that long. Not unless someone has died. And also, I smelled him, Nora. I took a really long, deep breath, and I smelled him, and he smelled good. It did weird things to my insides and it made my head feel fuzzy."

"I don't see the problem," Nora says. "That sounds like attraction to me."

"But it can't be. It's something else. It was a jazz club, so maybe someone at the next table was smoking something and puffing their waste products in my direction. Maybe I was under the influence."

Nora laughs. "Yes, you were under Garrett's influence. Just admit it, Meg. You like him. You've developed feelings for him. That's not surprising, given the fact that you spend every free moment together."

"But I'm seeing Adrian."

"You've gone on two dates with Adrian. You're not committed to each other."

"But we're so similar. We get each other. Plus, Adrian doesn't possess a single deal-breaking trait."

"Does he make your head feel fuzzy?"

The breath slowly fizzles from my lungs like air from a leaky balloon. "No, not yet. I'm hoping those feelings develop soon. But so far, when I'm with Adrian, I feel like I'm with a good friend—kind of like when I'm with you, only he dresses less colorfully."

"Then why are you still pursuing things with him? And why are you running away from Garrett?"

I slump down in my chair, shaking my head. "Garrett

is…perfect. He's amazing. I know I make fun of him for being an accountant, but I realize now the only reason he's an accountant is because he's a genius at math. He's smart, he's funny, and he's gorgeous—and I am *so* not his type."

"You don't know that," Nora says.

I huff a breath. "Of course I do. I've only ever felt this way about one other guy, and that was Braxton. The entire time I was with him, I couldn't believe we were dating. I remember thinking he was too good for me, and I kept waiting for him to figure it out, to realize that he and I weren't even close to being in the same league—and then he did, and that was that."

Nora places her hand on my shoulder. "Come on, Meg, you're not being fair to yourself. You're way too good for Braxton."

"Why? Because I can direct you to the juvenile fiction section of the library? I can look up a book on a computer and tell you if it's checked in, and if it isn't, I can put it on hold? What makes me impressive, Nora?"

She frowns. "I've never heard you talk like this. Why are you putting yourself down all of a sudden? You love your job."

"It's not just my job," I say. "It's me. Garrett deserves someone as amazing as he is. I know what I'm like. I'm opinionated, I'm argumentative, I complain—I'm just like my mom, and she drives me absolutely bonkers."

"Garrett knows all of this already, and he still likes you."

"Yes, as a friend. Because he has to."

"He has feelings for you, Meg. I can tell. And you need to tell him how you feel because I don't think he knows."

I pull my lower lip between my teeth, pondering. "I have another date with Adrian next weekend, and I think I owe it to him to figure out my feelings for him first before I move on to someone else. I've already made such a big deal about how well-suited we are and how well we get along. I can't just end things with him for no reason."

"It wouldn't be for no reason," Nora says. "It would be for Garrett, and he's worth it. Milo is hosting another cookout tonight at five. I assume Garrett will be there, so it might be the ideal time for you two to talk."

My gut clenches at her words. "That sounds terrifying." But if I don't tell Garrett how I feel and I end up old and alone, I'll only have myself to blame.

By the time five o'clock rolls around, I'm nothing but a big, bulging bag of mixed emotions. I've relived the moments with Garrett at the club a hundred times. Each time I try to imagine what I would've done if he'd tried to kiss me. Not that he would have. But let's just say he had. Would I have kissed him back?

Heck yeah, I would have.

But then what would've happened? Would he have apologized for it? Said that he got carried away or that he wasn't thinking? Or did he have feelings for me? And does he still, like I seem to have for him?

If only Adrian hadn't come. Then I would already know the answers to all my questions.

I follow Nora through the back door into Milo's kitchen. Garrett's not here yet, and I'm relieved. I need to prepare myself. What will I say? It might be awkward to see him at first, knowing how close we got last night, but I refuse to avoid him. I will make the first move and approach him if I have to. I'm a big girl.

I help Nora assemble a veggie tray while she mixes

together some dip using sour cream, mayonnaise, and dill. Then the back door slides open and Milo pops his head inside. "We're about ready to eat. Are you coming out?"

"Be right there," Nora says. She sets the dip in the center of the veggie tray, then turns to me with a questioning look. "Help me with the door?"

"Sure." I slide it open and then follow Nora outside. Garrett still hasn't arrived. I really hope he shows up soon, because I won't be able to think about anything else until we talk things out. No matter what he says or how he feels, I'm sure our friendship will survive. Even though we almost —well, maybe almost—kissed. Or not. Only Garrett knows what he would've done had Adrian not shown up, and I'm sure not planning on asking him *that*. I just want to tell him how I feel, and then put all of this behind us.

Milo says a prayer to bless the food, and I close my eyes. When he's done I open my eyes and scan the backyard. No sign of Garrett. The fact that he's late is odd. He's one of those perpetually early people, which used to drive me crazy, except now that I know him better, it seems appropriate. It's so very "Garrett" of him to arrive ten minutes early to anything.

Holding my can of sparkling water, I wander to the fence and push open the gate. Maybe he just pulled up and is still sitting in his truck out front. Maybe he's as nervous about seeing me as I am about seeing him.

But when I survey the curb, his truck isn't there.

Huh. I wander back into the yard and catch up with Milo just as he's removing another slab of spare ribs from the grill. "Hey, Milo," I say. "Do you know why Garrett's late? Do you think maybe he got held up at work?"

"It's Saturday."

"Oh, right. Maybe he's stuck at that intersection—you know, the one by the gas station near his apartment? That's always a busy place."

Milo's brow scrunches in doubt. "I don't think so. That'd be one really long red light."

I nod. "That's true. Something probably came up at the last minute. Maybe he got caught up rescuing kittens from a tree, or maybe his dishwasher overflowed and flooded his kitchen, or a tree was struck by lightning right in front of his building, and he can't get out because the door is blocked—"

"Meg, stop." Milo balances the plate of ribs in one hand while replacing the grill lid with the other. "He's not coming. He texted me over an hour ago."

I lower my gaze to the grass surrounding my sandaled feet. "And did he tell you why?"

"Not in so many words, but I got the gist."

I look up to meet Milo's gaze. "Did the gist have something to do with me?"

He shakes his head. "Look, you know how guys are. We don't like to talk about personal stuff. Just give him some space. I'm sure he'll get over it, move on, and then he'll be his old self again." He starts to walk toward the picnic table.

"Wait." I grab his shoulder, stopping him. "Do you mean to say he's not himself right now? Is he okay? Is he sad? Did he say anything about me?"

Milo's eyes widen as he inhales sharply through his nose. "If you need to know, you should call him. You two can work it out between yourselves."

I huff a breath. Guys are no help at all.

~

When I get home that night, I plop onto my bed and text Garrett. I have to do something because I'm pretty sure I messed up our friendship.

I missed you tonight at the cookout. Milo made ribs.

He doesn't respond right away like he normally would. I stare at my screen for several minutes, waiting. Maybe he went to bed already. It is after ten. But eventually, three little dots form below my message. His reply comes a few seconds later.

Sorry. I had other plans.

Other plans? Since when? And with whom? Garrett never does anything if it's not with us.

I stare at my phone, not sure what to do. I really want to talk to him. I'm not going to be able to sleep or eat—and I definitely won't be able to concentrate if Adrian tries to message me—until I figure out where Garrett's head is at. But this is a conversation we need to have in person, using real words. I need to hear his voice, not just read a bunch of letters on a screen. I type back.

Can I come over? I really want to talk about last night.

The dots reappear, followed a moment later by his reply.

It's late, Meg. Let's just talk another day.

What? No way can I wait an entire day—or longer—to fix this.

I'm sorry for telling you to go last night. Maybe you should have stayed? I was confused.

It's all right. I shouldn't have pressured you to make a choice. Let's forget about it, ok?

Forget about it? As if I'll be able to do that. But for now, it's clear forcing the issue isn't going to help. I'll have to wait until he's ready to talk.

Ok. Good night, Garrett.

Tears well in my eyes as my words are followed by nothing but silence.

twenty-eight

ON TUESDAY, I take the afternoon off so I can spend a long, late lunch with Nora. She blocked off two entire hours with no appointments so she could slip out for a while. I really need this. Things have been so bizarre lately. I haven't talked to Garrett since Friday night, and that's not so bad, given that it's only been four days. I just wish I could send him a random, weird text to lighten things up like I normally would—but I don't think we're in a place right now where we can send texts about nothing. Everything seems to have shifted to a more serious level, and I don't like it. I miss the good old days before the dancing and the closeness and the skin tingles made everything so complicated.

Ugh. But I miss that stuff too. I didn't get nearly enough before it was gone.

Nora and I are in Uptown, eating at our favorite Asian-fusion Japanese restaurant. Nora spends most of the time telling me why she thinks Milo is going to propose soon. Apparently he's been dropping hints and saying all kinds of mysterious things.

That's just what I need, another wedding to find a date for. I was hoping Braxton's would be the last one I'd have to worry about.

When we leave the restaurant, Nora still has another hour before her next appointment, so we wander up and down the streets, peering inside gastropubs and window-shopping at hip boutiques. We round a corner, and I see the sign above Sylvie's French Bistro. I elbow Nora and point up at it. "I really want to try this place sometime."

Her eyes light up. "Me too. Michelle says they make the best *Croque Monsieur.*"

I don't know what that is, but anything French has to be delicious—except *escargot,* but that's a given. "I think Adrian would really like this place," I say. "He's been to France several times. I bet he would know just the right thing to order. He would tell me all about it in his best French accent."

When I think about Adrian, I smile because he makes me happy. And that's good, right? But when I think about Garrett, I have this soul-deep, insatiable longing, like I'll never be satisfied with anything or anyone else. As far as I know, that's not good. Not if we're barely on speaking terms.

Nora and I slow our steps as we approach the bistro's front window, which is flanked by twin ferns in hanging baskets and sheltered by a classic striped awning. We pass the main entrance door and then approach the second enormous window. I glance over my shoulder and peer into the dining room, almost jealous of the couples sitting at the round tables beneath strings of white bubble lights. One couple in the back of the dining room catches my eye—and for good reason. I gasp and throw my arm out to stop Nora, like my mom used to do at every stop sign when I was a kid riding beside her in the car.

"What?" Nora glares at me.

I sprint past the window, pulling Nora with me, and lean against the brick façade. "Garrett is here. With a woman. A beautiful woman!"

"So?"

"So he's with a *woman*." I lean sideways ever so slightly so I can see inside once more. I put my nose to the glass and cup the sides of my face with my hands to block the sunlight. "Who is she? I've never seen her before."

"What does it matter? I thought he was too good for you."

Touché.

I stand there, transfixed, until Nora grasps me by the shoulders and pulls me away from the glass. That's when I notice I'd fogged it up and left two hand smudges.

I run my hands through my hair as mild panic sets in. "He didn't mention anything to me about dating someone."

"Does he have to tell you? I'm sure he feels no obligation, especially after you chose Adrian over him."

She's right. I had allowed this to happen. If I'd only figured out what I wanted a bit sooner, maybe it would be me sitting in that bistro across from Garrett. Seeing him laughing and talking with someone else, I'm experiencing some big-time regret. I exhale in a huff. "I'm going in. I have to talk to him."

"No way!" Now Nora's the one to throw her arm against me. "You are not going in there."

I pull away. "Why not? He's my friend, right? I'm both surprised and excited to see him, so the friendly thing to do would be to say hi to him."

"Maybe, if we were in the bistro already and you

happened to run into him. But we're not in there. We're out here, spying on him."

I lift my chin. "Fine. Then I'll go inside and act like I just happened upon him."

Nora takes two giant steps back. "You'll be going in there alone. I will not be party to this insanity."

I shrug my shoulders at her. "Suit yourself." I spin around toward the door, pull on the handle, and walk inside. I keep my head held high with confidence I don't feel and try to look like someone who is completely oblivious to anyone else who may be in the bistro as I make my way to the counter. No one is there at the moment, so I blink several times because it seems like something an oblivious person would do. I put my head on a slow swivel, pretending to scan the wall art while waiting for the hostess. There's a black-and-white photo of the Eiffel Tower on the back wall. How lovely. Oh, and next to it is a painting of the Arc de Triomphe. Exquisite. And then—*gasp*—there's Garrett! Sitting in a booth with a woman I don't know. What an unexpected turn of events.

I place my hand to my chest and open my mouth the slightest bit, like I'm surprised. Then I casually make my way toward his table. I stop when I reach his side of the booth and smile. "Fancy meeting you here." Yes, I say that. It's all I can come up with. "I'm glad to see you were able to tear yourself away from another boring nature docuseries long enough to enjoy lunch."

He leans back in his seat and scratches the side of his chin. "You do know it's Tuesday, right? I've been at work. No time for TV." He smiles at me, but the squint of his eyes tells me he's not in the mood for my comments.

"Ah, but you do have time for lunch, I see."

He nods. "Yep. Every day my firm is gracious enough to

give me an hour off. Today I went crazy and actually left the building."

"Wow." I smile at him. "I am impressed by your ambition. You might be impressed to know that I took the entire afternoon off, which I almost never do. Nora and I were just taking a walk downtown. We thought we'd stop and grab some macarons and croissants."

He cranes his head to look around me toward the door. "Where is Nora?"

What? Oh, right. She didn't come in with me. I feel like smacking myself in the forehead. "She had to...take a phone call. I told her I'd grab the pastries to go." I hate lying—partly because I'm terrible at it—but I don't know how else to get out of the mess I'm making.

Garrett bobs his head toward the pretty blonde across from him and smiles. "I should probably introduce you two. Meg, this is Julia Yeager. You remember Milo mentioning her? She owns a consignment shop next door to our office."

"Ah, yes, that's right." The woman I encouraged him to ask out. Because it wouldn't bother me at all to see him with someone else. Man, I hate being wrong.

Garrett swings his hand in my direction. "Julia, this is my friend Meg. She doesn't share my affinity for nature shows, and she's not afraid to tell me."

What? That's it? He could choose any way, any combination of words, to describe who I am and what I mean to him, and that's what he says? That I don't like his television viewing preferences? Nothing about our unique friendship, not a word about how we understand each other like no one else, how he comforts me whenever I have a bad day, or how we almost kissed at the jazz club just a matter of days ago?

"It's nice to meet you, Meg." The petite blonde holds

her hand out to me. Her perfectly white teeth glisten in the late afternoon sun shining through the window across the room.

"I'm glad to meet you too." All I can hope is that I don't have a piece of seaweed between my teeth. Stupid Asian fusion food! Why does so much of it have to be green? I join my hand with hers and am impressed by her firm, confident handshake. It's feminine, yet strong.

Garrett lightly touches my arm. "You should really stop by Julia's boutique sometime. I think you'd like her style. She only takes items that are gently used."

"Oh, does she? So you've been inside her store? You've shopped there?"

"Oh, no," Julia says with a laugh. "I only sell women's clothing. But he did ask me all about my store on Saturday night when he took me out to dinner." She gives him a pointed look. "Finally." Then she winks at me, like I'm on her side. And maybe I am, since I'm the one who pretty much insisted that Garrett ask her out.

I realize my mouth is hanging open, and that means that at some point while Julia was talking, my jaw must've dropped. As soon as I can compose myself, I clear my throat and attempt a smile. "So you went out on Saturday?" I swivel my head to look at Garrett. "And that's why you weren't at the cookout?"

As soon as I say it, I wince. I shouldn't have asked. I know how it probably came across. So jealous! But I couldn't help it. The words just fell out of my mouth, unbidden.

"That sounds nice." I attempt to recover my pride. "I'm assuming that wasn't a business dinner. You didn't hire Garrett's firm to handle your accounts or anything like that. Or maybe you did?"

Julia's face wrinkles in confusion. "No, it was just a regular dinner date." She shifts her attention to Garrett. "I've been hinting at him for weeks to ask me out, but he always had too much going on. Or so he said."

I cough. "Huh. Well, it's nice that your schedule has suddenly opened up, Garrett."

His eyes widen as his head turns in my direction. "You would know more about that than I would, Meg."

Uh-oh. *Abort! Abort!*

I can feel an emotional outburst rising up the back of my throat. *But I didn't know this would happen when I told you to go ahead and ask her out. I didn't think you really liked her!*

That, followed by immense amounts of tears and self-deprecation. I have to get out of here before I say something I'll regret. So I toss my head back and laugh, as if I've just heard the funniest joke, and then I sigh wistfully. "Well, my pastries are probably ready." Even though I never ordered any. "I hope you two have a lovely rest of your lunch."

With a smile on my face so wide it challenges the elasticity of my cheek skin, I turn and make a beeline for the door, bypassing the checkout counter entirely since I have no actual pastries to pick up. I can see Nora's head poking out on the other side of the window. The look on her face is both reprimanding and inquisitive at the same time.

Oh, I will answer her questions, all right. But first I have to reprimand her for leaving me alone to face such an uncomfortable situation. How could she?

Hurrying through the doorway, I cringe when the bells tinkle above my head. Why do people have to tie bells to doorways? It makes it so hard to leave without drawing extra attention in situations like these.

Nora rushes over to me. "What happened? Did you talk to him? Was she nice?"

I fist my hands and clench my jaw. "That's Julia, the woman from the clothing shop next to his office. And yes, she is very polite. This is actually their second date. They went out Saturday night."

Nora wrinkles her nose, then pats me on the arm. "I'm so sorry. Milo hasn't said anything more about her to me, other than that first time. Does it seem like Garrett likes her?"

"I don't know. He looked happy, but that doesn't mean anything. Does it?" I lower myself onto the black iron bench on the sidewalk and squeeze my eyes shut. This is my fault. I rejected Garrett. I couldn't acknowledge my feelings for him, not with Adrian clouding my focus, so I pushed him away, and pushed him toward another woman. I didn't expect him to actually ask her out, I just didn't want him to think it would bother me if he did. Now that he has, what's going to happen to our friend group—Nora and Milo, me and Garrett? We're a foursome, not a *fivesome*.

What will our double dates look like? Will it be Nora, Milo, Me, Garrett...and Julia? Or will Garrett come without her? Or will I eventually be pushed out of the way? Replaced?

Another tinkling of bells sounds from the door. I turn my head as Garrett steps outside onto the pavement. He directs his gaze right at me. "Can we talk?"

I feel a lump form in my throat. A giant, gelatinous lump that will choke me, block my airway if I try to swallow. I can't breathe. Somehow, I manage to croak out the word, "Sure."

A look of panic flashes across Nora's face. "I think I'll just walk around the next block and check out the theater showings. I won't be far."

"Thank you," I mouth.

Garrett waits until Nora is out of earshot before lowering himself onto the bench beside me. He runs a hand through his hair and stares down at his feet. "What am I supposed to do, Meg?"

"I don't know what you mean." I really don't. Is he talking about his lunch? Is he supposed to get a takeout container for his sandwich? Should he pay with cash or credit? He really shouldn't ask vague questions like that.

He looks over at me, his face about six inches from mine, his eyes boring holes into my soul. "On Friday night, I think I made it pretty clear how I feel about you, and even so, you told me you wanted to pursue things with Adrian. I took that as a closed door. You've been pretty clear from the start that you don't want our relationship going beyond friendship. You encouraged me to ask Julia out, even when I asked you if that's what you really wanted, and you said yes. But now that I have, you act shocked, hurt. Like I've somehow betrayed you."

"I just...I never thought you'd actually go through with it."

He scoffs. "Why wouldn't I?"

"Because it's only been four days."

"Four days since what?"

"Since the club, where we danced. Where we almost..." I shake my head. I can't finish the sentence.

"Where we almost *what?*" he prods.

"I don't know. I thought maybe...I wondered if you might have..."

"What, kissed you?" he says. "Then you'd be right. I would have, if Adrian hadn't walked in. But he did, and you couldn't get away from me fast enough. So I guess it was probably a good thing we were interrupted. It obviously wasn't something you wanted me to do."

"You don't know that."

His head falls to one side. "Maybe not, but I don't think you know what you want either." He laughs an almost sad-sounding laugh. "Look, I'm not sure if you're scared, or if deep down you really don't like me, and everything I think you feel is actually in my head. Maybe I'm reading you wrong." He runs his hand through his hair. "I don't know what you expect me to do. Wait for you to figure things out? Hope that after you've exhausted every other possible option, you'll realize I'm the best you can do, and you'll finally come running to me?" He shakes his head. "I don't want to be your last and only choice."

I blink fast, staving off the tears that are welling in my eyes. "You're not my last choice, Garrett."

"I'm not? So you *do* want me now? Or is it only because I'm here with someone else and you think you can't have me?" He sniffs. "Maybe I should remain unattached so you can keep me in your back pocket and use me for companionship when your dates go south or Nora's not available."

"That's not fair," I say. Now my lip is quivering.

He shakes his head. "No, it's not. It's not fair that I've been there for you every time you come home feeling rejected, yet somehow, you can't see what's right in front of your face."

"Of course I can see it." I reach for his arm. "Garrett—"

"Please let me finish." His lower lip disappears between his teeth, and for a moment I'm not sure if he's going to continue or get up and walk away. But then he straightens, and I can see a change in his expression as his resolve strengthens. "I realize that my asking Julia out the day after you rejected me might seem a bit rash. Okay, it was a knee-jerk reaction, but it just felt so good to be with someone who wanted me. She's been hinting around for weeks. I knew she was interested, but I was waiting to see where things were going with us first. Once I knew it was a lost cause, I asked her out. And do you know what? She said yes without any hesitation, and we went out that night. We had a good time together too." He shakes his head. "I don't know what to do now."

"I'm sorry, Garrett," I say between shaky breaths. "I didn't think you liked me that way."

He huffs a short breath. "My feelings are so far beyond *like*, Meg. But I'm not the kind of guy who would purposefully lead a woman on, and Julia has done nothing wrong. I don't want to hurt her." His chest heaves as he works his jaw. "I think I need to take a step back and think things over. While I do, it's probably best if we don't see each other for a while."

"You don't mean that."

"I don't?" He quirks a brow, stands, and then strides back toward the door. He gives me one last look, and with it I can feel the unspoken words that hang in the air between us as he reenters the bistro.

Watch me prove it to you.

twenty-nine

TODAY HAS BEEN the most unproductive day I've spent at work in weeks. I've been meandering through the biography section, aligning book spines along the edge of the shelf for at least ten minutes. There's only one other person working with me today, and since she's stationed at the circulation desk, there's no one to reprimand me. I don't get paid to align book spines, but who cares? It's not like the library is a happening place on Friday afternoons. That's one of the reasons there're only two of us. The place is totally dead, and that's good because I can't seem to focus.

Adrian's coming over for supper tonight. It will be our third date. I don't know how I let him talk me into cooking for him, since I've never been a fan of cooking. It just doesn't excite me. Cooking, cooking magazines, cooking shows on TV—I don't understand the appeal. Personally, I can't imagine anything more boring than watching other people cook and listening to them talk about the ingredients and the measurements, step by boring step.

Oh wait, there is one thing that's more boring—nature documentaries.

Ugh. And now I'm thinking about Garrett. And missing him.

Honestly, I think what got me into this situation is guilt, plain and simple. That night at the jazz club, I felt so guilty about what Adrian walked in on—or what he almost walked in on—that I was just thankful he wanted to go out with me again. So thankful, in fact, that I was willing to agree to anything he suggested, and he suggested a stay-at-home date, complete with a home-cooked meal. Cooked by me. At my apartment.

When four o'clock finally arrives, I log my time in the computer and leave work. I have two more hours until Adrian shows up at my house for supper. As I pull out of the library parking lot, I can't even think about food because my stomach is in knots. I've decided to ask Adrian to be my date to Braxton's wedding, and I'm doing it tonight. Finally, all of my efforts—all of the miserable, mismatched blind dates, the constant messaging, the see-through tights—it will all be worth it because I won't have to show up at Braxton's wedding alone, looking like I never moved forward in life after our breakup while he went on to meet the love of his life.

So I should feel pretty darn happy right now. Ecstatic. Only, I don't. There's a joy-killing, relief-squelching road-block standing in the way of my happiness, and that's the fact that Adrian isn't the one I want to go to the wedding with. Garrett is. But that can't happen now because he's seeing Julia. Oh, and also because he doesn't want to talk to me.

Obviously I need to move on, but I'm finding it extremely difficult to do so. There's only one way I can think of to get Garrett out of my head, and I have to do it now before Adrian comes over or I won't be able to give him my full attention like he deserves.

I put my blinker on and merge into the right lane, and find myself heading in the opposite direction from my apartment. Before long, I'm turning onto Garrett's street, and then pulling into the parking lot of his apartment building. Garrett might not even be home from work yet. Or maybe he's getting ready for a date with Julia, and I'll be in the way and it'll be awkward.

My gut clenches at the thought. But since I'm already here, I have no choice but to knock on his door, ask if I can come in, and do what I need to do to—extinguish my feelings for him. Hopefully.

I wait only a few seconds before he opens the door, and my mouth instantly goes dry at the sight of him. He's wearing joggers—my favorite joggers, the ones he was wearing when we went on our walk around Lake Harriet. His hair is wet like he just stepped out of the shower, and it smells freshly washed too. His whole body smells like soap and men's shampoo and spicy deodorant. All the things that make my head swim and my heart beat faster.

"Meg." He scratches his head. "What...what are you doing here? I thought we were going to give each other some space."

"We are. This doesn't count. I just...never see you anymore." I smile at him as if that isn't the most pathetic thing I've ever said to him.

"Well, I did ask you not to." He shakes his head. "Never mind. Can I help you with something?"

"I hope so. Can I come in? Just for a second?"

"Uh, yeah. Sure." He steps back and opens the door

wider for me to pass. "But you can't stay. I'm getting ready to leave—"

I hold up my hand to silence him. "Don't worry, I won't be long."

"So, not to be rude, but why are you here?"

How do I explain my reason for being here? I'm on a fact-finding mission of sorts. I'm here to find out facts which I hope will completely turn me off from Garrett for the rest of my life. But he can't know that. And he can't be around when I'm doing the actual fact-finding. I have to think fast.

"Um, actually I came to bring something to you. It's a surprise. I left it in my car. Would you mind getting it?" I hold out my key chain and point to my car. "It's parked just over there."

"You want me to get it? Whatever *it* is."

"Yes." I nod.

"How will I know when I see it?"

Good question, since I don't actually know what *it* is either. "You'll just know."

"Oh-kay." He draws out the word in obvious annoyance. "I guess I'll be right back." He takes my keys from me and slips past me and out the door.

I watch until he's halfway across the parking lot. Then I creep down the dark hall and enter the room that I hope is his bedroom. The light is off, but from the sunlight filtering in through the window blinds, I can see my way around good enough. I head straight for a tall dresser against the far wall. I figure he, like most people, probably keeps his socks in one of the top two drawers. I try the top one. Boxers. I quickly slam that drawer shut and move down to the next one.

Jackpot. Socks in both dark colors and white are...*balled*

up in the drawer. My hand stills, one round ball of cotton clenched in my fist. I can't breathe. He balls his socks. He balls his—

"Meg?" The overhead light clicks on. "There wasn't anything in your car." I turn, sock in hand, to face Garrett and his confused stare. "What exactly are you doing? Are you...going through my dresser?"

I don't know what to say. "We're friends, so this isn't weird."

His brow creases. "It's not?"

"No. This is totally something I would do in any of my friends' bedrooms."

"You rummage through their dresser drawers?"

I nod.

"Did you need to borrow a pair of socks or something?"

"No."

"Were you looking for money?"

My jaw drops. "Of course not! I would never do that."

He points to me, then the dresser. "You're going through my sock drawer! What am I supposed to think?"

I let my shoulders relax, then I lean back against the drawer, closing it with my elbow. "Look, I just needed to know how you fold your socks, okay?" I hold out the sock, still clenched in my fist, and wave it at him. "You ball your socks."

He shrugs. "That's how my mom taught me."

"Well, she taught you wrong." I shove both of my thumbs into the opening of one sock, once I *find* the opening, and demonstrate the amount of effort it takes to separate the socks that have been so tightly bound together. Then I hold them out in front of him. "Did you see how difficult that was?"

"Not really."

I throw my head back and groan, then chuck the socks onto his bed. "Never mind. No one understands." I stomp out of the room, sliding past him in the narrow doorway. But that's as far as I get, because Garrett grabs my upper arm, preventing my escape.

"Why do you care how I fold my socks?"

I stare up at him. What can I possibly say that won't make me sound like a neurotic, weirdo stalker? "I..." I press my lips together, garnering the courage to give him an honest answer. "I *don't* care," I finally say. "I really, really don't care." And, weirdly enough, that is the absolute truth.

Garrett balls his socks. And I. Don't. Care. It's the deal breaker of all deal breakers, and I still want him just as much.

Since when does a deal breaker not break the deal? This was supposed to work out the way I wanted it to. I was supposed to come here, find out once and for all how Garrett folds his socks and, hopefully, if he balled them, I would be so turned off that all of my stupid, unwanted feelings for him would vanish instantly. But they didn't.

This has never happened to me in my entire life. I guess the saying is true—love is blind, at least when it comes to sock-balling.

"I have to go," I say, and he releases his grip on my arm. "I have supper to cook. For Adrian, who's coming over." I take a deep, somewhat shaky breath. "Tonight I'm going to ask him to come to Braxton's wedding with me."

Garrett presses his lips together and nods slowly. "I see. So he's the one then?"

What can I say to that? I decide I have nothing to lose and go for the truth. "No. But I'm thinking of asking him as a friend."

"I thought you wanted more than just a wedding date with a friend."

"I did. I do, but I'm out of time and out of options. So now I have to settle."

He lowers his chin almost to his chest. "Meg. You promised me you wouldn't settle."

Tears sting my eyes. "Well, you made that pretty much impossible, Garrett."

He takes a step toward me. "I think we should talk about this."

"I don't have time. Adrian's coming. I have to go." I flip my hand through the air in a careless, haphazard wave. "Have a nice evening, whatever you're doing. And tell Julia I said hello."

thirty

IT'S after five when I get back from Garrett's, and that leaves me very little time to prepare dinner. I don't know what I'm going to say to Adrian. I'd hoped I would have a sense of closure with Garrett by the time Adrian arrived, but I'm no better off now than before I went to Garrett's apartment.

Since Adrian never knew about the wedding, he won't be disappointed if I don't ask him to be my date. But it's not just the wedding I'm thinking about now. It's the entire future of our relationship. He's a great guy, but I just went over to Garrett's and discovered that he balls his socks, and it didn't bother me one bit.

What in the world is going on?

I don't actually need to ask, because I already know. I've forgiven a deal breaker for a man because the man is more important to me than the deal breaker, and that can only mean one thing—I'm in love with him. I think I've always suspected it, but tonight I'm sure. And I can't continue dating Adrian when I'm in love with someone else, even if that someone is dating another woman.

I brace myself with a hand on either side of my kitchen sink and shake my head. How did I get myself into this mess?

There's no time to sort out my life. I have to cook dinner first. I rummage through my refrigerator, then my cupboards. If I'm ending things with Adrian tonight, there's no need to go out of my way to impress him. That will only cause him to regret our breakup more than he already will. So instead, I go out of my way to be unimpressive. I decide to make macaroni and cheese and hot dogs. I'll even cut the hot dogs into chunks like my mom used to do for me when I was little.

Adrian arrives a minute before six. I pull open the door to let him in, and I want to cry at the sight of him. While I may have worn ratty jeans and a T-shirt, he looks like he put actual effort into dressing for our date. He's wearing dark jeans and a dark gray long-sleeved, button-up shirt.

I smile, not quite ready to drop the bomb on him, then I step back to let him into my kitchen.

"I hope I'm not late." He hands me a dark green bottle with a gold foil-wrapped top. I didn't notice it when he arrived. I take the bottle and examine the label. It's sparkling cider.

He shrugs. "I didn't know if you...you only ordered water at the club, so I wasn't sure how you felt about..."

I pull the bottle to my chest. "This is great, thank you. This will pair nicely with what I've prepared for dinner." I set it in the middle of my table, between the pot of macaroni and cheese and the platter of cut-up boiled hot dogs.

Adrian looks down at the pot, then the platter, and then at his bottle. His brow lifts. "Um, yeah. No problem."

Feeling like a first-class idiot, I run to my cupboard, stand on tip-toe to reach the top shelf, then pull down two wine glasses. I return to the table and set one at each of our places. "There we go."

He shakes his head. "I'm sorry, I don't know why I expected this to be a little more..."

"Mature? Grown-up? You can say it."

He makes a wiggly-fingered gesture with his hands. "We'll go with grown-up. But it's fine. I love mac and cheese."

I side-eye him. "Do you? Or are you just humoring me?"

"No, I'm serious. I love comfort food."

"Great. Because that is pretty much the only kind of food I know how to make."

Our dinner conversation isn't quite as comfortable and free-flowing as it has been in the past, and there's a really good explanation for that—I'm distracted. I know I need to tell Adrian how I feel, and it's not going to be easy. I'd hoped to put that discussion off a little while longer and at least let Adrian enjoy the home-cooked meal he came here for, but I can tell he's not into it. I'm pretty sure it's because he can sense that something's bothering me, and not because the meal itself is kind of lame.

Once we've finished eating, I clean the plates from the table and then I offer him dessert. "I think I may have some ice cream sandwiches in here," I say as I dig through the freezer. "Or there's ice cream, but only vanilla. We could add chocolate syrup and make our own milkshakes. I can show you how to use my industrial-strength mixer."

"I'm actually not hungry for dessert," Adrian says.

"Oh?" I turn my head in his direction, and when I see the serious look on his face, I shut the freezer door.

Adrian puts his hands on the table and presses down like he's about to get up, but then he relaxes and slumps back into his seat with a defeated sigh. "Meg, what's going on with you tonight?"

I angle my head to the side. "What do you mean?"

He presses his lips together and stares at me for a moment. "I don't know. Ever since I got here, you've been acting really weird, making macaroni and cheese with hot dogs like I'm a five-year-old, dressing like you just got back from a week at summer camp. Please tell me what's going on. What's going through your head?"

My shoulders drop as I exhale. I guess it's time to lay it all out there. "Fine, you're right. There is something that I need to talk to you about." All I can do is tell him the truth, even though I know the truth is going to hurt his feelings. I return to my chair across from him at the table and look into his eyes. "I like you a lot, Adrian. You and I have everything in common that matters, and if I could picture the perfect person for me, it would be someone like you. But unfortunately, I think my heart has made its own decision without running it by me first. And even though I did not grant it permission, my heart has chosen someone else."

He nods. "Garrett."

I jerk my head back. "How did you know?"

He chuckles. "It's pretty obvious, Meg. I had my suspicions when I walked in on you two dancing. I wondered if maybe you guys had a history. If not, there must be a really good reason why you aren't together."

"There is. Her name is Julia."

"Ah, I see."

"I wanted to want you, believe me. But I just couldn't force it, no matter how hard I tried. I can't seem to think about anyone but Garrett." I hold my palms out. "I'm so sorry, Adrian. You're an amazing guy and I had no intentions of leading you on. I won't blame you if you want to slander my name all over social media."

Adrian laughs and reaches across the table for my hand. "I would never do that, Meg. Dating is hard. We're all trying to figure things out as we go. And as far as Garrett is concerned, I wouldn't worry too much. These things have a way of working themselves out. You just need to give it time."

That's true, but he doesn't know anything about Braxton's wedding. Time is something I don't have.

"Thanks for understanding and being such a great guy. If I meet any single girls, I'm going to send them your way."

"Please don't," he says, laughing. "I don't need referrals."

"Gotcha." I do my best to wink at him, but I've never been good at winking so it probably looks more like I've got something stuck in my eye. I shrug it off. "Well, it's still early, and although this night probably hasn't gone the way you'd imagined it would, I still want to be friends. We could watch a movie or something. I'll even let you pick which one."

The smile falls from his face as a sigh escapes his lips. "Can we...not? I'd rather go, if it's all the same to you. I feel like I'd be stepping on some other guy's toes."

"Oh, yeah. Sure. If you'd rather call it a night, I understand." The feeling inside my chest is one I've never experienced before. It's like a pang of disappointment mixed with a swirl of sympathy and a tiny bit of nausea. I've had to let guys down before, but it's never been this hard. Adrian is someone I actually like. He and I could be really good together, had I not already met Garrett. But now that I have, no one else compares.

I walk Adrian to the door and tell him goodbye. When he's gone, I lean against the door and close my eyes, praying to God that I haven't just made a mistake I'll regret for the rest of my life.

~

One hundred and forty hours have passed since I ended things with Adrian—not that I'm counting—and I still haven't heard a word from Garrett. I haven't seen him since the sock drawer incident. The stress of the situation is eating me alive. I have to talk to someone. Normally I'd go to Nora. But I already know what she'll say—in fact, she's already told me, "I told you this would happen."

And obviously I can't talk to Garrett about my problem because he *is* the problem. I feel like I'm spinning around in circles, being pulled under by a whirlpool of my own making and I have no one to pull me out. I have no one else to turn to except...my parents.

I've never been this desperate before.

Braxton's wedding is next weekend. At this point, I don't even care if I go. I really wish Garrett could be my date, but now he and I aren't even friends, and nothing matters more than fixing what has gone wrong between us. Braxton can elope for all I care.

I drive to my parents' house after work on Thursday. They have no idea I'm coming. I pull into their driveway at around five, and just as I step out of my car, my mom walks out the front door. She stops and her eyes grow wide.

"Meg? Is everything okay? You were just here on Sunday."

I frown. "Am I only allowed to come over once a week?"

She scoffs, waving a hand through the air. "Of course

not. I'm just surprised, that's all. I'm on my way to pick up pizza. Do you want to stay for supper?"

I can feel my shoulders relax. "Yes. I'd like that."

"Wonderful." She clears her throat. "Now, would you like to move out of the way or should I take your car?"

I hand her my keys. "Just take mine." It's quite a down-grade from her Acura, but I hope she'll be able to survive the ten-minute round trip without leather seats and satellite radio.

Inside, I find my dad in the kitchen preparing a salad. "Hey, Dad," I say. "I hope you don't mind splitting that salad three ways."

When he looks up and sees me, he smiles. "Meg, what a surprise. I didn't expect you twice in one week."

Apparently no one did.

I sit down at the kitchen island and watch him create his plant-based masterpiece. "I was free tonight, and I thought I'd stop by. Mom invited me to stay for dinner."

He chuckles. "What did you expect to happen when you show up here at suppertime? That was your plan all along." He gives me a wink.

"I guess I just didn't feel like going home after work."

"Are your friends busy tonight?" He tosses in a few tomato slices. "Not that I'm complaining about you being here. You can come over any time. You know that."

"Thanks, Dad." I scratch my head. "Things are a little tense between me and some of my friends right now." Garrett's silence speaks volumes, and Nora keeps giving me *I told you so* looks. Would it ever get better? I open a bag of sunflower seeds and reach for a few. "Speaking of friends," I say, "I have a problem and I need advice." And I'm asking my father. About my love life.

"What's going on?" He sets down the salad tongs and gives me his full attention.

"I think I messed things up with Garrett."

"How so?"

"I think I want to be more than friends with him."

Dad's eyes light up, and he holds out his knuckles for a fist bump. That's a show of affection as far as my dad is concerned. I press my knuckles to his. "Meg, that's wonderful," he says. "Your mother and I were really impressed with Garrett. After the picnic we talked about how well you two seem to get along, and we were both surprised to learn you weren't already a couple. Why would it be a problem if you want to make things official?"

I cringe. My dad would never understand my perspective, not after that reaction. "Because I think I figured that out just a little too late. Turns out, he's seeing someone else."

"Is it serious?"

I shrug. "I don't think so. It's pretty new. But I hurt his feelings, and he's kind of mad at me. Things were a lot easier when we were just friends."

"I don't think you and Garrett could ever be just friends. I've seen the way he looks at you. I say marry him. If he asks for my blessing, I'm giving it to him."

"Dad, please. We're not there yet. Not even close." I press my lips together, mulling over my next words, wondering how to phrase them without sounding cold and unfeeling. "Can I ask you something, and will you promise not to think I'm a terrible daughter?"

"Of course."

I hold my breath a moment, then release it, the question flowing out with it. "Out of all the eligible women in the world, why did you choose Mom?"

His brows knit together. "Come again?"

I inhale to quell the nerves building inside me. "You know she can be a bit...prickly. She's a little judgmental at times, she's very blunt, and she has so many pet peeves."

He smiles at me, and the laugh lines around his eyes deepen. "And you're like your mom in some of those ways. Do you want to know why I love her because you feel unlovable?"

How does the man know? Sometimes I don't give my dad credit for being as insightful as he is. "I'm starting to doubt whether or not I should pursue Garrett. Maybe he's better off without me. I mean, I love Mom. But she's my mom. Why did you choose her? Why have you stayed with her all these years, even when she can be so difficult?"

Dad moves to sit on the stool beside me and puts his hand on my knee. "I met your mom when we were in high school. I know you think the world of your grandfather, and he has grown to become a very warm, friendly man, but he wasn't always like that. Nothing Janice did was ever good enough. I witnessed that firsthand, and my heart broke for her. Believe me, she wasn't always as bad as she is now. She spent so many years listening to her father's criticism, I think she started to believe it. I guess she finds fault in others just to make herself feel better." He gives my knee a squeeze. "And I see you doing the same thing. It breaks my heart."

A tear trickles down the side of my nose. "So you put up with it because you love her?"

He shakes his head. "I know her heart. I know who she is when you take all that insecurity away. And that's the woman I love."

"Don't you want her to change? To stop being the way she is?"

"I pray for her every day—not that she'll change into a completely different person, but that she'll realize how special she is, that God didn't make any mistakes when he made her. I would love for her to get out more and have fun, enjoy life. But I can't force it. She needs to recognize what's happening and ask for God's help. I'm here for her as a supporter, just like she's there for me when I need her."

I smile through my tears. "Dad, you're a good man."

"And Garrett seems like a good man too."

"He is. I think he deserves better than me."

Dad takes my hands in his. "Do you know what I've prayed for your entire life?"

I shake my head.

"I've been asking God to bring into your life a man who loves you like Christ loves the church. That's what any Christian father should want more than anything for his daughter. You don't want a man who loves you only when you behave perfectly. Thank goodness God doesn't only love us when we're perfect, right? When we do everything right, say the right things, don't lose our temper. If God only loved us when we were deserving of his love..." He shrugs. "None of us would make the cut."

I know I wouldn't.

"Meg, do you know why God loves you?"

I press my lips together and shake my head. "Honestly, Dad, I don't always understand why or how he could."

He holds our joined hands up between us, giving them a little shake. "Here's the simple truth of it, and I want you to really hear this."

I blink. "Okay."

"God loves you because you're his. That's it. He paid for you with his son's life, his blood. You belong to him, and he loves you. That's it. And that's what I want for you in a husband. I want someone who loves you like God loves you, like I love you—because you're his."

More tears trickle down my cheeks, and I pull a hand free to wipe them away. "I want that too."

Dad smiles. "I wish you could see yourself through God's eyes. I have a feeling Garrett can. Give him a chance, honey. Don't make the decision for him. Talk to him."

"I'll try, if I can even figure out where to start."

"You'll be able to. I'll be praying for you and him."

"Thank you." I wrap my arms around his shoulders. "Dad, you're a great man. I don't tell you often enough."

He rubs a hand across my back. "I love you, Meg. More than you could ever know."

"I love you too."

I honestly can't remember the last time I told him that. It's not that I didn't realize it, but I'm not sure if I've ever fully appreciated how blessed I am to have a dad like mine. Maybe I needed to go through the humbling experiences of the last few weeks in order to realize how many wonderful people I already have in my life.

thirty-one

BRAXTON IS GETTING MARRIED TODAY.

He hasn't thought better of it, hasn't called the wedding off, and the only thing I can think about is the fact that I haven't heard from Garrett in two weeks. Not since I barged into his apartment and went through his drawers. Last night I called my parents and asked if they'd pick me up on their way to the ceremony. Going with them isn't my first choice—or second or third—but it beats going alone.

I've chosen a simple dress for the occasion, a blue one that Nora says compliments my auburn hair and fair complexion. Earlier, I tried to recreate a hairstyle that I saw Nora do on herself, but she's a professional and she made it look so easy. There aren't enough bobby pins in the world to hold my fine, straight hair in place, so I pulled them all out and opted to wear it down.

I look out the window and see that my parents have arrived. I grab my phone, the card I got for Braxton and Talia, and run out to meet them.

"Thanks for picking me up," I say as I climb into their back seat.

"No problem," my dad says.

Mom sniffs. "It wasn't exactly on our way."

That's my mom. Always more concerned about gas mileage than my feelings.

I notice my dad place a hand over hers on the center console, and then she turns around in her seat. "It's nice to have you along for the ride though." She gives me a slight smile.

Whoa. That's definitely a change. Did my dad talk to my mom after he and I had our conversation the other night? I chuckle to myself. Maybe it is true you should never give up on a person you love. There's always room for growth, for change.

Once I buckle up, my dad pulls away from the curb. He drives about two feet, then stops.

"What's wrong?" I look around the interior of the vehicle. "Did you forget something?"

He glances up into his rearview mirror and shakes his head. "No, but I think you might have."

I turn around, peering through the narrow window behind my seat. Garrett's truck has pulled up behind us. Panic fills my chest. I swallow. "What should I do?"

Mom turns around and narrows her eyes at me. "Get out, Meg." Then she winks, letting me know she's not trying to be as mean as she sounds.

I click the release button on my seatbelt, then hand them Braxton's card. "Here. You guys take this with you, just in case." If Garrett's here to talk, there's no telling how long it might take.

"Are you sure?" Dad asks. "We could wait for you."

I glance back at Garrett, who has gotten out of his truck and looks absolutely incredible, and decide I'd rather not have an audience when I talk to him. "I think I'm good. You guys go ahead."

"All right." Dad winks at me. "Good luck."

"Thanks." We fist bump, and I scoot toward the door and step out onto the street. After my parents pull away, I take a few steps toward Garrett. He's dressed in khakis and a button-down oxford shirt, similar to what he wore on our first date. His hair is combed back and he looks like he just shaved. He looks amazing. "What are you doing here?" I ask.

He stares at me like the answer should be obvious. "You still need a date to Braxton's wedding, don't you?"

Heat infuses my cheeks, and I force a laugh. "I don't know where you got that idea. I was all psyched to go with my parents, until you showed up and ruined our plans."

"Really?" He tilts his head to one side. "That's funny, because it was actually your dad who told me what time to arrive here today. He thought you'd be relieved not to have to go with them."

My dad knew about this? "When did you talk to him?"

Garrett shoves his hands into his pockets and walks toward me until we're standing a mere foot apart. "Last night. I had a few things to ask him, so I called him." He presses his lips together and stares into my eyes.

My heart does a crazy jig in my chest, like an Irish step dancer somehow got trapped inside. Who would've thought I'd actually be thankful that my dad gave Garrett his number?

"The thing is," Garrett continues, "I've spent the last two weeks trying to figure out how you and I move forward as friends, knowing that we both have stronger feelings for each other. I came to the conclusion that I'd have to avoid you at all costs because seeing you with someone else was far too painful. I couldn't handle it on a regular basis. It gutted me seeing you with Adrian at that club."

"I'm not dating Adrian anymore," I say.

"I know. And I'm not seeing Julia anymore either."

"Oh?" I fight the urge to start a cheerleading routine right there in the street. "I'm sorry things didn't work out with her."

"No you're not." He grins. "And neither am I. I'm only sorry that I pulled her into this at all. It wasn't right. It was selfish of me to ask her out when my feelings for you were so strong."

"Is she okay?"

He nods. "We had a long talk. Needless to say, she probably won't be stopping by our office any time soon."

Ouch. "I guess I can't blame her." I stare at him for a moment while replaying his last few sentences in my head. "So where does that leave us?"

He reaches for my hands and holds them, his thumbs brushing against my knuckles and his gaze fixed on mine. "I thought I might leave that decision up to you. Since we're both currently unattached, and you haven't secured a plus-one for a wedding that starts in less than an hour, maybe we could go together."

"We could." My lips are itching to turn upward in a smile, but I press them together. I'm not showing my hand just yet.

"I do have one stipulation," Garrett says.

"Which is?"

"If we go to this wedding together, we will not be going as friends."

I narrow my eyes. "What will we be going as?"

He places one of his hands against my cheek and leans in close. "You tell me."

My breath hitches. "Well." I swallow, then clear my throat. "I will match your stipulation with one of my own. Since I just sent my parents away, I do need a ride to Braxton's wedding, and you're here, so you would be the convenient choice...but I want to go with someone who makes me happier than I've ever been. Someone I care deeply about, someone I can see myself with for a very, very long time. My stipulation is that I need that person to feel the same way about me." I stare up at him. "Do you think you qualify for the position?"

He squeezes my hands. "I care about you more than you know. You are the only person I want to be with, and I don't plan on leaving your side anytime soon. In fact, that's exactly what I told your dad last night when I told him my intentions toward you."

My stomach somersaults. "Oh."

He angles his head to one side. "Is that a good *oh* or a bad one?"

"It's a good one." I nod. "A very good one."

"That's what I hoped you'd say." Garrett's hand slides over to cup my chin. Then he lowers his lips to mine until we meet in a sweet, tender kiss. I can't help but smile against his mouth as it moves over mine, his soft lips convincing me of his feelings, erasing my doubts.

My heart rate accelerates and my breathing shallows. I have never been kissed like this, and I never want it to end. But eventually, it does, only because I need to catch my breath. I step back and cover my mouth with the back of my hand. "Oh, my."

Garrett laughs as he brushes a lock of hair away from

the side of my face. "You know, we could just skip this wedding and go for a walk around Lake Harriet instead. I feel like we have a lot to talk about. Besides, I don't even know Braxton or whatshername."

I pull my bottom lip between my teeth and look him up and down, from his perfectly styled hair to his brown leather shoes. "But you got all dressed up. It would be a shame for no one to see you looking so good."

"Are you saying you want to show me off, Miss Rowland? Are you going to parade me around the reception like a prized pony?"

I smile up at him. "Heck, yeah. I put way too much time and effort into finding a date to this wedding, and I'm not wasting it. I'm introducing you to every single person there."

"Even the people you don't know?"

I shrug. "Why not? I promise I'll make it up to you. I'll dance with you at the reception, even though I'm self-conscious."

His lips spread in a sly smile as he pulls me close and wraps his arms around my back. "I would love to pick up where we left off at that club. I remember, I was just about to..." He bends down and presses a kiss to one corner of my mouth, then the other, and my head feels so fuzzy I can't tell which way is up.

"We should probably get going so we're not late," I say, even though moving from this spot is the absolute last thing I want to do right now.

"All right." He tugs on my hand and leads me to his truck. "You know, this will be our first outing as an official couple. Do you think we'll get through it without arguing? I'll try not to push any of your buttons, at least not until after the wedding." He winks at me.

"You can push all the buttons you want, Garrett Atkinson. There's nothing you can do to get rid of me now."

He presses another quick kiss to my temple. "Is that a promise?"

thirty-two

OCTOBER

Busyness surrounds me as Nora and Milo's few remaining family members disassemble the amazing engagement party that ended not too long ago. Nora's mom walks past me, picking up discarded paper plates while her dad folds up lawn chairs and puts them away. I do plan on helping, really—I'm just trying to process it all.

Nora is engaged, and I couldn't be happier for her. I only wish it didn't mean that our time together as roommates is coming to an end.

"Tonight was perfect," Nora says as she comes up beside me. "Thanks for all your help."

I look over at her and smile. "Nothing caught on fire, and we didn't run out of food. I'd say it was a success."

"Not bad for two amateur party planners." She places her hand on my shoulder. "You looked a little sad when I walked up just now. Is everything okay?"

I nod. "I'm fine. It's just hitting me that you and I won't be roommates much longer."

"We have six more months."

"That'll go fast. I should probably start looking for a cheaper place because moving back in with my parents is not an option. Although Milo's spare room is still open, so at least I won't be homeless."

Nora angles her head to the side. "Nice try. I'll help you find another place. But to be honest, I don't think you'll have to worry about that for too long. If what Milo says is true, you might already have your next apartment lined up. And your next roommate."

"What do you mean?"

She leans in closer. "Milo told me that Garrett's been dropping all kinds of hints lately, like asking him where he got my ring and how he knew what size to get without giving away the surprise."

Really?

Across the backyard, Milo waves at us, pointing toward the back of the house and making all kinds of hand signals and gestures. I turn my head slightly and notice that Hercules, Milo's new puppy, has gotten into the trash. He's torn into a black garbage bag, shredded plastic tablecloths and napkins, and strewn them all over the back patio. His adorable chocolate lab face is covered in white cheesecake. I would laugh, but I can tell Milo wouldn't appreciate it.

Nora touches my arm. "Oh, brother. That dog. I'll go take care of it."

"Are you sure you don't need help?"

She shakes her head. "Puppy training hasn't been going very well, but it'll be fine." She winks at me and jogs toward the chaos in her shimmery pink dress.

I follow her with my gaze and smile. Even with the dog destroying Milo's yard, Nora's happy. Why wouldn't she be?

When Nora asked me to be her maid of honor, I couldn't

have been more excited. Another wedding! And this time I'm not dreading it. I don't have to stress out about finding a date.

Garrett and I have only been officially dating for about two months, so I'm not expecting him to drop down on one knee tonight or anything. This is Nora's night. But any night after tonight is fair game.

I hear the sound of grass crunching beneath shoes, and I turn.

"There's my little librarian." Garrett takes my hand and laces my fingers with his.

"Hey, handsome. Where've you been? I was starting to think you left without me."

"No way." He pulls me into a hug and starts rubbing circles on my back. "Tonight was fun," he says into my hair. "Milo and Nora looked happy."

"They did." I love the way I feel in his arms.

After a minute, the circles slow a bit. "Do you ever envision having an engagement party of your own?" Garrett asks.

"Sometimes. I mean, I've thought about it. Maybe a little."

"When you picture it, am I there?"

My heart thumps in my chest. "You are, actually."

"Am I just a guest, or do I have some kind of place of honor?"

It takes a bit of willpower, but I pull away from him and look up into his eyes. "What are you hinting at, Garrett Atkinson? Are you testing the waters?"

He takes a step back and holds his hands up like he's under arrest. "Nope. I'm just curious, that's all. I've never actually been to an engagement party. It's all new to me. I find it fascinating."

Hmm. Sure he does.

"I promise when and if I do propose, you won't see it coming."

I scoff. "I highly doubt that. You're so predictable. Typical accountant, does everything by the books."

"Not when it comes to this." He shrugs. "Of course, you still have five, six years until you need to worry about an engagement, so try to put it out of your mind. Don't give it another thought."

"Five years? Nora predicts it'll be sooner than that. Much sooner."

"She's wrong. I hope you can be patient."

I am so close to telling him what Nora told me, but I wouldn't betray her trust. So instead, I play along with his little game. "I wouldn't wait too long if I were you, Garrett."

"Really? And why is that?"

"Because I might start looking for other options. I'll go back to my dating app and start making matches with guys the algorithm thinks are well suited for me."

He folds his arms across his chest. "Go ahead."

"You act like you don't believe me. You're a little too confident for someone who is barely qualified to be my boyfriend."

He tosses his head back and laughs. "Oh, now I'm *barely* qualified? How so?"

"Well," I say, poking him in the chest, "you have two deal-breaking qualities which I've chosen to overlook in order to be with you."

"Wait, two? I know I ball my socks, although I still don't understand why that's so bad. What else do I do that bothers you so much?"

"Your handshake. Didn't I tell you?"

He tilts his head. "What's wrong with my handshake?"

"It's weak. It's like shaking a baby's hand. Or a person who's asleep."

His jaw drops. "No one has ever complained about my handshakes."

"They probably didn't want to offend you."

"Unlike you."

I chuckle. "You already know I'm not afraid to offend."

"Okay, Meg." Garrett stands up straight. "How about I list off a few things you do that drive me absolutely insane. First, you're a little too—"

"Garrett, I don't think—"

He silences me with a finger to my lips. "I'll have to add *interrupts me when I'm talking*." He pretends to pull something from his pocket, then proceeds to write on his palm with an invisible pen. "All right. Now I have a *complete* list of things that you do that annoy me to no end, and why they are just what I need to become a better person."

"Huh?"

"You heard me. Meg, you drive me mad. I find myself losing my temper more often when I'm around you than with anyone else."

I blink. "And this is a good thing?"

He nods. "Weirdly enough, it is."

"Interesting."

"Also, you're a little self-focused."

"I'm working on that—"

He raises his hand, and I press my lips together. Right. Interrupting is something I will try to stop. He continues. "You find fault with everyone. You complain if I don't eat all my food. You don't like what I watch on TV, how I fold my socks, the fact that I don't hunt. You wish my truck was an automatic."

"That is actually true."

He smothers a laugh. "But you also probe deeper, beyond the layers, to get at what's bothering me when you can tell something's wrong. You ask the questions that need asking, not just the ones that are polite. You challenge me to reach for my dreams, to be more than I am, to find my true calling and passion in life." He smiles, and the skin around his eyes crinkles. "No one has ever done that for me."

"I want you to be happy."

"I know. And I love you for that." He half-laughs, half-sighs as he pulls me against his chest. "Ah, Meg. Life with you is going to be very interesting." He lowers his face until our lips meet, and he kisses me slowly, gently. I place my hand to his neck and pull him closer and—

"I hope I'm not interrupting anything." Nora stands beside us, grinning like a five-year-old who's just lost her first tooth.

"Nothing that can't wait," Garrett grumbles.

"Good." Nora excitedly grabs one of my hands and one of Garrett's. "It makes me so happy to see you two together." She turns to me. "I told you he was perfect for you, didn't I?"

I fight the urge to roll my eyes. "You did."

And she was right. I can hardly believe how much my life has changed and how far I've come since only a few months ago. To think I put so much weight in what Braxton thought of me. He made me doubt myself, and those doubts influenced so many of my decisions. But the last few months have taught me a lot. Now I understand what it means to find my worth in Christ, and I don't need to look any further. I'm his, and that's all that matters. Why did it take me so long to figure that out?

Because I'm stubborn and foolish, that's why. But thankfully, God loves me anyway. And so does Garrett.

"I'm so excited for you guys," Nora says, squeezing my hand. "I hope someday when you're old and gray and you're celebrating your fiftieth wedding anniversary, you still remember I'm the one who fixed you up."

I groan a little as I smile at Nora. "As if you'd ever let us forget."

about the author

Jessica Leigh Johnson lives in Northern Minnesota with her husband and three of their five children. She wrote her first book, *Do You Trust Me?* in 2012. That book told the story of her grief journey following the death of her young son, Ethan, to complications of primary immunodeficiency. Since then, she has written dozens of articles on the ins and outs of parenting children with chronic illness.

While that first book, along with the articles, are non-fiction, Jessica's passion is writing Christian romance, especially romantic comedy. *Fixed Up* is her first full-length fiction novel. It will not be the last.

When she's not writing fiction, Jessica can most likely be found at the lake or in the sauna, trying to be a true Minnesotan. She also enjoys working in her flower gardens, apple orchard, and blueberry patch.

She graduated with a degree in Christian Education from Crown College and currently serves as her church's librarian. You can follow her at jessicaleighjohnson.com.

 facebook.com/JessicaLeighJohnson

 instagram.com/jessicaljohnson_writes

Made in the USA
Monee, IL
20 April 2023

32112349R00173